AF413438

Meet Me at Midnight

BY BRIANNA BOURNE

You & Me at the End of the World

The Half-Life of Love

Meet Me at Midnight

Meet Me at Midnight

BRIANNA BOURNE

DELACORTE PRESS

Delacorte Press
An imprint of Random House Children's Books
A division of Penguin Random House LLC
1745 Broadway, New York, NY 10019
penguinrandomhouse.com
getunderlined.com

Editor: Kelsey Horton
Designers: Liz Dresner and Trisha Previte
Interior Designer: Cathy Bobak
Production Editor: Colleen Fellingham
Managing Editor: Tamar Schwartz
Production Manager: Liz Sutton

Library of Congress Cataloging-in-Publication Data is available upon request.
ISBN 979-8-217-22555-2 (hardcover) — ISBN 979-8-217-22557-6 (ebook)

The text of this book is set in 11-point Warnock Pro.

Manufactured in the United States of America
1st Printing

The authorized representative in the EU for product safety and compliance is Penguin Random House Ireland, Morrison Chambers, 32 Nassau Street, Dublin D02 YH68, Ireland, https://eu-contact.penguin.ie.

For all the daydreamers

Eros never hesitates to say, "Better this than parting. Better to be miserable with her than happy without her. Let our hearts break provided they break together." If the voice within us does not say this, it is not the voice of Eros. This is the grandeur and terror of love.

—C. S. Lewis

And I wake with your memory
Over me
That's a real fucking legacy
To leave

—Taylor Swift, "Maroon"

CHAPTER ONE

THE FIRST MIDNIGHT

The first time it happens, I wake in a dim lavender glow, a thick layer of mist curling over the ground like smoke.

I jolt up, blinking into the night, eyes wide in the half-light. Trying to take it all in. Trying to make sense of what I'm seeing. I'm sure I fell asleep in my own bed, in my own house. But now I'm—

Where *am* I?

The bedroom I share with my twin sister, Cady, is gone, replaced by a forest of towering, otherworldly trees.

Sequoias. The sight of them calls up fluttering images of long-ago field trips: lunch boxes and buddy systems, a line of yellow school buses trundling into the foothills of the Sierra Nevada. It's a fifteen-minute drive from my town to a stand of giant sequoias like this one, so maybe I could have sleepwalked here. But I've never heard of anyone sleepwalking more than a mile.

I rise on unsteady legs and turn in a cautious circle. There's something hypnotic about the purple-blue light—something whispering that this is no ordinary forest. No ordinary night.

I check my watch, a delicate gold bracelet with a pearl face that belonged to my grandmother. The minute and hour hands both point firmly to twelve. Midnight exactly.

At my feet, a ribbon of red dirt winds deeper into the woods. A path. And because it feels like an invitation, I begin to walk.

The scale of the world is fever-dream warped, and I am a dollhouse version of myself weaving between the sequoias. I should be feeling a low simmer of apprehension—forests at night are not safe places to be—but fear seems like a faraway, impossible thing.

Am I dreaming? It doesn't feel like it. My dreams are usually disjointed and nonsensical and almost always end up morphing into a nightmare featuring my deepest, oldest fear: facing something new without my twin sister at my side.

But this forest, this night . . . it's more lucid than any dream I've ever had. I can smell the peaty bark, the green newness of the leaves overhead. I can dig my bare toes into the dirt and feel the dark, rich damp hiding underneath.

Inside my chest, in a place I thought had been hollowed out, something stirs. Something I haven't felt in so long. My pulse becomes an eager throb in my neck, beating out one thought over and over: *beautiful, beautiful, beautiful.*

All my life, I have been a dreamer. When I was a little girl, my mom's friends would murmur about me, things like *Oh, she's off with the fairies again* or *Gosh, her head is in the clouds, isn't it?* My sour-faced second-grade teacher called me "spacey," and my favorite grandma called me her "starry-eyed daydreamer" right up until the night she slipped away from us. I didn't mind the murmurs. I loved being a dreamer. The world was prettier in my imagination, and I loved sliding into my own spin-off realities. It was always easier there than in real life.

This strange forest feels even better than those daydreams.

The ground slopes downward, and the trees start to thin. If these are the same sequoias from those childhood field trips, I should spill into the valley that leads to my hometown. People think of beaches and surfboards when they think of California, but I live on the eastern edge of the Central Valley, where the forests grow thick and the mountainsides are dotted with log cabins and stony mountain lodges.

But instead of breaking into the valley, the forest suddenly opens onto a wide, empty clearing. The sequoias here stand sentry in an almost perfect circle, leaving the sky open to a strangely bright, blue-violet moon.

When I see what's in the center of the glade, the night stutters.

A grand piano.

For a full minute, I stare at it, too stunned to move. And then, slowly, as if the piano is a creature that might spook, I step into the clearing.

The moonlight shines down on the piano like a ghostly, diluted spotlight. The wood is soggy, blanketed with tufts of emerald moss and laceworks of lichen. The keys are more yellow than white, broken like teeth. I touch one carefully. *Middle C,* I think, calling up the brief run of piano lessons I took when I was ten. I press the key, but no sound comes out.

I peer under the propped-open lid and discover a tiny, mossy world growing over the strings. Softly rolling hills, the shiny marching carapaces of june bugs. And flowers: prairie smoke and chokecherry, skyrocket and mallow. I know their names the way I know the names of every fabric I've ever run through a sewing machine: chiffon, organza, bombazine.

As I run my fingertips over the velvet petals of the nearest bloom, a smile spreads across my face. For the first time in three months, I'm able to breathe without the crushing weight of real life sitting on my chest.

My smile falters. Just thinking about that weight has it settling back over my lungs, pressing the air out of me. Reminding me of my life outside this dream.

Real life is the subtle but unmistakable rattle of everything falling apart.

I wish I could be the sort of person who can handle it, but I've never been strong like that. Not like Cady.

I slip my hand into my dress pocket and find the double penny that comes with me everywhere. It's two pennies melded together, side by side. As strange as an egg with double yolks. My dad has always wanted to sell it; says it will get hundreds, maybe thousands, of dollars on the coin-collector circuit. But Cady and I found it on the boardwalk in Santa Cruz when we were eight, and we've taken turns carrying it around ever since. I pull it out, rubbing the bright copper with my thumb.

Cady.

My breath catches, and I force myself to focus on the moon-light, the forest, the piano. I'm not there. I'm here.

As the mist curls around my ankles, the weight on my chest lifts again, replaced by a stillness so deep it almost makes me cry. Whatever this night is, I love it. It's . . . frictionless.

"Thank you," I whisper, letting go of the double penny in my pocket so I can lay a hand on the mossy piano. This gorgeous, undemanding calm . . . I need this. All I've ever wanted is to escape, and this place can be that for me. My forest, my glade. Nothing and nobody to remind me of reality.

I run my fingers over the silent keys again. If I dreamed of this place three months ago, I would have whirled wide-eyed and carefree into the glade, drinking up the magic and letting it inspire an entire flock of daydreams.

Now I start to spin, slowly, with my face tipped up. Maybe I can be that girl again, just for a little while, just in here before I wake up.

The sound of something thrashing through the underbrush sends my heartbeat skittering. I stumble out of my spin, but be-fore I can run or hide or grab a stick to brandish like a sword—someone surges into the clearing.

He stops short when he sees me, surprise flaring in his eyes. For a moment, we are two pulsing, startled people locked in a standoff in the woods, both of us too shocked to speak.

My heart lurches. Because this person—this *boy*—

He's everything my hopeless romantic heart would have dreamed up.

In the blue light, he seems etched out of something harder

and more valuable than skin. A precious stone, quartzite or marble. Everything else about the night feels soft, but this boy is cut in high definition. His nose is a noble, almost haughty thing. Two thousand years ago, they would have called it aquiline. The slow way he blinks—those large, lucid eyes—it's as if a Roman emperor stepped out of the pages of a book and into a pair of jeans. The only thing tempering all that hard dignity is the reckless, playful softness of his curly hair.

My heart climbs into my throat.

Escape.

He's the first to move, striding toward me with a loose, easy confidence. Something about his unhurried saunter reminds me of East Coast royalty: summer in the Hamptons and trust funds and boys clapping each other on the back after a game of polo. Maybe it's the sharp navy-blue blazer he's wearing, the sleeves pushed halfway up his forearms, or the gleaming watch on his wrist. The forest has to take a breath to wrap around the space of him.

I take a step toward him, dizzy with anticipation.

My foot catches on something—a gnarled loop of root I swear wasn't there a second ago. I lurch forward, my arms wheeling for balance, but it's hopeless. I go down.

I land sprawled flat on the ground, knees and palms stinging.

It's like a record scratch, the way the fantasy falls apart. I press my eyes shut. *No, no, no.* My body curves inward on a full-body cringe. I don't know why I'm surprised—for a hopeless romantic, my track record around boys is appalling. I just thought I'd be smoother in my dreams. The unfairness of it stings worse than my scraped knees.

The boy reaches to help me up, the heavy, expensive-looking watch on his wrist glinting in the purple light. I think he's asking if I'm okay, but my ears are roaring with embarrassment.

It takes every shred of courage I have to raise my chin and meet his eyes. Behind him, the light changes from that electric violet to a grayer, flatter hue. The fog retreats, stirred away by his steps. The glade around us is just a little less beautiful than before.

He tucks his hands into his pockets and looks down at me. A boyish, disarming grin blooms over his face. "Well," he says, "my dream just got a hell of a lot more interesting."

I bristle. His dream?

No.

This is mine.

And God, what a line. *My dream just got more interesting*?

"You've got to be kidding me," I mutter, rolling my eyes.

The left corner of the boy's mouth turns up, and an amused sparkle lights in his eyes. "Can't say I've ever had that reaction before."

Annoyance flares in me, then grows even hotter as the boy's eyes scan me from my tangled hair down to my bare toes. I run my hands over the lacy white dress I wore to school today, now smudged with dirt, and I'm fairly sure there are twigs in my hair. I can feel myself clamming up, my defense systems kicking in.

The boy's eyes skate to the side, to the space behind me. "I'm sorry, I have to ask—is that really a piano?" Before I can reply, he steps around me to investigate.

"Sure, just stomp into my dream, make yourself at home," I grumble under my breath.

He makes the same circuit around the piano that I did a few minutes ago, bending to study the flowers growing up through the copper strings. *My flowers.*

"How long have you been here?" he asks.

"Half an hour maybe." I flick my wrist to check my watch. That's strange—the minute and hour hands are still pointing to twelve. I tap the glass, then hold the watch up to my ear. It's ticking, the second hand continuing its industrious march around the clockface. But it's still exactly midnight.

The dream was beautiful, but now it feels all *wrong,* and I want to wake up.

With my hands over my face, I take a deep breath and hold it. It's a surefire way to turn a dream into a suffocating underwater nightmare, and those are the ones that always have me jerking awake in bed.

Seconds tick past. The blood rushes to my face, and the air in my lungs starts begging to be let out.

"Uh . . . what are you doing?" The boy's voice is closer now. I ignore him.

My lips purse with the effort of trying to keep my breath held, until I can't take it any longer. It explodes out of me in a rush.

I find the boy standing in front of me, one eyebrow raised. "What was that about?" he asks.

"If you must know, I was trying to wake myself up. This has to be a dream."

The grin that erupts on his face makes me want to throw things. "I've been called a dream boy before," he says, "but I think you might be the first girl who's meant it literally."

Before I can argue, he chuckles, wandering back to the piano. He hesitates there for a second, then slides onto the bench and rolls his shoulders back. I try very hard not to notice the defined tendons in his forearms as he positions his fingers, touching the keys with a confidence that tells me he knows his way around them. His thumb presses the same key I pressed a minute ago—middle C—but this time a cold, clear note rings out.

With a frustrated huff, I spin away. There's a whole forest here, and I don't have to stay in this glade. I can find another one, one without a piano, one without a boy trying to take my escape from me. I'm halfway to the trees when the music spills into the air.

My footsteps falter. It's complex and immaculately structured. Classical. It must be one of the old composers, because it's vaguely familiar, even to me. The fog, now necklaced around the trees circling the glade, seems to . . . react. Like it's perking up, edging closer to the source of the music.

I can't help it—I have to turn back. I have to see how he's making this ethereal sound.

The boy's eyes are closed, and his hands . . . they're mesmerizing. His fingers are long and elegant, moving fluidly over the keys.

That's when I feel it: A surge of emotion, unexpected and intense. An inexplicable . . . *fondness* for him?

It must be the music, the skill with which he plays. Whatever it is, I can't seem to look away. As if in a trance, I watch him play until the piece finally tapers to an end. The boy waits until the last chord fades into silence before lifting his fingers from the keys.

He opens his eyes and looks up. Directly at me, like he knew exactly where I was all along.

Our eyes lock.

His eyebrow rises, as if daring me to say something.

My lips part.

And then, just like that, it's over.

The forest and the boy and the midnight are gone.

CHAPTER TWO

Third-period study hall is even more unbearable than usual.

My latest Photoshop project stares up at me with accusatory blankness. I pick at the unraveling edge of a fabric swatch, one of a dozen I've laid out around my tablet. Once, the swatches would have been enough to spark a neckline or a silhouette, but they're not anymore. I haven't drawn a new dress in weeks. Which is not ideal, because I'm supposed to be working on my final project for art. Technically there's no fashion design course at our school, but my art teacher lets me tailor my assignments to dressmaking, because that's what I want to do after graduation.

No—it's what I *wanted* to do, I remind myself. Past tense.

Defeated, I drop my head to my desk. I promised myself I'd focus on school after spending all of first and second period in a daze, obsessively thinking about last night's dream, but . . .

I never was very good at self-discipline.

My eyes flutter closed. It's so easy to slip into those midnight thoughts again, letting them take me away from the classroom, away from the blank white screen on my desk.

The forest. That light . . . it had to have all been a dream, right? But dreams dissipate when you wake up, the specifics vanishing like smoke the moment you try to hold on to them. And last night . . . I remember every detail. Every word.

My mind drifts as I recall the way the mist swirled around my ankles, how the moonlight pooled bright around the piano.

How the boy looked at me right before I woke up.

The boy. He was so—

The bell rings, snapping me harshly back into the classroom. So much for daydreaming.

I shoulder my way through the crowded main hallway, then peel off into the quieter, carpeted history hallway to swap my binders out at my locker. When the next bell rings seven minutes later, I'm one of the last ones lingering. I have lunch next, so there's no rush to get into a classroom.

I click my lock closed and twirl the dial. I start toward the cafeteria but stop when I hear familiar voices by the drinking fountain around the corner. Heart thumping, I swerve and plaster myself to the wall just outside the door.

It's Britt Coleman, from Cady's varsity volleyball team, and AJ Ranganathan from the swim team. I don't feel like talking to them. It'll be all awkward silences and pitying glances and that surface-level kind of friendship I've always had with most of the people Cady and I hang out with.

I try to breathe as soundlessly as possible. If they see me, I'll have to face the dark thing in my chest I spend every waking moment tiptoeing around.

I'm about to slide back toward my locker when Britt's voice wafts into the hallway.

"Is it bad that I'm kind of glad she doesn't eat lunch with us anymore?" she says.

Instantly I know: She's referring to me. My blood slows with the sick, swooping feeling of hearing someone talk about you behind your back.

"I mean, it's kind of bad," AJ says. "But I can't say I disagree with you."

"Have you noticed, though? She hasn't latched on to anyone new in months. Wonder who her next victim will be."

I can picture Britt so clearly, rolling her eyes under her high, white-blond ponytail.

AJ snorts. "At least we don't have to read any more letters."

"Oh God, the letters."

My face flushes red as shame spills through me. That was in *eighth grade.* And yes, in retrospect, it was a really bad call to hide in the bathroom while I had Cady deliver my three-page declaration of love to Austin Chen, but I was *twelve.*

A heavy ache lodges behind my collarbone. I know that most people don't have unrequited crushes that last years, and they certainly don't write cringe-fest letters to the objects of their daydreams professing their feelings.

My whole life, I believed I was built for some special love. Maybe it was the old-school Disney movies I watched over and over, or the romance novels I started sneaking into my room when I was too young to be reading them, or the folk ballads my grandma played in her car when we stayed at her house in the summer, but I knew I had this well of love in me, and I wanted to give all my attention to someone who would give just as much back. Maybe that's pathetic. Maybe I should have had my eye on some greater purpose in life. But I really thought that was it. *Romantic love.* The pinnacle of existence.

Later, this manifested as . . . I can probably only call them *obsessions*, with a series of boys. In my head, they morphed into the people I wanted them to be, and I'd imagine scenes from a whole beautiful love story. We'd have tickle fights. We'd spoon-feed each other chicken soup when we were sick. We'd touch under blankets until we were dizzy with it. I would convince myself I was the only person who could be exactly what they needed.

My feelings were never once requited.

The first time was seventh grade: Ollie Pålsson, the new student from Sweden, stocky and blond and smelling like snow. Finally—I had a focal point for all my daydreaming. And I *loved* being in love. I stared at Ollie's perfectly curved, peachy-soft cheek for forty-seven minutes every day in our one shared class, and it was *everything*.

Freshman year it was Austin Chen. That one felt more serious, and the pining, God—it felt so good. With Austin, maybe it wasn't completely unrequited; his hand slid under my sweater during a movie night at Clary Adler's, and I thought I was going to pass out.

And then there was Dean. More serious still, so intoxicating

I could barely think of anything else for all of sophomore and junior year.

Now, for the first time in a long time, I'm not pining for anyone. I wish I still believed I was built for a grand love story, but lately I've been wondering if it's childish to hold on to that hope.

"You're too attached to the *idea* of people," Britt said once. She was always so blunt, always more Cady's friend than mine. "You make them up in your head to be something they aren't." After Austin, she patted me derisively on the shoulder and said, "Don't worry. You'll be obsessed with some other guy who doesn't know you exist soon enough."

She wasn't wrong.

I frown. Is that why that boy was in my dream last night? I ran out of real people to cling to, so I made one up in my head?

My phone buzzes in my pocket. My heart rate cranks up another notch, terrified that the noise will alert AJ and Britt to my presence. But even as I'm digging my phone out to shush it, their voices move away down the hall.

The screen glows with a text from my mom.

About to leave the house. Are you coming with me this afternoon?

A sickening wave of guilt washes over me.

I should say yes, but . . . I can't. Just thinking about going *there* has my mind clamping down like a steel bunker door.

My fingers are unsteady on the keyboard as I tap out my reply to Mom. It's almost impossible to lie to her face—her bullshit meter is distressingly strong—but I've recently discovered that I can lie in my texts to her. I do it almost every day.

Too much math homework tonight. There are a few problems I don't understand so I'm going to see Mrs. Rutkowski after school.

I swear I can feel her disappointment, even though her reply is bland.

Hope your teacher can help. There's some soup in the refrigerator, or you can make yourself a grilled cheese for dinner.

Okay thanks.

I slump against the wall, exhausted already and only halfway through the school day.

CHAPTER THREE

The streetlights cast a thin yellow glow into my bedroom, stretching into the long space between Cady's side of the room and mine.

Cady's bed is made up neatly. The stuffed seal on her pillow—creatively named Sealy—beams her sweet, vacant smile up at the ceiling, unperturbed by the voices traveling up through the floor. My parents are in the living room right below me, stuck in the loop of another tense "discussion."

I try to tune them out, but snatches of their conversation make it through.

"You know how I feel about it, Michael," Mom says, cold as iron.

A familiar knot gathers in my chest, the one that's always there when my parents are in a room together. Dad's been sleeping on the old leather couch in the garage, and he's shifted his work hours so his path never has to cross Mom's. A carefully choreographed dance.

Cady was always the one to smooth over our family tensions. She was always the one between the two of us to take charge while I stared out the nearest window, daydreaming. I could levitate slightly off the ground because I could count on her to pull me around behind her like a balloon.

Don't think about that. *Don't think about her.*

I roll over to face the wall, pressing my pillow over my ears as I squeeze my eyes shut. I force myself to start listing colors.

Cornflower blue. Magenta. Copper.

I started doing this three months ago. I had a book of fabric samples in my bag, and an ugly slice of real life that I didn't want to face. I turned through the pages of swatches, over and over, worrying each square of color like a rosary bead. *Wisteria. Dusty rose. Ivory.* I pretended I was floating through each vast expanse of color. As if ignoring the whole situation would mean it wasn't real.

Goldenrod. Evergreen. Sapphire.

My parents' voices become a lulling murmur, then fade out as I start to drift off. But just as I'm about to succumb to sleep, the atmospheric pressure . . . changes. My skin goes clammy and warm, as if I'm in a sauna, and then I hear something I've never heard in the quiet of my bedroom: an exotic bird call.

My eyes snap open.

My bedroom is gone, and I'm standing in a thick, dripping-wet jungle.

For a moment, all I can do is stare as my sluggish mind processes what I'm seeing. Compared with the silence of the sequoia forest, this place is a lush symphony of noise. If birdsong is the dawn chorus, this is the night chorus: the rhythmic, throaty rumble of frogs, the vibrating underlay of a thousand cicadas, rain from the last storm *drip-drip-drip*ping onto wide leaves. Humidity clings to my skin, and somewhere nearby there is a white-noise rush of fast-moving water.

I can't believe I'm in a *jungle.* The awe of it fills my bloodstream, sparkling like gold flakes in a vial.

The moonlight is a bright ultraviolet, just like it was in the sequoia forest. This has to be another dream—surely the moon could never glow this color in real life. But this place feels so much more solid than a normal dream.

I lift my arm to check my watch.

Midnight.

A strange thrill runs through me. Delight and suspicion and awe all at once. What *are* these dreams?

Eager to see more, I push through the choked underbrush, a thousand glossy leaves licking at my arms. And then I'm shoving one last enormous waxy leaf aside, and— *Oh.*

The scene is overwhelming in its perfection, like an old master's painting or a photo from a travel brochure. A waterfall drops like a hazy white ribbon into a deep, dark pool. A small black-sand beach slopes down into the water.

God, it's all so beautiful I can barely breathe. And just like before, the pressures of my waking life seem faded and far away. I hear my heart whispering: *Just stay here, where nothing hurts.*

But then I see the figure standing at the edge of the pool, limned in jungle moonlight.

Shock roots me to the spot, hidden in the fronds like a jaguar lurking in the underbrush. I *know* those shoulders. That crisp navy blazer, that perfect posture, that glinting, heavy watch.

I don't understand.

Why am I dreaming of *him* again?

I squeeze my eyes shut. *Mint green. Orchid. Salmon pink.*

When I open my eyes, he's . . . not gone.

Well, I have no intention of letting him derail this dream too. I'll just slink away before he notices I'm—

"Hey, wait—girl from the piano glade!" he calls over.

Too late. With a dejected sigh, I emerge from the underbrush and join the boy at the edge of the pool.

"You again," I say, scanning him for any differences. If this is a dream, wouldn't my mind have edited him in some small way? But he looks exactly the same.

A wry smile tugs at the corner of his mouth. "Nice to see you too."

He looks up, scanning the lush orange flowers bursting from the mouth of the waterfall. "Pretty cool place, I guess," he says, shrugging a shoulder. "If you haven't been to Bali, or Saint-Tropez."

Wow. Pretentious much? "Not all of us get to jet off to places like that," I say. It burns in my chest—that same feeling from last night, like he's ruining everything. I wanted—*needed*—this to be my escape. Maybe I'm being unfair to him, but he's grating on my nerves in a way I don't understand.

I press my eyes shut. "I can't do this," I murmur.

"Can't do what?" he asks, puzzled.

"I need—I'm just going to go, okay?" And with that, I turn on my heel and swivel away.

"Wait, what? Where are you going?" He hurries after me. "Seriously, can you just wait a second—"

I whirl. Trying to clamp down on the upsurge of emotion. Trying not to cry. "Look. This place is big enough, so let's just hang out in different parts of it and leave each other alone, okay?" My voice wobbles dangerously at the end, but I keep it together.

Hurt flashes over his face, but he covers it quickly. He stiffens, tucking his hands in his pockets. "Fine," he says. "Have a nice night."

We stalk away from each other, and that's when the most bizarre thing happens.

The ground *moves.*

With a deep, heaving groan, the earth slopes up in front of me. Before I can process what's happening, I'm flat on my stomach sliding down the slope. I dig my fingers into the black sand, but there's nothing to hang on to. The incline gets steeper and steeper, and I slide faster and faster—

My back slams into something firm and warm. My elbow digs hard into the boy's stomach, and he grunts. His knee bashes into my lower back.

And just as abruptly as it started, it stops.

We're a tangle of limbs, both breathing hard. We've tumbled to the bottom of a V—the ground on his side sloped up at the opposite angle to mine, as if some godlike being took the entire world and closed it like a book. Above our heads, the tops of palm trees clash against each other, their leaves interlacing to block out the moonlight.

For one long moment, everything is still. Then the earth

moves again, slower now, in reverse, as graceful as a butterfly's wings unfolding.

Once the ground is flat again, the cicadas resume their chirping. The waterfall continues rushing. The jungle beats on as if that whole impossible thing didn't just happen.

The boy's eyes meet mine. They are saucer-wide. "I think we can safely assume that something doesn't want us to split up," he says.

I wrench my leg out from between his. I'm shaking, the adrenaline coursing through me making me feel edgy and sick. "This is ludicrous." I crawl to a boulder and hug it as if it can anchor my reeling thoughts. The boy stands and paces, hands on his hips, blowing out hard breaths to shake off the shock. My confusion reaches fever pitch as my brain desperately tries to comprehend what just happened. The way my stomach flipped as I slid, the pain in my kidney when his knee slammed into it? That felt real.

What the hell is going on?

The boy shakes his hands out once more, then crouches in front of me. "Are you hurt?" He touches my shoulder to comfort me, but I flinch away.

He freezes, hand hovering in midair. "I'm sorry. I didn't mean—"

I look down at the ground.

"Shit," he says, and then he's lurching up, pacing again as he rubs a hand over his mouth. He turns back to me. "I don't know what I did to upset you, but I'm not used to—" He closes his eyes for a moment, gathering himself. When he opens them, there is hurt there, and desperation. "I'm not used to people not liking me, okay? In fact, I'm kind of a pro at making sure they do like me. So why don't *you*?"

I press my eyes closed. I hate confrontation. Anything hard, anything ugly. I'm about to say, *No reason,* or *It's me, not you,* but there's something about the jungle, about this strange light, drawing the honest answer out of me.

"It was because you said it was *your* dream," I whisper.

His brow furrows. "In the forest?"

I nod, eyes on the ground. The moment stretches out uncomfortably. It doesn't seem like a good enough reason, but I really did feel like he was taking something from me, something I was desperate for.

After a long silence, he slides down to sit with his back against my boulder, keeping a few feet between us.

"You know, I get it," he says, so quiet I almost don't hear him over the sound of the waterfall.

In the space between us, something goes still.

"You wanted the escape, right?" He tips his head back against the boulder, eyes closed. "I get that. Sometimes I want that too. My dad . . . Usually I'm okay with taking care of him, but lately it's been exhausting."

The moment stretches out, so starkly *real* it starts to pulse between us. If I were someone else, I'd know what to say. Something soothing. But I'm not that person, so my mouth stays glued shut.

Suddenly he blinks, shifting as if coming out of a trance.

"Wow. Let's forget I said that. I had a real violin moment

there, huh?" He's trying to joke it away, rolling his shoulders as if he can shake off not only the admission but also the weight of what's behind it. "I need to cool down. That whole earthquake thing freaked me out." He shudders visibly. He glances up at the waterfall. "In fact—I'm going to go banzai off that thing," he says. He starts wriggling out of his blazer.

"Wait—" I blurt, but he's already peeling his shirt off over his head. I flush at the sight of all that bare moonlit skin, but then my focus burns to a point on the right side of his body, and everything in me goes sickeningly still.

"Stop." My voice comes out in a harsh bark.

He glances at me, eyebrow cocked. "Don't worry, I'm not going to strip naked. Although I don't usually get that reaction when I—"

"Where did you get that scar?" I demand.

He looks down. "What, this?" His fingers trace the angry ridge over his ribs. "It's no big deal. Skateboard accident, when I was twelve."

I have a scar on my side too. Running right over my ribs, same as his. Only mine's on the opposite side of my body.

I order my pounding heart to calm. His scar is a jagged zig-zag curve, not scalpel-straight. Puckered and pink, not the silver sheen of the one on my skin. I try not to think about how it's on his right side, or how, if I stood next to him, our scars would line up the way Cady's and mine do. It's just my subconscious at work, I tell myself. My brain's electric circuitry stitching all this together as I sleep. Clearly I need to have a word with my subconscious.

I'm too rattled to protest as he skirts the pool and disappears into the ferns next to the waterfall. There's a tugging sensation behind my breastbone, dragging me a step closer to the edge of the pool. The ground isn't rising up to smash us together again, but it's definitely not going to let him get too far from me.

A minute later, he comes back into view at the top of the waterfall, bare-chested, white water lashing around his calves. He inhales, his chest broadening with it—and then he lets out a joyous, reckless whoop.

He jumps. There is one weightless, falling moment where I feel as if I'm jumping too.

But when he surfaces from the dive, my mouth drops open, and all thoughts of scars and scalpels and sisters flee. Because under the water, a shimmering gold mist radiates from his skin.

He looks up at me, his eyes burning with a silent question: *Are you seeing this?*

Without saying a word, I tiptoe to the edge of the pool. I lean down and draw my fingertips in a swirl on the surface, and there—a matching, delicate gold shimmer follows wherever my skin touches the water. Wonder swells in my throat. I wade carefully into the pool, not caring that my dress is getting soaked and heavy, mesmerized by the luminescent whorls that follow my movements.

We stay there for a long time, trailing our arms and legs through the water. The glowing particles curl around us in wispy tendrils, never radiating more than a few inches from our skin. It feels fizzy. It feels like magic.

I watch as he draws his hand in a slow arc, watching the gold glisten and vanish. Something's different about him when he thinks I'm not looking. A little bit of the charming, cocky, polished boy falls away, and I like him more for it.

When our fingertips start to prune, we finally drag ourselves out of the water. I turn and watch as our fairy-dust glimmers fade away until the pool is flat and black again.

Side by side on the shore, we stand in reverent silence.

What *is* this place? It feels so real, but at the same time, it's too perfect to be real. And pools in the jungle don't usually *shimmer.*

And this boy. Two midnights, and he's been here both times. *Why him?*

He turns to look down at me, and suddenly I'm caught in the amber of his eyes. They're the exact same cinnamon brown as his hair.

"I'm sorry we got off to a bad start," he says gently. "Do you think we could try again?"

He looks so sincere. In this sliver of a moment, despite what Britt said, despite the fact that I fell flat on my face the first time I saw him . . . maybe I don't *totally* hate the idea of this handsome stranger sharing these quiet, intimate spaces with me.

I swallow hard. "I—I guess so. Yeah."

The corner of his mouth tugs up, just a fraction. "I don't even know what to call you. We should have started with that. What's your name, Girl in the Piano Glade?"

"Aria."

His next blink falters, as if his brain's just tripped on a jagged stone. For one sharp moment, the way he blinks reminds me of something—but I can't think what.

"That's seriously your name?" he asks.

"Yes, seriously. Why?"

"I just—you know it's a musical term, right?"

"Sure. But I'm no opera singer."

"Okay. What are you, then?"

"I . . . I don't know."

I know what I *used* to be. A dreamer. A hopeless romantic. Although that term has always seemed like an oxymoron to me. No one is more full of hope than a romantic. We hope that life will be beautiful, bursting with love and full of people who rise up to meet our starry-eyed expectations.

But three months ago, I realized that real life isn't beautiful. It's hard and ugly, and I'm so tired.

"What about you?" I ask. "What's your name?"

"Strat," he says.

"Strat," I repeat, testing it on my tongue. "Is that short for something?"

"Yes," he says, but he doesn't elaborate. He just grins, and *oh*, there is a dimple tucked into the soft fullness at the corner of his mouth.

I roll my eyes, but there's an annoying tug at the edge of my own mouth.

That must be the moment the hands on my watch flick over to 12:01 a.m., because suddenly I'm back in my bed, in my house in California, and the waterfall is gone. My hair is bone dry, and my heart is swollen with something I can't name.

CHAPTER FOUR

The locker room buzzes with activity, but none of it touches me as I sit, dazed, on the hard wooden bench before fourth-period PE.

Strat.

The boy I dreamed of twice has a name.

Will it happen again tonight? And if it does, where will I wake up this time? I've been imagining possibilities all morning.

The bell rings, crackling from the locker room's broken speaker. I sigh. Only PE has the power to derail my looping obsessive thoughts about the dreams.

I unzip my strawberry-print dress and pull on our school-sanctioned PE uniform: a pair of baggy black shorts and a yellow shirt that faded to the color of baby puke after the first wash. Then I push through the door at the back of the locker room, squinting in the sun as I follow my classmates onto the field. Our teacher, Coach Kapoor, jogs over. Apparently he was a big track and field star in his twenties, when he competed internationally. He barks out instructions for a few warm-up stretches, then he orders us to run four laps—*four laps*—around the track.

The next ten minutes are a special kind of torture.

Halfway through my third lap, Coach Kapoor blows his whistle. "Aria Lendell!" he yells. "If I see you walking again, twenty push-ups!"

I wilt. I can't even do one push-up. My feet plod as heavily as an elephant's footfalls. Even though my run is slower than most people's walk, I make it to the finish line.

Coach Kapoor is waiting for me there with crossed arms. He pitches forward onto the balls of his feet, his calf muscles flexing as if he could sprint off at any second. I frown—does he *oil* his legs, or is he just really well moisturized?

"Ms. Lendell, I will fail you if you can't run a whole mile without walking by the end of the year."

I nod, but my eyes sting.

"Cut her some slack, Coach K," Tahirah Watkins says, adjusting her Nike hijab. She's on the volleyball team with Cady. "You know what she's got going on. Her sister—"

"Was able to run a mile in under seven," Coach Kapoor snaps. "And they're identical twins, right?"

As soon as my brain processes that past-tense *was*, something in me shuts down. Blood roars in my ears and my eyes slam shut to block the world out.

Don't talk about her please don't talk about her.

"Aria?" Tahirah touches me on the shoulder. Coach is waiting for a reply, but there's a burning pain in my lungs that makes it impossible to speak. I nod instead.

Fed up, he waves us off. I guess class is dismissed.

In the locker room afterward, I collapse onto a sticky wooden bench.

"I say this with love, but maybe you should get your lungs checked out," Tahirah says as she swings open her locker.

I groan. "After this year, I'm planning to never run again in my life."

She laughs. "Fair enough."

You'd think some of Cady's athletic prowess would have rubbed off on me, but no. Over the years, I've sat through hundreds of my sister's volleyball games. For her, I woke up early and dragged myself into the back seat of our car, nursing a grande latte as Mom drove us all over the county, then the region, then to state finals. I went to Cady's volleyball summer camps with her and played in dozens of impromptu beach volleyball games, hating every minute. I never once scored a point.

I roll up stiffly and start to change.

"Thanks for having my back out there," I say. Of all the volley-ball girls, Tahirah's my favorite.

"Anytime," Tahirah says. "Love the dress, by the way. What's this one called?" She knows I name all the dresses that I design and sew.

"'Strawberry Shortcake,'" I say, tying the green ribbon around my waist and sliding a clacky plastic strawberry bracelet onto my wrist.

"Wicked."

I stuff my atrocious PE clothes into my bag, breathing a

little easier now that I'm in my dress. I sling my white eyelet backpack over my shoulder and wave bye to Tahirah before the conversation turns inevitably to things I don't want to talk about.

In the airy, double-story main hallway, I fall into step behind two juniors.

"Did you hear about Jacob C. from our biology class?" the taller girl, a redhead, asks.

"You mean about how he puked all over that senior guy he has a crush on?"

"Yeah, well, apparently he was so mortified he went to ArEx and got a Mini."

"No way, seriously?"

I frown. They're talking about a memory erasure.

The word *ArEx* immediately calls to mind the silvery, trapezoidal Aracen Exradere clinic buildings dotted all over town. When I was little, the fledgling biotech company became a wildly popular nationwide chain, and now its distinct buildings are as recognizable as a McDonald's or a Starbucks. On the sides of their buildings, bright LED screens stretch two stories high, cycling through clips of shiny, happy people advertising Aracen Exradere's sole service: memory erasures.

Once, on a family road trip, we stayed in a hotel across from an ArEx, and I sat by the window for hours, watching people coming and going from the building. They'd shuffle up to the sleek revolving door with slumped shoulders, knuckling away barely suppressed tears. When they left an hour later—and that's all it ever takes, no recovery time necessary—they were always smiling. Lighter, brighter, unburdened.

The LED screens burned their message into my eyes: *Ask your doctor about your ArEx erasure today!*

"It's the only thing that makes sense," the girl in front of me says, tugging my mind back into the school hallway. "This morning someone teased Jacob about the puke incident and he looked totally blank, no blushing or running off to cry in the bathroom or anything."

When Aracen first opened, people would notify their friends and family that they were about to have an erasure, and ask them not to bring up in conversation whatever was about to be erased. But now erasures are so common that if you ask a question and the person just looks at you blankly, you both assume an erasure is involved and you move on. The world is an onslaught of information, and it's impossible to keep track of it all anyway.

"But you can't get an erasure until you're eighteen," the shorter girl says. "Plus, how would he have paid for it?"

"I don't know. It's just what I heard."

I consider it. Maybe they've changed the age limit for a Mini? They're less intense than a full wipe. The technician goes in and blitzes one single memory, instead of something more complex like a whole person or a repeat source of trauma. Minis only take five minutes under the proton beam. My aunt in Virginia has had six, and there's a famous singer who's had a record number of them—twenty-seven, according to last week's *People* magazine.

The girls peel off toward the cafeteria, and I make my way to my art classroom. Inside, I weave through the tables to the one in the back corner, the one no one else wants. Underneath the sharp scent of solvent, it always smells like moldy sewage back here, from years of paint being washed down the industrial sink by my desk.

Across the room, Arissa Myung pulls her art supplies out of her cubby. Her eyes catch mine, and she tucks the ends of her sharp-edged black bob behind her ears and gives me a little wave. I wave and smile tentatively back. I want to tell her that I like her lime-green corduroy overall dress, but we don't talk that much anymore. I feel a little stab of regret. Last year I helped Arissa pattern and sew an Elizabethan dress for the spring play. I didn't have to be at rehearsals, but I started going to a few after school, sitting with Arissa in the audience, helping her mend things that had been ripped in rehearsals the day before.

I liked hanging out with Arissa. It was nice talking to her about dresses and sewing. The two of us would chatter excitedly for hours about the evolution of nineteenth-century bustles or the classic elegance of 1950s shoes. I never have nearly as much to talk about with the volleyball girls.

I don't know what I did wrong, but our friendship seemed to taper off after her birthday last semester. She said she was going to invite me to the epic ski lodge sleepover she was planning, but then she never sent any details.

I slide into my seat. Even after four years in the art hallway, I still feel like an imposter. Some of the art kids have *real* talent—they can turn a blank sheet of paper or a stretched white canvas into something profound. I've tried to do my designs by hand, with colored pencils or watercolors, but it's so much easier on my tablet, where I can search for a photo of a dress close to the one I'm imagining, import it, and trace lines over it. My art teacher says that if I practice enough, I'll eventually be able to draw decently from scratch, but the underlying context was there: I'd never be able to bring a lush landscape to life like Javi Lopez, or draw with graphite like Jenna Albert, so realistically that it looks like a photograph, or, like River Ness, be able to shape a lump of clay into something that tugs at your soul.

River is at their table now, beaming, surrounded by a cluster of their friends. "I got in," I hear them say, squealing as they bounce up and down. River holds up their acceptance letter to show everyone, and I think of my own mailbox at the end of my driveway. I checked it this morning—empty except for a dead beetle. Nothing from the art school *I* applied to, Sciarra Academy.

I sigh, tugging my fabric swatches out of my backpack. None of it will matter if I can't pass my last semester of high school, and I'm currently flunking every class. Art should have been my easiest A, but I'm starting to get a heavy, dreadful feeling that I'm not going to be able to pull even that off.

I never should have applied to Sciarra in the first place.

Later that night, I sit at the desk in my bedroom, trying to muster up the energy to do at least an hour of homework. I'm behind on everything, and it's only a matter of time before my teachers start requesting parent conferences.

Noises blur through the walls, coming from the garage this

time—it sounds like canned laughter from a sitcom rerun. Dad's in there, set up on the lumpy foldout couch. The thought of him out there, miserable and alone—

My pencil tip breaks, ripping a hole in my otherwise blank sheet of notebook paper.

I ball it up and flop back on my bed. It's no use. I'm not getting anything done tonight.

All I can see from here is the ceiling fan, and the row of books on the highest shelf of our bookshelf. Next to the unicorn mystery series I loved when I was a kid, there's a framed photo of Cady and me in formal dresses, hers sleek and mine flouncy, our arms looped around each other's shoulders, against a gaudy backdrop of black and gold streamers.

There's a buzzy sensation behind my left temple, and suddenly Strat's face flashes into my mind. I've been replaying scenes from my two dreams all day, but this time it feels different.

Strat isn't in the forest or by the jungle waterfall—he's sitting at a glossy black piano in the dimly lit rotunda of my high school.

He's playing just as gorgeously as he did in the glade, long fingers working elegantly, lost in the music as he sways over the keys. The rotunda is decorated with black and gold balloons, and a disco ball spins above the darkened cafeteria behind him. *Homecoming.*

I blink rapidly, trying to clear the vision. I rub my forehead, but the tingling feeling's already dissipating.

I slide into bed, shaking my head at myself. It was only a

matter of time before I started inserting Strat into scenes from my real waking life.

As I snuggle down beneath my comforter, I glance at the numbers glowing on my clock: *11:43 p.m.*

I can't help but feel a surge of excitement.

Will he *be there again?*

CHAPTER FIVE

I wake in a room thick with heat.

Ahead, a low fire crackles in an ancient stone hearth, and the room's rough-cut walls glimmer in the firelight. There are no corners, only smooth curves.

Strat's already here, standing at the hearth with his back to me, inspecting a heavy silver goblet. Seeing him a third time—three dreams, three nights in a row—feels impossible.

My wonder builds as I take in the thick fur laid out in front of the fire, the heavy pewter candlesticks on a long oak table. Everywhere I look, old-world romance whispers to me. It's an altogether different kind of beauty from the sequoia forest and the jungle waterfall, but I'm just as eager to run my fingertips over every detail. Maybe *more* eager.

"Oh, I think this is my favorite one yet," I say, marveling at it all.

Strat turns then, clocking me. He smiles. "I had a feeling you'd like it."

I run a fingertip over a velvet armchair. This place . . . it's a perfect re-creation of a room in some enchanted medieval castle keep but without the chamber pots, brutal weapons, and deadly diseases. A version with a glowy filter laid over it—which is just the way I like things. I'd put a glowy filter over my entire life if I could.

Strat sets the goblet back on the mantel. I can't decide how I feel about him tonight. Something loosened between us at the waterfall.

He reaches up to test the sharpness of the blades of two crossed halberds mounted on the wall, sending muscles shifting under his blazer. He really does look good from the back, tall and lean, with a pristinely straight spine and broad shoulders.

"Has anyone ever told you that you have an extremely straight spine?"

I clap my hand over my mouth. Did I really just say that out loud?

He turns, looking as if he's trying to bite back a smile. "I can't say anyone has ever told me that, no."

I swallow, trying to hold on to a scrap of dignity. "Well, you do."

Heat sparks in his cinnamon-brown eyes. "Straight spines are one thing, but you . . . I mean, Christ, look at you," he says, waving a hand over my general existence.

I eye him suspiciously. "Me?"

"Yeah. The romantic hair, the ethereal dress, the huge dark eyes. You're like a Godward painting."

That catches me off guard. "You—you know Godward?"

He's one of my favorite artists. He painted his models in diaphanous silks, lying on sun-warmed marble benches somewhere in the Mediterranean. Their hair was always like mine: thick and unmanageable and a brown so dark it's nearly black.

"Sure, I know Godward," he says.

"But . . . how?"

He shrugs. "School."

I frown skeptically. But I'm secretly a little pleased. By design, and years of refining my aesthetic, my hair *is* dark and romantic: two strands from each side loosely twisted and tied back with a silk ribbon, the rest cascading in waves against my dress. I named this dress Jane Eyre's Honeymoon, and even though the color is more muted than I normally like, a gray with shimmering lilac undertones, the cut is undeniably romantic: square neck, ruched bodice, cap sleeves with three fluttering layers. The chiffon shines like spiderwebs in the candlelight. Maybe I do look like a Godward painting.

"Have you seen the door?" he asks.

When I turn to look where he's pointing, my heart gives a giddy thump. The door is like something out of a fairy tale: a slab of impossibly thick wood set in a stone arch, wrought-iron hinges curlicuing over it like ornate bookbinding. And best of all, it's ajar. Warm candlelight flickers beyond, illuminating the first few steps of a winding staircase.

"Lead the way," he says, gesturing for me to go first.

We start up the tight spiral staircase. I run my hand over the rough stone walls as we ascend, and I marvel at the dips worn into each narrow tread by centuries of footsteps. At one point,

I pause by a narrow leaded window and press my palm to the glass. It's freezing cold; the night outside must be deep and dark.

My imagination skips away from me, wondering what this climb would be like if I hadn't tripped on that root that first night. Would we have fallen straight into a fairy-tale dream romance instead? Maybe now I'd be tugging Strat up these stairs, laughing. Maybe he'd stop and catch me by the waist, press me against the rough wall to steal a quick kiss, and—

I shake the vision loose, heat rising in my cheeks.

"Why did you stop?" Strat asks.

"No reason," I say, flushing harder.

The stairs become narrower, and my legs start to ache. Can legs ache in dreams? Finally we reach the last step. The door at the top swings open into the night as soon as I touch the handle.

The wind sings over the open doorway like breath blowing over the mouth of a glass bottle.

Carefully I step onto the roof of a magnificent old-world turret, towering high above the world, ringed with dark battlements.

"Oh my God," I whisper.

The room below was a small, warm world in itself, but here, the world is vast. The moon glides out from behind a cloud, shining with that strange, iridescent purple light. A wild ocean breaks over rocks far below. It must be cold, but I can't feel it. It's only a dream, after all. A very vivid dream, but still a dream.

Strat props his elbows on one of the crumbled crenellations. We watch the ocean churn for long minutes, the wind whipping salty strands of hair across my cheeks.

"It's so gorgeous," I murmur.

"I don't know," Strat says, scanning the rooftop. "There's nothing to . . . do."

"Yeah . . . I think that's what I like about it."

He frowns, as if he can't comprehend why I'd like a place where there's nothing to do.

"What would you play if there were a piano here?" I ask.

He cocks his head thoughtfully. "For this? I think I'd play . . . 'Un sospiro.'" At my questioning glance, he clarifies: "It's Liszt. I learned it for my last competition. It means 'a sigh' in Italian."

"That sounds perfect."

"Un sospiro." I should probably be wondering where all these small, specific details are coming from. They must have been buried deep in my subconscious. I've maybe heard of Liszt, but I don't think I'd know the names of any of his pieces or what their names mean when translated. But minds are powerful things, and I know this dream is all woven from the millions of threads of my seventeen years alive.

Speaking of woven, my eyes snag on the insignia on the breast pocket of Strat's blazer: an embroidered shield. I'm sure it didn't have the school name underneath it before. Now, in block capitals in yellow-gold thread, are two words: *St. Swithun's.*

I know it; it's an all-boys private prep school in Sacramento, less than an hour away from where I live. Suddenly, so many pieces of him click together. Why he seemed jaunty and even a little entitled that first midnight. Why I felt the instant urge to associate him with yachts and country clubs. But why Swithun's? Why is my mind layering *this* detail into the dream, of all things?

Did I see the name on the big marquee at my school, the one that announces upcoming games and which schools our teams are playing?

Something moves in my peripheral vision, and I tear my attention away from Strat to see a sweet little green vine creeping up over the lip of the wall. Frowning at the impossibility of it—vines can't grow that fast—I peer over the edge. A dozen more vines are growing up the castle walls, so fast it's like I'm watching a time-lapse video. My breath catches in delight when the vines begin to flower, bursting with hundreds of five-petaled blossoms, softest cream with a buttery-yellow tint wheeling out from the middle.

Strat picks one with a bruised petal and tiny nibbles serrating the edge of the leaf.

I frown. "Why did you pick that one?"

He shrugs. "It seemed more . . . real. Flaws are interesting."

I scan the vines for the most startlingly beautiful flower, the one that's so large and creamy it looks unreal. "Well . . . I like this one." I like it when things are soft and beautiful and easy.

He smiles, and I swear there's a touch of fondness on the curve of his lips. "Of course you do." He takes the flower from me, and before I can process what he's doing, he's stepping close to tuck it behind my ear.

His fingers are warm as they brush my hair aside. I go very still, every cell in me suddenly humming. My heart thuds with startling power, and I'm unable to do anything, too afraid to move in case it beats right out of my chest.

"There," he says softly when he's finished. "Beautiful."

This is when he's supposed to drop his hand and step back.

But he doesn't. He looks . . . caught. Staring at where his fingers are still curled around my ear.

He's so close. The magic of the night, cloying and sweet and heavy, wraps around me, the pure romance of the moment making my head light. I tilt my head back just a little, sway forward so I'm a millimeter closer into him.

His eyes shift to meet mine. A shiver runs through me, unfurling along every nerve ending.

A thought: *It feels like we've been here before.*

We move at the same time. Closing that small distance for the sweetest, softest kiss. An exquisite moment, so delicate the world tilts.

There's something a little blurry about it, something that makes me feel as if I'm floating somewhere just above my body.

He touches my face, and the kiss deepens, tender and dreamy and dizzying. I'm lost in it, spiraling, thoughts drifting so far away there is only this, only him.

We're kissing like we're experts, like we've done this before. My brain isn't in control—something else is. My fingers wind their way into his hair, and his hands drift to rest on my waist, warm through my dress, before sliding to splay at my back, pressing me closer to him. His fingers drag some of the fabric into a bunch in his fist, clenching me closer, and something tugs hazily behind my belly button.

A thought tries to push through—*We shouldn't be doing this*—but the kiss is too dazzling, and there's another voice saying, *It's just a dream. Melt into it. Do what you want. What feels right.*

He stops for a second to catch his breath, a stunned look

on his face that mirrors mine. "God, I'm so sorry, Aria, I didn't mean to—"

"It's okay," I whisper, touching my lips, reeling. "It's just a dream."

That's why it happened. He's just a figment of my imagination, and maybe I shouldn't be dreaming about this, or liking it, but *oh*, I liked it so much and—

And that's why I stand on my tiptoes and kiss him again.

CHAPTER SIX

In art the next day, I paint the flower Strat tucked in my hair. Five detailed studies on thick watercolor paper, using real paints and real paintbrushes.

A small, secret smile ghosts my lips. I have a full day of torture ahead of me, but it's fine because no matter what happens, the midnight will be there at the end of it. The weight will ease up off my chest again, just enough for me to breathe, my secret weapon for making it through tomorrow.

And if there are more kisses like the ones last night . . .

Ms. Marley pauses at the side of my table, wooden bracelets clacking at her wrists.

"Oh. That's . . . that's actually lovely, Aria." She doesn't quite manage to mask the surprise in her voice, but I'm just glad she didn't ask me what I'm doing screwing around with this instead of working on my final textile project.

She moves on, peering over more shoulders. The classroom

is quiet this morning, as if a spell has fallen over the room. The only noises are the soft scratches of graphite on paper, the tap of a brush against the rim of a water cup. I can't stop glancing up at the clock, calculating the minutes I have left until I can slip away again. It's as if half of me is already dreaming and the rest of me is just waiting until it can catch up. Living one foot in fantasy, the other in reality. How hard would it be to take one more step and slide all the way into a midnight?

I'm dipping my brush in my water cup, watching my coppery-brown paint swirl through it, when my thoughts unfurl.

In my imagination, Strat and I are on my front porch. It's dark outside, and he's looking down at me, that maddening smile quirking up the corner of his mouth. One loose copper curl falls forward, and I reach to tuck it back up, staying a second there just to feel the silkiness of it.

He leans down and brushes his lips to my cheek, sending tingles skittering through my whole body. I shiver as his mouth skims up to my ear, and when he murmurs, *Goodnight, Aria*, it shimmers through every nerve in my body.

"Aria? Are you okay?"

My eyes fly open. Arissa Myung is beside my desk, touching my shoulder. "You look a little flushed," she whispers, careful not to disturb our classmates. "And you were doing a creepy thousand-yard stare. Are you feeling all right?"

I can't speak. My pulse is thudding so loudly I'm sure she must be able to hear it.

"I'm going to go get Ms. Marley," Arissa says.

"No," I croak. "No. I'm fine. Really."

She's skeptical, but thankfully Ms. Marley interrupts us, breaking the room's silence with a clap and an announcement that it's time to start cleaning up. Our classmates stir out of their own reveries.

"Let me at least clean up your stuff for you," Arissa says gently.

I can only nod, staring down at my watercolor petals. There's a grinding buzz behind my ear. I press my hands against my cheeks, trying desperately to cool them. First that devastating, flawless kiss in last night's dream, and now this?

I can't help the little thrill that sparks inside me. I haven't had a real daydream in so long.

It feels amazing.

The moon is high by the time I finally drag myself up to my bedroom. I flop onto my bed, starfishing out on top of my comforter. I reach up and brush my fingers over my cheek, where Strat kissed me so softly in my daydream.

It's 10:35 p.m., and suddenly it feels like midnight can't come soon enough.

It's astonishing, how clearly I can call up his image in my mind. Every detail is etched there, from the rich tones in his hair to the shape of his fingernails to the embroidered crest on the breast pocket of his private school blazer. *St. Swithun's.*

It's the only written word I've seen in the dreams, and suddenly it's bugging me like a rock in my shoe.

On a whim, I lift my phone and type "St. Swithun's" into the search bar. The school's website is slick, full of action shots of vigorously healthy-looking boys. A year's tuition there is more than most people make in a year, and the names of the alumni are staggering—this is where the state's richest people send their sons.

I've only interacted with St. Swithun's boys once before, at a party in Sacramento that Cady dragged me to, and I can't say it was a wonderful experience. At one point, I remember going out into the hallway to catch my breath, and there I overheard two boys talking.

"Some of these volleyball chicks are smoking hot, and I bet they're way less high maintenance than the girls our moms want us to date."

"Don't get attached, Stew."

The boy—of course he had a name like Stew—scoffed. "I'm not an idiot. But hey, nothing's stopping us from having a little fun with them for one night, right? Did you see the abs on that blonde?"

I shake my head to clear the memory. Of all the types of boys my mind could weave into my dreams, why did it have to be a St. Swithun's boy?

Absently, I type in a new search, adding one word to the string: *St. Swithun's Strat.*

The results take a second to load. I almost click my phone off—this isn't important, and I need to get to bed—but then the images load and my hearing goes flat and fuzzy.

The earth seems to slide sideways.

It's him.

Strat.

I don't understand. His face. Four times. On the image search results screen. His hair. His eyes. My pulse starts to throb: *That's him, that's him, that's him!*

The boy I've been dreaming of . . . exists in the real world?

No. That's absurd. There must be some other explanation.

Logic rushes in. My heart and lungs kick-start, and I gulp in a breath. Of course—I must have seen his face somewhere, in the school paper or at a football game or in a restaurant or at that party two years ago, and my brain pasted his face into my dream.

But if he made that kind of an impression, wouldn't I know where I'd seen him? Surely I'd remember something about him. Who is this boy? *Where* did I see his face?

Riding the sudden, intense wave of curiosity, desperate for an answer, I click on the first photo. I'm swept into an article penned by a small-town news site. His name glows on the screen.

Strat Madigan, of St. Swithun's School in Sacramento, has been named the winner of the Eleventh Central Valley Youth Piano Competition.

He looks exactly like he did in my dreams. Curly mop of copper hair, lucent cinnamon-brown eyes. Same blazer, same tie. He's standing on a stage beside a glossy grand piano, holding a shining trophy.

Strat Madigan. *He has a last name.*

I click further into his life. No Instagram, or at least not one under his real name. A TikTok with videos of him playing the piano, wearing the St. Swithun's blazer in most of them. He starts every one staring soulfully into the camera. I tap on the latest video, posted three hours ago. He's in a small practice room with a scarred, weathered upright piano. Like in the other videos, he leans in as if the viewer is an old friend. Or a person he's flirting with.

And then he speaks. Seeing his face on my screen already stunned me into a frozen numbness, but hearing his voice is a million times more shocking.

"So, here's the thing: I've been exhausted lately, because I've been having these wild dreams. And I haven't played this étude in over a year, but I dreamed of a place last night that reminded me of it, so here you go."

He's not about to play what I think he's about to play.

That's impossible.

Dread settles in my stomach as I tap to expand the video's caption: "Un sospiro" by Hungarian composer Franz Liszt. LMK what you think. #piano #pianocover

I start to shake.

I don't understand.

He's real.

That's what this means, right? He's a real person. He said he's having dreams, and he's playing the piece he talked to me about *last night*, the one he told me he'd play when we were looking out from the top of the medieval turret.

I am trembling all over. About to burst into a million splintery pieces. This can't be—this isn't possible. It's not possible, right? You can't dream *with* someone.

Hold on—maybe I'm in one of our midnight dreams already. Yes—that has to be it, even though the moon outside is white instead of purple. I give my head a vigorous shake. Hold my breath. When none of that works, I leave my phone on my bed and go to the bathroom to slap cold water on my face.

This isn't real. He isn't real. I'm dreaming. I mutter it over and over and over as I stare at myself in the mirror. *Wake up.*

My room is silent when I get back. My phone screen's gone dark. I give it a wide berth and crack open my laptop. I'll type in the same search, and this time there won't be any sign of a boy named Strat, no TikTok with flirty piano videos. Everything will be back to normal.

My finger hovers over the Return key. I've never been so afraid to press a button in my life.

I nearly vomit in the split second it takes for the page to load.

No no no no.

I sink into my desk chair. Reeling.

It's all there. His face on the larger screen, twenty times over instead of four. Shakily, I click on the link to his videos. There's the one from three hours ago, with the "Un sospiro" caption.

I press Play and start to unravel.

"So, here's the thing: I've been exhausted lately, because I've been having these wild dreams."

His voice. Even his voice sounds exactly like his voice in the dreams.

I stare at the screen for so long the video burns itself into my retinas. I can't move my neck. Can't move anything. My pulse feels like molasses, like I'm sick or broken or dying.

My mind spins with the magnitude of what all this means. Strat is a real person. A person who lives thirty miles away. He has friends and a school and a last name and at least one fancy piano competition trophy, and I *kissed* him.

I've been dreaming about a boy who's real.

No—I've been dreaming *with* him. How is that possible?

My cursor hovers over the watermelon-colored Follow button. I almost laugh from the absurdity of it. I can *DM* him. The boy in my dreams is real, and I can fucking DM him.

I blow out a hard breath and shove back from my computer. I can't just message him out of the blue. No; this is the sort of news you have to break in person.

Or maybe I shouldn't tell him at all. We were just getting comfortable, and I was so close to getting what I wanted: a back door out of reality. In the forest, I resented his being there, getting in the way. I can't pinpoint the exact moment when I decided he could be part of the escape; I only know that I don't want that to change now.

Telling him I'm real is only going to mess everything up. Part of me wants to keep everything just as it is.

It's 11:13 p.m. If the pattern holds, I'll see him in less than an hour. No matter what I decide, if I tell him or I pretend he's still just a dream, I know one thing for certain.

Nothing will ever be the same again.

CHAPTER SEVEN

I slide back into awareness in a train terminal made entirely of stained glass.

The vaulted ceiling soars high over the cavernous space—bigger than a football stadium but a hundred times more ornate. The roof is a rolling wave of glass in a thousand shards of color, and there must be a hundred railway tracks running through the station. There are no benches, no information boards . . . and no exits.

I'm still a mess of stunned disbelief. *Strat is real.*

Suddenly the glossy green art deco tiles under my feet start to vibrate. I hear an infernal roar behind me, but there's no time to turn around before the train powers past me. It's enormous and deep green, polished to a gleam. The sucking backdraft knocks me off-balance, and then there is smoke, thick and black. Hot orange sparks crackle inside it. It's beautiful, all power and fury and fire.

It takes a full minute for the smoke to clear, but the orange sparks stay hanging in the air. The train chugs into the night, disappearing into the distance. It's like my brain is trying to give me Second World War kiss-your-soldier-goodbye-as-steam-blows-around-you vibes. In the modestly tailored 1940s dress I wore to school today—the one I named Allie Hamilton—I'm certainly in the right clothes for it.

I scan the platforms. Strat's not here yet. Relief mixes with apprehension in my belly. I don't want to tell him. I have to tell him.

Three more trains come and go, rumbling out of nowhere and vanishing into the ether. I pace up and down the platform, gnawing at the skin at the edge of my thumb. "Come on, come on," I whisper. "Where are you?"

When I turn back, I see him stepping out of the smoke.

He looks the same as always. Blazer, tie, beautiful hair, beautiful face, heavy watch. That easy, charming smile, just like in his piano videos.

Real, real, real.

The last time I saw him, we were on top of a castle, leisurely, decadently *making out.*

My cheeks start burning. He's real. We kissed, and he's real, and what am I supposed to do *now*?

His smile falters when he sees me. "Aria? Is everything okay?"

I shake my head no. Nothing's okay. This is impossible.

His brow furrows with concern, and he takes a step toward me. I take a step back.

"Aria?"

"You're not my dream boy," I blurt.

He raises an eyebrow. "I thought we'd already established that."

"No, I mean—you're not a dream at all. I thought you were, but you're not. I don't know what any of this is," I say, waving my hands ineptly at the space around us, "but you—Strat, you're real."

He frowns. "Of course I'm real."

Tears of frustration gather at the corners of my eyes. "I'm trying to tell you something, damn it." I press a shaking hand to my forehead. "Okay. Let's try this—what do you think *I* am?" I ask.

"I—" He stops. "You're . . . part of all this. You're a dream."

"No. I'm not. Strat, I'm real too. You wake up and go to school and live in the real world, and I do too. It didn't click until I saw this," I say, stabbing a finger at the badge on his blazer pocket. "You go to St. Swithun's, right? Well, I go to Ridgecroft High, Strat. I'm a senior. I'm real."

He's gone completely still, trying to pick apart what I'm saying and put it back together in some way that makes sense.

"I live on the north side of Ridgecroft," I continue, reeling off whatever facts I think might land, whatever might convince him. "My address is 1616 Tall Trees Way. And two hours ago, I googled you, and *found* you. I saw your videos, Strat. I saw you talking about how you've been having weird dreams. I watched you play 'Un sospiro.'"

He drags a hand over his mouth. "But if you're just part of my dream, you'd know all that. Because my brain knows all that."

Another train whooshes by, thundering behind him. I watch him, worry and nervousness wringing themselves together in my stomach.

He scoops a hand through his hair. "Just—give me a minute. Let me think."

All traces of the jaunty, easygoing guy who likes to grin down at me and tuck his hands so coolly in his pockets are gone.

When he speaks, it's careful and measured. "If you're right and we're both real—what are we supposed to *do* with that?"

"I don't know." My eyes sting. This is impossible. I turn away, but his hand shoots out, grabs mine.

"Wait. Aria. I want to see you."

I blink down at our hands, then back up at him. His eyes burn with a sudden intensity. "In real life. If you're right, and we're both out there, I want to see you, Aria."

"To prove it?"

"No, not to prove it. Well, maybe partly. But that's not the only reason." His gaze pins me so I can't look away. The sparks from the soot hover in the air between us, glowing like embers. I swallow hard at what I see in his eyes. The memories of our castle-top kisses shimmer between us.

The platform vibrates again. This time, two trains approach from opposite directions. But instead of hurtling past us at terrifying speeds, they both slow and glide to a stop. The doors slide open as if they're waiting for us to board.

Strat jumps onto one, then turns so he's facing me.

"What are you doing?" I ask, panicking. "You can't leave."

What will happen this time? Another earthquake? I look

at the glass dome high above our hands and imagine it raining down in glittering, deadly shards.

He holds his hand out. "Come with me, then. And meet me tomorrow in real life."

The moment pulses between us. The whole midnight waits for me to make a decision.

What will happen if we meet? What if he doesn't like me in real life? What if he realizes that kissing me was ridiculous, that we hardly know each other, that what was okay in a dream is really not okay in real life? What if our meeting breaks the whole world, in some impossible collision of reality and fantasy? Will it break *me*, just when I needed this escape the most?

The train doors start to close, but Strat doesn't budge. I bite my lip, hard enough to draw blood.

I should let him go.

I don't want to let him go.

At the last second, I leap.

The sliding door clips my shoulder as I tumble into the compartment, a flurry of noise and breath and rattling motion. Strat catches me by the waist, steadying me as the train roars down the tracks. I wish I didn't love the pressure of his hands so much.

"All right." I set my jaw. Straighten my spine. "Meet me tomorrow. In real life, in the daylight."

CHAPTER EIGHT

I wish I hadn't suggested *here* for our first real meeting.

Last night, when I pictured the long stretch of road between my mountain-fresh town in the foothills of the Sierra Nevada and the brittle-grass flatness surrounding Strat's city in the valley, the only thing I could latch on to was Ron's Roller Rink.

Now I lean against my car door and stare at the chipped pink facade. This place probably had its heyday in the nineties. A broken beer bottle rolls on the sidewalk, and a pile of swollen black trash bags slump against the wall. *Ugly, ugly, ugly.*

This is stupid. And possibly dangerous. I should have told Mom the truth about where I was going instead of telling her I was going to the library to work on a group project for my Digital Design and Media Production class.

Twice I've almost gotten back in the car and left. There is a deep, aching sense that this isn't where I should meet him in real life for the first time, but it's probably just a shadow of the old Aria, thinking this isn't a very romantic spot for a first date.

I wince. This is totally not a date.

For the tenth time, I scan the cars in the lot. Maybe he got here even earlier than me and he's already inside waiting. Or, you know, maybe he's not going to show up, because he's A FIGMENT OF MY IMAGINATION.

I feel like an idiot. I haven't been getting enough sleep, and it's entirely possible that I've finally snapped. Had some sort of psychotic break. I'm about to open my door and get back behind the wheel and go home when a car trundles into the lot. An old brown station wagon, its suspension rattling. I'm about to turn away—something that old and janky can't be what a boy from St. Swithun's private school drives—but something makes me pause.

I shield my hands to block the burn of the sun on the horizon. When the driver gets out and starts walking across the parking lot, silhouetted against the fiery-orange glow, I feel it instantly: *recognition*. So deep it rattles my bones. I know that long-legged lope, that explosion of springy hair.

Strat.

His steps falter. He lifts a hand in a small, unsure wave.

Nerves swarm in my stomach. A normal person would wave back. Take a few steps forward, maybe. But I stay rooted to the spot, as if the weeds growing up through the cracks in the pavement have twined around my ankles.

There is no turning back now. I told a boy I met when I was asleep and dreaming to meet me in a real place, at a real time, and *he showed up*.

He stops three feet in front of me, and I feel an inexplicable, overwhelming urge to cry. My body goes woozy and light, like the time I got heatstroke at my grandmother's lakeside ash-scattering ceremony and everything went vast and white for a moment.

He's real. He's here.

And—

He is in *Technicolor*. Too much for my eyes to take in. Things that seemed blurry in the glowing, bizarre midnights are now diamond clear: a silvery-pink scar by his left eyebrow, an imperfect fold at the top of his ear, an irritated patch of skin on his jaw from shaving. He seems taller in real life. He's still stupidly gorgeous, but there's something—more.

I didn't realize just how airbrushed the midnights were until this moment. I feel like I've swallowed one of those plasma balls from the science museum and its blue-violet tendrils are electrocuting me from within. My body is humming, buzzing at a pitch a hundred volts stronger than it did in the midnights.

He's taking me in too, looking as shell-shocked as I feel. He studies my dress, my mouth, my hair. The moment our eyes meet, it's a sudden, powerful punch.

"Hi, Aria," he says, the words crumbling like he hasn't used his voice in hours.

"Hi, Strat," I whisper.

He clears his throat. "You were right. We are real."

"Seems so."

His eyes drop to my mouth. Just for a millisecond, but in it, I know he's remembering what happened at the top of the castle. Are we going to talk about it, or pretend it never happened?

"The whole drive here, I was convinced you wouldn't show

up. This is . . ." He shakes his head but doesn't take his eyes off mine. "I think I need to sit down. Do you need to sit down?"

I nod inanely. I can't stop looking at him. *This is mind-blowing.*

We walk the few steps to the rink, and he opens the door. "After you," he says.

The interior is as worn as the exterior and smells of stale Fritos. Strat leads the way, the fine navy fabric of his blazer swishing. The world became unsteady the moment I saw him step out of his car, but crossing this psychedelic, confetti-flecked carpet makes me feel even more unbalanced.

We slide into a booth. The cheap laminated bench is cold on my thighs. Under the table, I hug my arms around my stomach. The last time I saw him, we were in a palatial train station, our skin glowing with shards of colored light, and now we're at Ron's Roller Rink with a smear of ketchup from the booth's previous occupants drying on the tabletop.

That's when I get my first good look at his watch: heavy, chrome, with a midnight-blue face and gold numbers, the tiniest crescent moon in the center.

"God, you really are real," he says, raking his hands through his hair. The curly strands don't separate or go frizzy like my hair does; they spring this way and that before they settle. My fingertips flex, yearning to touch. I shove my hands under my thighs.

A thousand questions suddenly form on my tongue. Now that I know he's real, I want desperately to know everything about him. He has a birthday and a home and a deepest fear and a greatest regret. Has he ever been in love? *Does he have a girl-friend?* That last question is a hard, sour knot in my stomach.

God. The algorithm in his music app probably knows him better than I know him. I wouldn't even be able to guess his favorite song.

But all those questions pale in comparison to the elephant in the room: How are we sharing the same dreams?

A waitress in a sunshine-yellow uniform skates over. She's in her fifties, scrawny, sun bed tanned, etched with smoker's wrinkles and a voice to match, but she's still got the peppy optimism of a teenager. She stops smacking her gum and asks us what we want to drink.

"Sprite, please," I say, my voice still a little unsteady. "With three maraschino cherries, if you have any." I look to Strat so he can order and find him staring at me. "What? It's not *that* weird."

"Trust me, that wasn't what I was thinking."

His eyes linger on mine for another second, then he turns and tells the waitress he'd like a black coffee.

"Aw, you kids look so nervous," the waitress says, beaming as she collects our menus. "First date?"

"Yes," I mumble at the same time that Strat says, "No."

My dignity curls into a ball inside me. The waitress shoots me a sympathetic look. "I'll get those out for you real quick." As she glides away, the wheels on her skates crush a tortilla chip into dust, grinding it into the confetti carpet. I kind of wish I was that chip right now.

Across from me, Strat shifts uneasily. "Sorry," he says. "I only said no because it doesn't feel like a first date. I mean, we've been swimming under a jungle waterfall together."

There's an awkward silence. There's so much to say, but I have no idea where to start. This is weird, right? I shouldn't be so on edge around him. It wasn't like this with Ollie or Austin or Dean. I'd get fizzy and daydreamy, but I wouldn't *physically* tremble.

Strat blows out another breath. "Sorry. I think my brain is melting a little. And it's not helping that you . . ." He rubs his hand over his face, like he needs a second to gather himself. "You were gorgeous in the dreams, but here in real life— God, Aria."

A wildfire sweeps through my body at the words.

So he's feeling it too. The punch of . . . whatever this is. I wish we were back in a dream, where the moonlight softens the edges of everything.

"I guess we . . . could get to know each other the normal way?" Strat asks, grasping for normality. "So . . . you go to Ridgecroft, and you're always wearing incredible dresses." He leans forward, laces his hands on the table between us like this is a dating app hookup and we're making small talk. "What else should I know about you, Girl in the Piano Glade?"

"I make them."

"Pardon?"

"I make all the dresses I wear. All the ones I've been wearing in the dreams—it's always been whatever I was wearing that day."

"That's amazing. They're beautiful."

The compliment makes me flush.

"And you—you really go to St. Swithun's?" I ask.

"I do."

"And you play the piano. As well as you did in the forest?"

"Better than that, honestly. I was a little thrown that night."

The conversation tapers, but the edgy buzz of sitting across from him doesn't fade by a single degree.

"So . . . what do you think they are?" I ask softly.

"The midnights?"

"Yeah."

"I have no idea," he says.

We are quiet for a long moment. It's baffling, what's happening to us. Too absurd to believe.

I pick at the chipped edge of the table. "Shared dreams are impossible, right?"

"Before today I would have said yeah." He pulls out his phone. "If this has happened to anyone before us, we can find it."

I shake my head. "I'm pretty sure the only thing we'll find online are whack jobs."

"Have you considered that maybe *we're* the whack jobs?" he asks. His teasing smile is back, and it loosens some of the tension in my body. "Oh, wow, I see what you mean, though," he says, raising his eyebrows at his screen. "This is—" He starts to turn the phone toward me, then hesitates. "Can I come over there?"

I blink. "Oh. Sure."

When he slides in next to me, my mind glitches. In the dreams, he didn't have a smell. Here? He's pine and cinnamon, and when his leg brushes against mine, thigh to knee, the contact has my vision going fuzzy.

Again, my stupid brain is cycling back to the castle kisses. What would it be like to kiss him here?

He taps through a few links. "This site's pretty bizarre. Oh God, there are terms. 'Linking'? 'Meshing'? This all sounds extremely dubious."

I force myself to focus on the screen: *Learn how to use astral projection to connect to someone.*

He shakes his head. "You were right. We're going to have to sift through more garbage than I thought."

I pull out my phone to bolster the search. There's got to be something here.

By the time the waitress skates back over with our drinks, grinning slyly at the sight of us sharing a bench, Strat and I are deep into our research, tumbling down internet rabbit holes. I shoot a surreptitious glance at him. It's interesting, feeling like we're suddenly . . . teammates or something.

The more we read, the more absurd the stories get, and none of the testimonials are even close to what we've shared. Finally Strat flicks his phone off and lays it on the table.

"I don't know. It sounds like with all this you have to be intentional about it. I definitely haven't been intentionally trying to astrally project myself to you, like holding a quartz crystal to my third eye or anything."

"Yeah, me neither," I say.

A humming quiet falls between us.

"Strat?" I ask quietly. "Should we tell someone?"

He scrubs at his jaw. "If we try to explain this to anyone, they'll either laugh in our faces or haul us off to a psych ward. So . . . maybe not yet?"

I nod. "Maybe not yet."

Our eyes catch again, hold.

The moment is broken by a burst of laughter and the slam of the double glass doors. A group of guys our age in letter jackets come in, hooting and punching each other's shoulders.

I stiffen, the outside world suddenly seeping in. Behind the group of guys, the sky is dark outside. "Crap. I need to get going. My mom thinks I'm . . . it doesn't matter. I should go."

He nods, then slides out of the booth and offers me his hand to help me up. I try not to let my whole existence narrow down to this one warm touch, but I fail miserably.

The air outside is hot and dry, but I'm grateful for the heat, how it thaws the shivering tension that comes with being so close to Strat.

He walks me to my car. The breeze lifts his hair as he looks down at me. "Can we keep doing this? Meeting up in the daylight, I mean."

Through his easy confidence, I see a tiny crack of uncertainty. Maybe nervousness. It's sweet.

My mind is still reeling. He's real, he exists, and we're dreaming together. I still haven't wrapped my mind around that. But every cell in my body is leaning toward him, chorusing *Sure sure sure yes yes yes. Kiss me again, the way you did in the castle.*

I'm not strong enough to resist the temptation of escape. And now it doesn't have to be just in the midnights. Wouldn't spending a little bit of time with this boy be a welcome distraction in real life too?

"I'd like that," I say softly.

He beams. "Awesome. Let me give you my number."

I tug out my phone, and he adds himself as a contact.

"Okay. See you in five hours, Girl in the Piano Glade."

"Bye, Strat."

He turns to go, then swivels back, his eyes meeting mine one last time with searing intensity.

"Hey, Aria? I'm really glad you're real."

The color rises in my cheeks. I nod.

After his junky brown station wagon trundles out of the lot, I have to sit in my car for a long time before I'm steady enough to start the engine.

CHAPTER NINE

When I wake up on Saturday morning, I feel better than I have in a long time. Sure, I'm sharing dreams with a boy who lives thirty miles away, which is bizarre and mind-melting, but it's also . . . kind of incredible.

Last night's midnight with Strat was on a covered bridge dripping with wisteria, purple light soaking everything and petals falling on his hair. I could hardly keep my composure, walking beside him on the endless bridge, elbows grazing every now and then, trying to act like I wasn't aching for another kiss like the one on top of the castle.

In a haze, I float to the kitchen table and sit down to the breakfast of champions: Fruity Pebbles and watching reels on my phone.

I zone out as the videos play, but my attention is snagged by a name I see referenced over and over. *Have you heard about Delilah Lane?* I must have missed something big. Delilah Lane's eighteen and the breakout star of a big Netflix series. I type in her name and click on the most popular post: *Delilah Lane erased her ex, and here's why you should too!*

Delilah's in her bathroom, no makeup, zit cream dotted on her forehead. I turn the volume up.

"I've been getting a lot of questions about why I made this decision," she says, staring straight into the camera, her eyes limpid blue pools. "And I'm glad we're talking about it. It's not like it has to be some big secret. I know that I dated him, I can't get the entire internet to erase that. There are pictures and articles everywhere. But the point is—and this is what's so beautiful about it—I don't have to remember any of the behind-closed-doors moments. So you can remind me about him as much as you want; it doesn't bother me. I got my erasure so no baggage has to come with me into my next relationship. ArEx forever, baby!" She flashes a peace sign and sticks her tongue out.

The comments are divisive, ranging from her fans supporting her—*Luv u Delilah!* and *Such an empowered choice!*—all the way to someone preaching: *You shouldn't erase a relationship even if it was bad. U learned something important and you'll devolve if you erase that.*

I back out of it and settle into the comfort of my FYP. The sun streams in through the back-door window, warm on my face.

Something about the sunlight sends my thoughts floating.

A scene forms in my mind's eye: Strat, sitting next to me on a blanket on a dewy lawn, in a plaid shirt that makes him look so soft and warm I want to nuzzle up to him and live tucked by his side forever. The shirt is woven in soft shades of raspberry and lilac, and it complements the dusty rose of my dress perfectly.

The sun rises behind him, flickering through the leaves of a tree over us like an artsy photo reel.

His eyes sparkle mischievously. "You know, this is the second time you've kept me out all night, and I only met you four days ago. I'm starting to think you might be a bad influence."

"Oh, I am absolutely a bad influence."

The teasing humor softens into something more sincere. "Seriously, though, I'm glad we stayed out. I couldn't bear to say goodnight."

"Me neither," I say, so soft only he can hear it. My body is full to bursting with—*everything*.

He leans in. A moment before his mouth touches mine, I press a palm to his heartbeat.

"I've never kissed anyone before," I whisper.

"Well, then." He brushes the tip of my nose with his. "We'd better make this stratospheric."

And then his parted lips touch mine, exquisite dizziness sliding through me at the softness, and then we're kissing, kissing, kissing. His hands come up to touch my face, and mine are running over his shoulders, over the raspberry-and-lilac plaid. It's so soft, and my hands are as hungry as my mouth.

My spoon clatters to the table, and the daydream scatters.

I stare wide-eyed at the wall, heart pounding, head buzzing. What the hell was that?!

I press my hands over my eyes, letting out a shaky breath. My daydreams don't usually feature quite that much dialogue. When I daydreamed about Strat in art, it was safe, because I didn't know he was real. Now kissing him *is* a real possibility. And adjusting to that paradigm shift is . . . a lot.

I take my bowl to the sink, then head for my room. Maybe a shower will loosen the ball of heat that's suddenly lodged in my chest.

I'm halfway down the hallway when I freeze.

Wait.

That shirt Strat was wearing—

My stomach drops out from under me.

I tear through my house. Run up the stairs, yank open my closet door, dig through clothes, clothes, clothes. Hangers screech. Piles of sweaters fall to the floor.

I've seen that shirt before. Last week I was rummaging through the back of my closet for my summer sandals, and when I saw it, I didn't think anything of it, even though I knew it wasn't mine. I thought maybe Cady had bought it, although it wasn't her style and I'd never seen her wear it.

I start trembling the moment my fingers close around the fabric.

No. It can't be possible.

I lift the shirt.

Raspberry-and-lilac plaid. Exactly what Strat was wearing when he kissed me on the dewy grass in my—

The world tilts on its axis.

Oh God.

They weren't just daydreams. That dizzy kiss on the dewy field, the soft touch of his lips to my cheek on the porch, him playing piano in the rotunda at homecoming—none of those were daydreams.

They were *memories.*

CHAPTER TEN

I lie on the floor of my closet, clutching the raspberry-and-lilac shirt to my collarbone.

This can't be happening.

Finding out Strat was real threw off my balance, but this . . . this feels like something precious has been ripped from me. I'd just gotten used to the midnights, and I'd finally accepted that he'd be there for all of them. I'd decided that I *wanted* him to be there. Now I have to reframe everything again.

Memories . . . I think of the Aracen Exradere buildings all over Sacramento. Delilah Lane's video. A television jingle starts playing in my mind. The commercials were all over TV when I was little. Big beaming smiles, doctors patting old ladies on their shoulders. *Enhanced targeted proton beam therapy. One hundred percent effective and one hundred percent safe. Ask your doctor about it today!*

The pieces finally click into place.

I erased him.

I erased him I erased him I erased him.

I press the shirt over my face to scream into it, but then the shadowy scents of pine and cinnamon buzz their way into the bones behind my ears. Short, sharp clips of memory hit, a reel almost too quick to process.

There I am, strolling with my hand tucked casually into Strat's, marveling at the newness of the feeling, the simple sweetness of it.

There he is, staring intently at me, leaning over a pristine white tablecloth. We're so deeply lost in each other that the restaurant around us may as well not exist.

There's his face, close to mine—so close—and my fingers are running through his hair.

His face again, in softer, bluer light. He's over me this time, the ceiling beyond, curls brushing against my temple, his eyes wide and a little scared and full of love.

In my chest, this feeling —

Building, building, building.

Love love love—

I scream.

I stagger up out of my closet. This can't be happening. It's impossible. I pace between my bed and Cady's, hyperventilating.

Strat and me. We were together. And judging by how many images just flooded my head, it wasn't for a short time, and it wasn't a casual thing.

I feel so stupid. The dots were all there, I just didn't connect them.

I erased him.

An erasure. I can't believe I've had one. Gingerly, I touch my head, as if I can feel the proof of it in some tangible way. Part of me feels stupid for not realizing it, but of course I couldn't have known. It's not like true amnesia, where entire months are blank. With ArEx erasures, only a specific person or event is surgically excised. And any moments where you're talking about them to others.

So of course I remember everything else—Thanksgiving and Christmas and every boring unremarkable day at school—just not him.

My head throbs. I have to tell him.

Normally it would take me forever to compose the perfect first text to someone, but I pull out my phone and dash out the words without giving them a second thought.

It's me, Aria. Can you meet me today?

He replies almost immediately. I can almost see his wry grin when he responds.

Not what I guessed your texting style to be. But sure. I can be back at Ron's this evening.

Not Ron's. There's a library about a mile from it. It stays open late.

My head starts to ache. There are too many questions ping-ponging around in my skull. How did I get an erasure? I can summarize all the rules about ArEx erasures: Parents can't erase their children unless the children are dead, and vice versa; kids can erase their parents if they make their case in a family court and are awarded legal emancipation; no erasures under eighteen without parental consent.

Would my parents really have consented to this? Did they drive me to ArEx and home again after? Surely not. I can't imagine their being on board with that. My head is spinning.

Wait—there's an even bigger question I should be asking: Why are my memories coming back? That shouldn't happen. I've never heard of anyone recovering the erased parts of their pasts.

I flip open my laptop and type in a search.

memory erasure gone wrong why can i remember

The results blare up on the screen. It's all trash; a handful of sensational gossip rag articles and websites regurgitating the same material. MY MEMORY ERASURE FAILED. Or even more clickbaity: ALABAMA MOM'S MEMORY ERASURE GOES WRONG— YOU'LL NEVER BELIEVE WHAT HAPPENED NEXT. Finally I find one scholarly article from the NIH determining that erasures are indeed as safe and effective as they claim.

Memories coming back are not a thing that happens. Except to me, apparently.

I don't understand. I couldn't have had an erasure without parental consent. Memory erasures are the second most common elective surgical procedure these days, only slightly less popular than boob jobs, and thousands are performed every day, but it's very hard to get one done as a minor. Unless . . .

Unless there's been some horrific trauma.

*　*　*

The moment I step into the library, the smell of sun-warmed books and nylon carpet envelops me. It should soothe me, but I'm too wound up to be soothed. I have to resist all those small things about Strat that I was starting to find charming, because he could have done something awful. It's an insidious thought, slithering through everything. All the horrific reasons for erasing him I can imagine—and my mind has been cycling through *dozens*—coil in my stomach.

My phone pings with a text from Strat.

> Just got to the library—assuming you wanted to research some more stuff about shared dreams, so I'm by the New Age/Occult shelf in the back right corner.

I navigate around the shelves until I find him. He stands as soon as he sees me. I falter at the sweetness of that small, chivalrous gesture.

"Hey, you," he says, all warmth and that loose, easy grin.

It feels so familiar, standing in front of him. We must've stood like this dozens of times before. It occurs to me—in most of those instances, the next thing we would have done was kiss hello. That's why kissing him on the castle roof came so naturally, and that's why it felt so electric in the roller rink. Why it feels so electric now. My mind doesn't remember him, but my body is screaming, *It's you it's you it's you.*

"You're not in your blazer," I say stupidly.

He glances down. "Oh—yeah. It's Saturday." He frowns. "Are you okay?"

I'm suddenly frustrated with myself. It must seem to him like I'm always in the middle of an emotional meltdown. Seventeen years with very little drama, and then it all hits at once.

"Let me take your bag," he says. "And maybe sit down—you look a little pale."

I slide into the chair he holds out for me.

He could be dangerous. He could have hurt me.

According to the ArEx website, even when memory cells are destroyed, the *emotions* connected to the memories persist. Like if someone had been abused, they'd still feel uncomfortable around the person who hurt them. If they'd been best friends, the feeling of warmth and ease and laughter would still be there.

Looking at Strat now, I feel a thousand different emotions all at once, tangled up. I don't think I feel danger, or *fear*, but how can I trust myself? I can't remember an entire relationship.

"Aria? What's going on?" He keeps his voice low, glancing at the librarian who's restocking shelves a few yards away.

I blow out a breath. "Strat, I've been having these . . . what I thought were daydreams. About you."

A flicker of amused light jumps into his eyes. "That doesn't sound like a bad thing, Girl in the Piano Glade." My panicked, unblinking stare doesn't shift, and his smile drops. "Sorry. Go on."

"It turns out they weren't daydreams at all." I pull my bag onto my lap, unzip it. Draw out the plaid shirt. "This is yours, right?"

He blinks. Frowns. "Yes—but how . . . ?"

"In one of my daydreams, you were wearing this. And something about it felt familiar, so I ran up to my closet. I had to upend the whole place, but I found it."

I stare at him, waiting for the pieces to click. He doesn't lift his eyes from the shirt.

"It means it wasn't a daydream. It was real. I think I *erased* you, Strat."

I see the moment it sinks in. He goes very still. Maybe he thinks I'm full of crap, or that he's gotten himself wrapped up with someone who's seriously deranged, and he's trying to figure out how he can get away from me.

"Strat?"

"Sorry. Just processing. It's a lot to take in." He rubs at his temples. "I've been having some weird daydreams too, but—"

"You have?"

"I mean, you're gorgeous. You're a Godward," he says, lifting his hands helplessly. "I thought I was just . . . you know. Fantasizing."

I blush scarlet.

He drags a hand over his mouth. "But you're saying maybe those were actually *memories*? From us before?"

"How else could I have your shirt?"

He shakes his head in disbelief, letting out a curse. The librarian glances over, and he looks chastened, angling himself in closer to me.

My mind is working. "Okay. So you erased me too. We erased each other."

"This makes no sense," he says. "Wouldn't we have needed our parents to sign off on it? I'm not eighteen yet."

"Me neither."

"I guess we could have forged the signatures. Or maybe we drove across the border?"

"Is that a thing?" I ask.

"I mean, I assume so. You can get other surgeries done that way, right?" He thinks for a moment. "Aria, how much do you think an erasure costs?"

"I have no idea. Is it the sort of thing insurance covers?" It's not something my parents would have paid for unless it was necessary. Especially my accountant dad, who's always been cautious with money.

I drop my head onto my arms. "You must think I'm unhinged."

"Aria, we've been having co-op dreams while asleep in bedrooms thirty miles apart. I don't think it's crazy that we had an erasure. That's the least crazy thing out of all this. I drive past an ArEx every day on my way to school."

"But Strat—the memories coming back—it's not a thing that happens. I googled it."

He frowns. "Not to anyone? Not even a tiny percentage, an unexpected side effect?"

"Nope. It just doesn't happen."

He stares at the table, deep in thought.

"Do you think this is why we're meeting in the midnights?" I ask. "Did something go wrong during our procedures that, like, tied us together somehow?"

He tugs his fingers through his hair. "That . . . might be the most plausible idea we've thrown on the table so far."

He shifts, and his knee brushes mine under the table. I'm so on edge that it makes me audibly gasp. Touching him—it's like lighting a match in an apartment with a gas leak.

"Whoa," he says, reaching out to steady me.

I flinch away from his hands. Tears prickle at the corners of my eyes. I wish I could rewind, forget that I ever googled his name, forget that I ever found his shirt in my closet. We could have just enjoyed our midnights. Enjoyed whatever this insane chemistry is. How much of it was there at the very beginning, and how much of this is something we built together?

"I hate this, Aria," he says softly. "I can feel you shutting down on me."

"I'm sorry," I whisper. "I have to be smart."

Understanding dawns on his face. "Oh. You think something bad happened. You think . . . I did something?"

"Maybe. I don't really know you."

He looks pained. "Aria, I would never—"

"How can you know that for sure? I've seen us kissing a few times, but who knows how long we were together, or how it ended?"

"Maybe it wasn't anything I did. What if it was you, or something outside of our control?"

I drop my head to the table and groan. "I wish we could go back to yesterday. Can't we just start over? Ignore whatever happened in our past?"

As soon as I say it, I realize how stupid and dangerous it sounds. Like something Cady would be mad at a character on a TV show for.

I should probably tell him we can't see each other again. The old Aria wanted to erase him, and she would have had to sign dozens of forms declaring it. I should respect that. I should trust her decision and say goodbye to this boy right now.

But the thought of walking away from him hurts in a way I don't expect. Somehow it feels deeply . . . *wrong*.

"What do we do?" I ask helplessly. I'm so torn. This feels like such a mess, and my feelings are so muddled and chaotic, and—

"Aria. Please. Look at me. Hey, Girl in the Piano Glade."

I shake my head, unable to meet his eyes. "It's too much."

He finally catches me, locks me into his serious, steady stare. He asks, very quietly, "Aria. The memories—did they seem good?"

My vision blurs. "Yes. They seemed good, Strat," I say softly. "Really good." Like a fairy tale. Like the kind of love story I've always wanted.

"Mine were really good too, Aria."

I take a breath. Maybe it's foolish, but I'm desperate to see more of them. Our history. The flashbacks have all been glittering, intoxicating. Addictive.

"I want to see more," I whisper. "I want to see what happened, before."

Strat nods, holding my gaze. "Me too."

I want our midnights. I don't know what they are, or how they're happening, but I can't lose them.

This too, being so near to him . . . I want more time with him. Even if it means steeling myself to face this instead of running away from it or sticking my head in the sand.

Maybe the only way back is . . . through.

"There's just one problem," Strat says. "*How* are we going to figure out what happened?"

The question feels unanswerable.

"We could look for more evidence of our previous . . . relationship," I say unsteadily. "I found your shirt in my closet. Maybe there's more, at our houses or in our deleted photos or something."

He nods. "And maybe our friends know something?"

"Maybe." But I feel miles apart from the volleyball girls. How much would they even know? How much would I have shared with them, with Strat and I going to different schools?

"I can try to figure out how much my dad knows," Strat says, "but I can't imagine I would have kept him looped in. He's . . . I just don't normally talk to him about what's going on with me, especially about relationship stuff."

I try to imagine asking my parents about it, but a lump rises in my throat. I can try, though.

His eyes widen suddenly. "Aria—I got a new phone a few months ago. Not just a phone but a new number too. All my social media accounts had been deleted. I thought it was a hack or something, but maybe it was part of us erasing each other?"

This is wild. The exact same thing happened to me. I tell him as much.

"So that's somewhere else we can look for answers." Strat pulls a notebook out of his backpack and starts writing a list.

1. Search our houses
2. See if we can recover anything—photos, texts—from our old phones
3. Wait for more memories to come back

I touch my finger to the third step of the plan. I guess it's the most accurate way to get the whole story, in vivid detail.

"It shouldn't be hard to confirm when we had the erasures, right?" I ask. "There'll be records, paperwork, bills and stuff?"

He pulls the notebook back. "That can be number four, then."

4. Find proof of erasure procedure. When did we do it?

He tears the page out and hands it to me. "See? We can handle this, Aria."

I stare down at the list. A plan. Steps to take, a puzzle we can solve. So why do I still feel like my life is going off the rails?

CHAPTER ELEVEN

On the drive home, I'm shaky. Spaced out. Other drivers honk their horns at me more than once for going twenty miles under the speed limit.

The dreams, the memories, the erasures—it's too much. I'm trying to handle this all on my own, and it's awful, because for the first seventeen years of my life, I was never alone.

There's an urge rising in me that terrifies me. I want to tell someone about Strat. And not just any someone.

I want to tell my sister.

It's in that moment, in that chest-tightening onslaught of *need*, that the car speakers ring with an incoming call.

Mom.

I have to answer her. I've been avoiding her too much lately, texting every day with some story about how I need to stay late after school, and every night pretending to be asleep when she looks into my room when she gets home.

The call connects, and I stumble through a few minutes of surface conversation about my fake group project meeting. I keep my answers short so she doesn't catch on that I basically snuck thirty miles away to meet up with a boy I don't know.

A boy I really do know.

"So you're on your way home now?" Mom asks.

"Yep."

"Well, I'll probably be here until around seven." She's quiet for a moment. "You really should come by today, Aria. It's been a while since you've seen her."

Eight days, I almost say. But we both know exactly how long it's been.

For a long, terrible moment, I can't speak. And then it all rises up in me, unstoppable after eight days of keeping it all bottled up. *I want to talk to my sister.*

"Okay," I say. "I'll head there now."

It makes my heart hurt to hear the extra buoyancy in Mom's voice as she plans what to get us for dinner.

I grip the wheel harder and steer into the left lane to do a U-turn. Instead of going home, I head for the hospital.

Thirty minutes later, I'm at my sister's bedside, watching her monitors track her heartbeat as the sun sets in the wide California sky.

Last week I overheard a nurse talking about how unsettling it was to see someone who looked exactly like the patient sitting vigil at her bedside, like a spirit peeled from a body. But there's nothing supernatural about it: Cady and I are identical twins. Of course I look like the girl in the bed.

The central fact of my existence—the thing I expend so much time trying to avoid thinking about, the black hole at the heart of me—here it is:

My twin sister is in a coma.

"Hey, Sleeping Beauty," I say quietly. I reach out to brush her hair from her temples, but my fingers curl back before I can make contact. It's hard to touch her. It makes it all more real. I know what her skin will feel like—a degree too cool, sticky with the clamminess that comes from three months of sponge baths and dry shampoo.

I glance at the whiteboard over her head, where her neurologist scrawled her name and basic info in green dry-erase marker: *Cadence Lendell—"Cady"—17—loves volleyball—Cerebral AVM.*

Three months ago, I had no idea what AVM stood for, but now I know it means arteriovenous malformation. A blood vessel defect in the brain. When I looked up pictures of it on my phone, the results were horrifying: Most of the veins webbing over our brain are thin and elegantly formed, but an AVM is like a tangled lump of overcooked spaghetti sitting on the surface, swelling and swelling and waiting to pop. Cady's doctors said she'd had the defect from birth, and that there would have been no way to tell it was there until it ruptured. Which it did, spectacularly. And when there's bleeding in the brain, it messes with important things like intracranial pressure and oxygen levels, and brain cells start to die. The surgeons operated on her for hours, then kept her in the ICU for five days. When they took her off the drugs that were keeping her in a medically induced coma, she didn't wake up.

She was supposed to wake up.

When I reach to tug Cady's blanket up over her shoulder, the skin on the left side of my body tugs tight. I've never been able to stretch fully on that side, thanks to the thick line of scar tissue that never quite grew as long as the rest of me. Before we were born, Cady and I were connected by more than just DNA: we shared blood and flesh too. We weren't really conjoined twins, medically speaking, but our skin had fused together, under the left side of my rib cage and under her right. The doctors said they'd never seen anything like it before. Just skin. No organs, no veins, no nerves.

It meant that we got lifted gently into the world instead of coming out in the usual squalling, violent push. Ten minutes later, the doctor severed the bridge of skin between us, cauterizing the place where we'd been connected. Burning my sister off me.

For the first thirteen years, even though we weren't physically connected anymore, Cady and I were the kind of twins people wanted to peel apart, just to see if one of us would start gasping for air as the gap between us widened. We slept in the same bed until we were nine, scar to scar. At that point, our parents gently suggested that people might think it was weird. Sleepover invitations were rolling in, and they bought us two separate sleeping bags, *Frozen* and *Tangled*, even though with our dark brown hair we look more like Belle on a bad hair day. We resisted at first, but what the world thinks of you seeps into everyone eventually. Sometimes it feels like it's been trying to force Cady and me apart our whole lives, but nothing has been as painful as this separation. For the first time, she's gone somewhere I can't follow.

The urge to tell her about Strat looms in my chest. I slide a chair close to the bed, but now that I'm here, the words catch in my throat. What am I supposed to say? *I met someone?*

Suddenly it feels wrong to tell Cady about the gorgeous places I've been going in my sleep, about the knee-melting memories and the midnight kisses and how much I want to kiss the real-life version of Strat.

Guilt swarms thick in my chest. I shouldn't be feeling these things right now. I shouldn't be daydreaming *or* night dreaming about a boy. Not while my sister is in a coma.

I flinch when a nurse bustles in, as if she can see my turmoil written all over my face. The nurse is followed by my mom, who's talking about a faulty light switch. *Not really the nurse's job, Mom,* I think, but she's become best friends with everyone who works on this floor and it'll probably be fixed by morning.

Something in me relaxes a little now that she's here, though. Mom's in a swimming-pool-blue coordinated yoga set and has her hair in a slick, high ponytail. Another mom might be a puffy-eyed wreck, barely scraping through the days, but not Meredith Lendell. It's not that she's untouched by the gravity of the situation—I saw her stunned fear during those five days that Cady was in the ICU. And then I saw her decide to buckle down and manage it as if it were a challenging business project to tackle.

When she sees me, she brightens. Comes over to press a quick kiss to the top of my head. "Glad you're here," she murmurs.

Later, after night has fallen outside the windows and whatever courage I brought with me to face this place starts to wear thin, the sequoia forest dream pushes its way back into my mind. Wouldn't it be nice if I could slide into it, so I wouldn't have to be here with all these ugly smells and sounds and sights?

Something in me loosens at the thought. Starts to drift.

Escape.

Immediately, I feel like a horrible sister. I don't deserve to flitter off to some dreamland when the most important person in the world to me is barely hanging on to her life. In my pocket, my fingers close tight around the double penny, feeling traitorous for that brief, intense desire to desert her. She would never leave me if I were the one in that bed.

I trace the ridge of scar tissue on my rib cage. I was born stitched to someone, and sometimes I wonder if whatever I had with Strat was just me trying to stitch myself to someone new.

CHAPTER TWELVE

There's only one low light on in the kitchen when I let myself in the back door. As I turn the deadbolt to lock out the night, I pause for a moment. Dip my forehead to rest on the cool glass. Anything to stop my reeling, scattered thoughts. I feel like a different Aria from the one who left the house this morning to drive to the library to meet Strat.

The only way back is through, I remind myself. Time to start searching for answers. We have to figure out what's going on.

I start with my laptop, running searches for the words *Strat* and *Madigan* and *boyfriend*, to see if they appear in any files. Then I move to my phone, combing through my texts for numbers or names I don't recognize.

Nothing.

I paw through my drawers, through piles of dried-up markers and stacks of half-full notebooks. I lift my corkboard off the wall to check the back. For a split second, I'm sure that I'll find an envelope taped there, but there's nothing.

When I put the corkboard back on the wall, I narrow my eyes. The photos look . . . more spaced out than usual. I lift a fingertip, tracing a paler square of exposed cork. Maybe there was something here before. A picture of Strat?

My parents both sleep like rocks, but I still pull on my thickest pair of socks before tiptoeing down the dark stairs to Mom's office. She started working from home only a few years ago, but the towering gray metal filing cabinet has stood tall in the corner for as long as I can remember.

The bottom drawer screeches on its rails when I tug it open. I cringe at the sudden noise, crouching in the darkness, but no one comes.

There are folders labeled MORTGAGE, TAXES, CAR, LIFE INSURANCE. I silently thank my mother's impeccable sense of organization. Finally I find one labeled MEDICAL—GIRLS and pull it out.

It's fat, bursting at its seams. The first document in the file is a hospital bill from our C-section birth. I have to stop for a minute, holding this piece of our history. I run a fingertip over my own name, *Aria Louise Lendell*, and then over hers, *Cadence Marie Lendell*.

I didn't know that our first names were musical terms until I was in middle school and the trend of the week was to look up your name's meaning. When I asked Mom about it, she shrugged and said she just thought they were pretty names. My parents aren't musically talented, and they passed their ineptitude on to Cady and me. Sometimes I wonder if some other babies deserved these lilting, musical names.

Strat liked my name, my mind whispers.

I set the form gently back where it belongs and flip the whole file folder over. If it's chronological, I need to start from the back.

For a while, there is only the whisper of paper and the low chirp of the crickets outside the window. But it doesn't take long to realize that there's nothing here about an erasure. I rifle through the middle drawer, then the top one.

It's not here. There's no proof of Strat in my room, and no proof in this filing cabinet that I erased him.

Nothing, nothing, nothing.

I slump back to the floor, shoving the folders away from me with a resentful push of my foot. I've fallen at the first hurdle, *again*. Even when it's something as small as finding a form, I don't want to keep trying if I think deep down I won't succeed.

Wait—if I had an erasure that my parents knew about, there would be proof here in Mom's office.

Which means they don't know about it. I have no idea how I got around the age limit, but now I'm *sure* I got an erasure without their knowledge.

It tracks: Mom's never been a big fan of the procedure outside of psychologist-recommended situations, and everything Dad's ever said about it makes me think he's morally against it. They would have never driven me down to ArEx and signed the papers.

So much for asking my parents about Strat. Maybe I can figure out a way to phrase the question that won't tip Mom off that I got an erasure, but if I make a misstep, I'll be in huge trouble. My parents are reasonable, and they trust Cady and me with a lot of stuff, but even they would draw the line at something against the law.

If I kept it a secret from her, I must have had a reason.

I clean up the files and tiptoe back up to my bedroom. Cady's stuffed seal stares unblinkingly at me from her bed.

"I know, Sealy," I sigh. "Believe me, I know."

There's not a shred of proof of my relationship with Strat left in here—on *my* side of the room.

It feels as if Cady's side is frozen in time, like there's a layer of dust settling onto everything, but when I swipe a finger over her bedside table, it comes up clean.

I slide down to kneel in front of Cady's bedside table. I pull out the bottom drawer and start pawing through a tangle of junk, mostly stuff we've had since we were little kids. Stretchy plastic necklaces, fidget spinners, a few of her favorite paperbacks about a group of girls in a horse club.

I'm not sure what I'm hoping for. A diary with all the answers I'm seeking? A single sentence with The Why? All the gory details laid out neatly, like: *Dear diary, Aria decided to erase her hot boyfriend today because he turned out to have the world's largest collection of Cabbage Patch Kids in his basement and he changes their diapers every day.*

There's nothing in her desk but school supplies and half-empty notebooks. Nothing in her dresser but clothes, even though my fingers were hoping to bump up against a hidden box of photos or the cold metal of a diary key.

Her backpack hangs on the back of the door. I take it down and pull out two brick-heavy textbooks: *Physics* and *AP US*

History. Here's her beach-themed pencil case, three flattened protein bars, a handful of spare hair ties. Her school-issued planner, the one with the cougar on the front, sharp teeth bared and ready to pounce.

My fingertips pause on the planner. A premonition, like a whisper over a grave. I had an identical planner, I'm sure. I remember sketching dress designs in its margins. But the one I've been using lately is purple and glittery. I don't remember throwing the old one away. It would have had mentions of Strat. So what happened to it?

I pull Cady's planner out and lay it open on her bed. The spiral binding creaks. Her bubbly, ultra-neat handwriting fills the weeks. The volleyball games stand out: *Ridgecroft Cougars vs. Camelot Gators*. I flip to October. She's written *HOMECOMING* in 3D block letters, surrounded by black and gold stars. After seeing the flashback of Strat at the piano in the rotunda, I know he was there that night, but there's no note about it in Cady's planner.

Halfway through November, the sad faces start appearing. They are pinkie-nail small, always at the bottom right corner of the days. Just two little dots for eyes and a downturned curve for a mouth.

Was she marking the days when she felt down? It doesn't make sense; the Cady I know is confident and resilient.

I turn through the pages, searching. The sad faces persist through November and December. On Christmas Day, there's a happy face. It's the only one.

And then, written next to the sad face on the corner of

December 29, in tiny writing I have to turn the planner on its side and squint to make out:

she's with S again ugh

I go still. The sad faces . . . could those have been the days I was with Strat?

Did she . . . not like him?

My thoughts churn. Something's not right here.

I hug Sealy to my chest. The world seems to warp, this one new piece of information reshaping the history of me and Strat, giving new context to everything else.

I sit there for a long time, staring at the words, feeling more confused than ever.

CHAPTER THIRTEEN

This time, my bed has been replaced by something colder and harder than dirt. White marble seamed with glittering veins of silver. I press myself up from the floor only to find myself hemmed in on both sides by towering walls, rising up to meet an impossibly high ceiling. No, not walls—

Bookshelves.

I dash to the end of the row and gasp. It's never-ending. Row upon row upon row, stretching into darkness.

What *are* these dreams? How are they happening? It's hurting my head to think about.

Instead of spines in muddy leather tones, the books are bound in pastel pinks and purples and blues. To my delight, dust motes float in the air. There's no moon here, but the blurry little flecks glow with the ultraviolet light I've come to associate with the dreams. I try to catch one on my fingertip, but it disappears without a sensation when it touches my skin.

Enchantment swells in my chest. This is a midnight made just for the little girl inside me, the one who watched *Beauty and the Beast* so many times I lost count.

It's as silent as velvet between the shelves.

"Strat?" I call out warily.

"Aria! Over here!"

I follow his voice through a twisting maze of shelves. It's still unnerving. Every night, without fail. Me and him and this purple-blue light. This impossible, inexplicable connection.

When I round the corner and see him, I wait for the nerves to hit like they did at the roller rink, but it's easier to look at him here, like whatever's connecting us in this place gets fuzzy having to travel over the miles between our sleeping bodies.

Only now I can't unsee those tiny words: *She's with S again ugh.*

Strat glances down at me. The scar by his eyebrow is a hazy smudge once again. I seem to forget how tall he is—every time I see him, I'm surprised all over again by it. "Everything okay?" he asks, frowning.

"Yep! Fine." I bite down on the urge to tell him what was written in my sister's planner. I don't even know if S is him.

"Did you find anything at your house?" he asks.

"Nope," I say. It's mostly the truth. One cryptic sentence isn't a clue to our past, no matter how sharp it feels under my skin. "What about you?"

"Nothing," he says, sighing. "I spent an hour on hold with my phone company, only to be told there was no way I could recover anything from my old phone without actually *having* my old phone."

We fall into step. The midnight is tugging me into that place of blurry peace, and I run my fingertips over the books as we walk. "Do you have a library like this?" I ask.

"What do you mean?"

"You probably have a really big house, right?"

He frowns, his eyebrows knitting together, and for the first time with him, I get the feeling I've said something wrong.

I turn my attention to the pastel spines, fumbling for a way to step out of the awkward moment. "Do you recognize any of these?"

"I don't think so." He searches the shelves. "Wait—this one. I think I read this one when I was in middle school. And this one here—this used to be one of my dad's favorites."

"Used to be?"

He swallows. "He doesn't read anymore. When I was little, he'd have stacks and stacks of books all over the house. Poetry, murder mysteries, sci-fi, whatever."

The conversation feels like it's stepping out onto thin ice. Whatever's weaving around us in these strange liminal spaces, it has real power if it's got me asking follow-up questions.

"You said your dad was . . . having a hard time," I say carefully.

"Yeah." He pauses, just a beat. "The anniversary of my mom's death is coming up, and it's always a hard time of year for him. Well, every time of year is hard, but this is worse."

Oh.

I wish fervently that I hadn't taken that step out onto this emotional ice. Now I really don't know what to say.

"It's fine," he says. "It's been twelve years, and I don't really remember much about her." He swallows, and I wonder how true that is. "I mean, it sucks. But it's okay now, for me. Dad, not so much."

"I think it's kind of lovely that your dad is still sad."

I'd like for someone to love me so much they're still wrecked twelve years after losing me.

"I guess it's better than jumping into the sack with someone a month later or whatever. I've always been kind of grateful I haven't had to deal with that. So yeah. Sad I can handle. But, like . . . twenty-four-seven wrecked? Kind of unhelpful, if I'm being honest. He probably should have been the one to get an erasure, not me."

These emotions lodge heavily in the air between us.

"God, this is so weird," Strat says, running a hand through his hair. "I *never* talk about my dad with anyone, and I've brought him up twice with you. There's something about these nights," he murmurs.

I know what he means. It's easier in here to be . . . honest.

We walk for a minute in a heavy silence.

Halfway down the next aisle, he touches my waist to move me a little to the left, studying the titles on the shelves. Even through the pressure of the midnight, it sends a tingling rush over my scalp, down my neck.

My instinct is to lean into it—but then I catch myself. *Don't be stupid, Aria.* I step away so he's not touching me. I catch the flicker of hurt and disappointment in his eyes.

Something in me withers. Three nights ago, I was ready to spend the rest of my life in a dream, kissing him as the world spun around us, and now I can't even let him touch me.

For the rest of the midnight, I make sure to keep just out of reach, and Strat doesn't smile again.

CHAPTER FOURTEEN

The cafeteria is a dull roar, a thousand voices bouncing off the hard tile floor. I scan the lunch lines for Tahirah and finally spot her at the back of the stir-fry line.

She grabs a tray when she sees me coming, passing it over with a smile. I ask her about last night's game, but the small talk peters out quickly, leaving us shuffling forward in the line in awkward silence. The question I really need to ask her—the reason I'm risking my digestive health on cafeteria stir-fry—is lodged in my throat.

All through second and third period, I struggled with how to phrase it. It's difficult when you don't know how much someone knows. Does Tahirah know I got an erasure? Were Strat and I even officially together? Maybe she doesn't know him at all; she might have seen him at homecoming, but all the other flash-backs have just been Strat and me alone.

I swallow. It's now or never. "Hey, T? Can I ask you something?"

"Sure, what's up?"

"That guy I was with last semester—I can't remember, did you ever meet him? Sorry if that's a weird question. Everything from before Cady's hospitalization is all a little jumbled."

Her brown eyes soften with sympathy. "That's totally understandable that things are shook up. It was a rough time. And yeah, I met Strat once or twice."

Okay. So she knows about him. She knows I was with him.

"Why not more often?" I ask. "Because he went to a different school?"

She shrugs. "I guess. You guys didn't really do stuff with the group. You were really into each other. Like, *really* into each other," she adds with a meaningful look.

My mortification must be splashed across my face, because she laughs and says, "I don't blame you, girl. He was cute AF."

I recover, picking my words carefully: "Do you remember that time I told you what happened between me and Strat, at the end?"

She frowns. "You didn't tell me. At least, I don't think you did," she says, trying to recall.

"Oh—I must be thinking of when I told Devyn or Britt," I say hastily.

"Mmm . . . I don't think you talked to any of us about it. We assumed something happened, obviously, and figured you'd called things off because you had so much to deal with once C was in the hospital and stuff."

"Um, yeah. That was it, basically."

We reach the front of the line and a lunch lady piles a lump of slimy gray noodles on Tahirah's plate. My thoughts spin. How does she not know anything? Were Strat and I really that removed, that wrapped up in each other? For the *whole* time we were together?

The fact that Tahirah doesn't even know I got an erasure is unsettling.

Lunch passes at a sloth's pace, me picking at my food while the volleyball girls talk nonstop. For once, the harsh buzz of the bell is a welcome sound.

This used to be one of my favorite parts of the day, walking from the cafeteria to the science wing on the other side of the campus, because it was one of the three times in my schedule that Dean and I passed in the wide tiled hallway.

My obsession with Dean started at the end of sophomore year, when I started helping Arissa with costumes for the spring play. Dean was a magnetic force onstage, and equally magnetic when he was off. He had his own little group who somehow seemed older and cooler than the rest of us.

Right on schedule, I spot Dean approaching with his regular cohort of friends. The sight of him in the hallways used to make me buzz with giddy energy. I hitch my backpack up, preparing for him to completely ignore me like he has every other time we've passed. But this time, when his roaming gaze glances over me, it stops. His eyebrows lift in recognition.

"Aria, hey."

I can only stare stupidly as the surging salmon stream of students carries me past him.

When it deposits me in the science hallway, I stop and lean

against the wall. Did Dean really just say hi to me? He's never talked to me before.

It's not the most outlandish thing that's happened to me recently, not by a long shot. But it's still deeply *bizarre.* I didn't think I could feel any more off-kilter, but that interaction has unbalanced me even more.

When I get to my desk in Mrs. Acosta's room, I pull out Cady's planner and stare at the small sad faces she penned in the margins. I don't know why I brought it with me today. Maybe to keep her near, or to remind me not to slip into any embarrassing daydreams about Strat.

I flip forward to this week. It's blank, of course. My own planner has a few scrawled assignments, and vines doodled along the borders. Proof of life. Cady's is empty, untouched since January first, the day she went to the hospital.

There is one page near the back, however, that's decorated wildly: Graduation Day. Cady clearly spent a lot of time on it. She's no artist, but the colors around the blocky GRADUATION! lettering pop, radiating her excitement.

A memory comes back to me—not the way the erased memories of Strat and me come back but just a normal memory that I've carried with me since I lived it.

It was last summer, and Cady and I were at our grandpa Dan's house, the one built on stilts on the North Carolina shore. We'd pulled our sleeping bags over to the big window at the back of the house. It's the most amazing part of having a twin: You always get to take your best friend on vacation with you, and every night is a sleepover.

"Hey," I whispered in the dark. "Remember that time we snuck downstairs in the middle of the night to play with our Shopkins?"

Cady shifted in her sleeping bag, instantly ready to play along. "I think it was maybe, like, nine-thirty, but yeah." She suddenly sat up, her hair matted on one side, mischief twinkling in her eyes. "Let's sneak down to the beach."

There was a little answering thrill of fear in me—we shouldn't, it might be dangerous—but when Cady got an idea, I could rarely resist. We giggled as we pulled on our flip-flops and unlocked the door.

The beach was beautiful at night. We slid off our shoes once we passed through the long beach grasses, then walked a little way down from the house. There was a storm off the coast—we could see the line in the sky where the dark sheets of rain started. The air smelled of rain and electricity.

"Man. Senior year," Cady said, flopping down to sit on the damp sand. "God, we're so old."

"I know. It's kind of gross, honestly."

"You excited for it, though? Being seniors?" Cady asked, burrowing her toes deeper in the sand.

My smile faded. "Sure, I guess."

It was a lie. All summer I'd been feeling more and more anxious. Something in me was railing against senior year, against graduation, against real life looming on the horizon. It was finally sinking in that everything was going to change. I would have to get tougher. Stop drifting along ineptly and start being an adult in a world that feels like it's on fire, and it felt unfair and terrifying.

I was scared, and I hated myself for my weakness.

"College is going to be amazing," Cady said, seemingly totally unaffected by the worries that clung to me.

Just the word *college* had the blood turning to acid in my veins.

Back when Cady and I were first researching colleges, I stumbled across the website for the Sciarra Fashion and Design Academy in Milan. As soon as the images loaded, I felt a bone-deep sense that I was looking at my future. They're one of the only schools that are open to more whimsical, fantastical creations, like the fairy-tale sketches I make on my tablet and the dresses I sew from those designs. I'd never been all that interested in haute couture, so when I saw that I could choose "Unconventional Wedding Dress Pattern-Making" as my capstone course at Sciarra, I fell in love.

Only problem? Cady didn't want me to apply.

It's the only thing I've ever done without telling her.

On the beach, I felt like a fraud—how could she not know? How could she not tell that every time she talked about our applications, it felt like a thousand needles were stabbing me all over?

"We'll be getting our letters soon," Cady said, oblivious to my inner tumult. "If we get into all three, I'm thinking we go to Sacramento State. But if we don't get in there, the volleyball team at Pepperdine is amazing. And then University of the Pacific in Stockton for our third choice, right?"

I swallowed hard. "Sure. Sounds good."

Images surged in my head: the Italian countryside, vineyard-laced hills, Milan, fashion, sewing gauzy conceptual fairy-tale dresses. I suppressed them.

"I might not get into Cal State or Pepperdine," I said. "My grades aren't your grades, Cady."

"Oh, don't worry," she said, waving a dismissive hand. "You'll get in."

The truth crawled up my throat, aching to be told. What if I just blurted it out? *I applied to Sciarra, and I want—*

A white-hot fork of lightning struck a mile out from shore. Another, another, until it became a whole light show playing out against the night sky, one electric fork every second.

"Wow," Cady whispered.

It was beautiful and surreal and felt like it was just for us. A warning to me, to keep my mouth shut about Sciarra.

The thunder growled overhead like a hungry belly.

"We should get back inside," I said warily, and for once she listened to me.

Our feet slipped in the sand as we climbed the dunes, barely outrunning the sheet of rain that pulled across the sky like a curtain. Back at the house, we zipped ourselves into our sleeping bags—the same ones we had when we were kids, Rapunzel and Elsa. Cady fell asleep quickly, but I stared into the dark, guilt writhing in me as I thought of my Sciarra application halfway across the world.

I swear I haven't always been an eavesdropper. But when it's your own parents, in the kitchen of your own house, I feel like you're entitled to stop at the bottom of the staircase, fingers tightening on the banister, barely breathing to keep your body still.

Especially when you hear the word *divorce* spoken by your mother in a clogged, weary voice.

A long silence follows.

Divorce.

The word sits there, growing heavier and heavier. It has its own gravity, like it's slowing down time.

I came down to ask Mom about Strat, stomach already heavy with nerves because that was an even harder question to frame than the one to Tahirah, and instead I'm getting . . . this.

A ceramic *clunk* as Dad puts down his coffee cup. "I don't know what to say, Meredith." His voice is shaky. "I don't know what you *want* me to say."

I feel the cracks running through the foundation of the house.

"Is this about those forms?" Dad's voice breaks on the last word, but I don't know what he's talking about.

"It's more than that, and you know it. Look," Mom says, sighing like she's never been so tired. "There's too much going on to be able to add lawyers and counseling and more paperwork into the mix. We don't have to do anything yet."

"But this is what's going to happen, is it?" Dad asks. "You've decided."

"Don't pin this all on me. You're miles away, Michael, and you have been for months. Maybe years. When shit gets hard, you just get further out of touch." Her voice cracks. "I need help here."

I know I'm not like Mom . . . but am I like Dad? I can't be. He doesn't have a creative bone in his body, and he lets Mom buy all his clothes, and he buries himself in work. Do *I* get further and further out of touch when things get hard?

"You're fine, though," he protests. "You have everything under control."

"I have to have it under control, because you're not doing anything! You didn't even go see her this week!" She reins it in, with effort, and when she speaks again, her voice is steady and low once more. "But I don't know why we're arguing about it. We can't do anything right now anyway. We can talk to a divorce lawyer when Cady gets better."

Divorce.

There it is again. The word I've been dreading. The word that splits families in two. Deep down, I think I knew it was coming.

Something dark and horrible crawls into my heart, and I feel like puking.

Divorce. Divorce. Divorce.

The shadow Mom's been casting into the hallway lengthens, and my heart jump-starts.

I am gone before she sees me.

Upstairs, I shut my bedroom door and sag down against it.

Crimson. Tangerine. Silver.

I press my eyes shut until the house is quiet and my eyes have stopped stinging.

It's nearly midnight, and suddenly all I want to do is dive headfirst into a dream and lose myself in it.

CHAPTER FIFTEEN

I come around sharply this time, ripping out of sleep and into the midnight on a gasp. I'm folded over a cold metal bar, staring at my bare feet, which are—

Dangling over a dizzying hundred-foot drop to the ground.

Adrenaline roars in my veins. I rear back and Strat's there, catching me, stabilizing me.

"It's okay, we're fine—Aria, we're safe," he says. "It's just a Ferris wheel."

Fingers still digging tight into his shoulders, I hazard a peek. He's right—we're at the top of a Ferris wheel in a red metal seat that's rocking back and forth from the force of my freak-out, suspended in an endless starry sky.

Now that I'm awake, it all floods back. The word *divorce*, spearing through my muscles, my heart.

Before I can control it, a strangled noise erupts from my throat.

Divorce divorce divorce—

I squeeze my eyes shut again. *Aquamarine. Prussian blue. Terra-cotta.*

"Is it the height? Aria?"

He must think I'm having a total meltdown. "It's—it's not the height," I manage to croak.

Divorce divorce divorce.

"What's wrong? Did I do something wrong?"

His arms around me feel like the only steady thing in the world, and, without thinking, I bury my face in his shoulder. I try to list more colors—*Charcoal. Magenta. Peach*—but a more effective distraction is tugging at my attention: the small circles Strat's rubbing on my back. I sink into them, my awareness shrinking down to the warm comfort of that small touch, settling every rattling fear in me somehow.

My breath finally slows. The fierce surge of adrenaline ebbs, and suddenly I become all too aware of how desperately I'm clinging to him. I wince, untangling myself. Self-consciously, I push my hair back from my face and try to make my hands stop shaking.

Strat looks a little bewildered. "Whoa. What was that?"

"I . . . I'm not—" I press my eyes closed again.

Normally I would offer some blithe response, anything to move past the moment. But in that strange way these dreams have, I feel the words burbling up out of me, unspooling from somewhere deep and dark inside me.

I tell him about what I overheard in the kitchen. About how my dad's been living in the garage for months. And I tell him about

Cady, because he doesn't know yet that I have a twin sister, or that she's in the hospital.

He listens quietly, never taking his eyes off me.

"Sorry I'm such a mess," I say quietly, once it's all out. "I just . . . suck when it comes to dealing with stuff that's difficult."

"It's no wonder," he says softly. "That's—holy shit, you've got a lot going on, Aria."

I look away sharply, clamping down on the tears that are threatening to come.

"I wish I wasn't like this," I whisper.

He's still got one arm around me, and those small circles are the only thing keeping me together. We're still wedged close together on the seat, and warmth radiates off him, soaking from him into me, thigh to knee.

I press my eyes closed. Did the midnight really have to strand us up here on this tiny chair, where I can't even put a full foot of space between our bodies?

"Guess the midnight didn't want us walking away from each other again," I say.

Strat smiles. "I find it a little disturbing that you think these dreams have intentions."

When I don't respond, he does a double take. "Wait—you're serious," he says. "*Do* you think they have intentions?"

I shrug. "How else would you explain the way the ground moved by the waterfall?"

These nights must be happening for a reason, right? I don't know what's pulling the strings, but it wants us here together.

A warning voice in my head cuts in, reminding me of the

words in Cady's planner. Strat and I erased each other for a reason.

I hate this. I hate feeling so confused, torn between being so thankful for how sweetly he handled my breakdown and trying to keep my defenses up. I want to sink into these midnights, into the warmth of the shoulder that's a few inches away from mine, without having to think about protecting myself.

We have to ramp up our efforts. Find out what happened to us before, so I don't have to feel so confused *now*.

"We should go to ArEx tomorrow, Strat. Try to get some answers."

"Sure. But Aria—have you noticed where we are?"

I was so busy having a meltdown that I didn't really *look* at the ground below us, or the city rolled out on the horizon. The streets look like a perfect little scale model. Jutting up from the neat grid of roads, the Eiffel Tower rises into the clouds.

"Paris," I whisper. I'm in the City of Love, and I'm a mess. I wonder what we'd be doing if I'd never googled Strat's name and found out he was real. He'd be tipping my chin up, and we'd be lost in each other, not a care in the world.

"I should have brought some champagne," Strat jokes, trying to cheer me up.

I smile weakly. "Is that a thing rich boys offer first dates? Private jet to Paris, champagne?"

Again, that almost imperceptible pause. "I imagine so."

I stare down at the streets of Paris. The city's beautiful, but there's something odd about it.

"It's so . . . still," I say.

Strat cocks his head, puzzled. "What do you mean?"

"I don't know. It's just . . . there's nothing extra. Like an impossible piano or shimmering gold mist in the water."

The words are barely out of my mouth when the first firework shoots up from the Champ de Mars with a high-pitched wail, bursting across the sky in streaks of blue and purple.

"Oh," I say, stupefied.

Three more fireworks pop, their sparks blooming in slow motion. They don't dissipate like normal fireworks; instead they layer over each other, blending into a blur of color and light until the whole sky is ablaze.

I jerk awake in my bed, plunged suddenly into darkness.

I stare up at my unremarkable bedroom ceiling as the afterimage of that flaring brightness fades. I can't shake the feeling that the midnights might have a . . . *personality*. They didn't like it when I said there wasn't anything extra, and decided to prove me wrong. Intentions . . . do the midnights have intentions? A goal? A *purpose*?

But that's absurd. I shake the thought away. It's bad enough that I'm meeting a boy in a dreamscape every night. I don't need an invisible sentient force in my life.

CHAPTER SIXTEEN

Strat and I stand on the sidewalk, staring up at the Aracen Exradere building. The mirror-like shard gleams in the afternoon sun.

"It looks like a piece broke off a spaceship and slammed into the earth," he says, propping his hip on a low decorative wall. As usual, he looks like a chiseled J.Crew model.

I hug my arms around me. I'm a little steadier than I was yesterday but it feels like I could unravel at any moment.

For a while, we just watch people coming and going.

"It really works, huh?" Strat says. "There's a big difference between the people going in and the ones coming out."

"It's so unsettling. Did we really do this?"

"We must have. But I'm still finding it hard to believe that I let someone go poking around in my brain with a laser."

"You know it's not really a laser."

"Close enough. Ready to go in?"

I sigh. "As I'll ever be."

It's awful of me to feel this way, but I'd rather be doing this than sitting in the hospital next door.

We shuffle through the revolving door and into a sunny, swanky atrium. The receptionists bustle around behind a huge ultramodern check-in counter, chatting to each other like friends. It feels like a trendy hotel lobby or an upscale coffee shop compared to Cady's ward, where the ceilings are low, the lights are harsh, and the staff's faces are all weary exhaustion.

I hover by the door, wondering if I really came here for a procedure. Shouldn't just being here trigger a memory? I concentrate, but nothing comes.

We join a line and wait for our turn to approach the reception desk. Off to one side, there's a whole area just for people who are considering the procedure. Attendants mill through, overly helpful, hoping to make a sell. I don't want to attract their attention, but I dart in long enough to snag a thick, glossy folder of information. I've been doing so much internet research on the erasure procedures, but there might be some new stuff here.

The Q&A flyers and colorful pamphlets inside are designed to convince customers to spring immediately for a service, but at the back, on plain photocopier paper, there's some technical information.

I've been wondering what happens when the proton beam hits a person's brain. Does it kill the cells that store specific memories? I have this image of laser blasters destroying asteroids, but memory storage must be more complicated than that. Can a single tiny particle of your gray matter really hold a specific scene from your memory?

Or maybe the procedure is more like placing a roadblock in my mind, and now my memories are pushing through the block and fighting their way back to me. That seems more plausible, but I did get a C in science last year. And the year before.

As we inch closer to the front of the line, I sift through the materials. I learn that it's not a block; tiny individual brain cells are fried into nonexistence. So how are my memories coming back? Are our brains the only ones that can regenerate those cells, like roses blooming the summer after you were sure they'd died in a frost?

"Look at these prices, Aria," Strat says, pointing up at a digital board behind the desk.

"Yeah. There's no way I would have been able to afford this on my own. Strat," I whisper, catching his elbow, "these receptionists look really competent. This place is like Fort Knox—we'll never get them to tell us if we were here. We're minors."

He rolls his shoulders back, sliding into his breezy I'm-handsome-and-I-know-it mode. "Have you no faith in me?"

"Next, please," the receptionist calls cheerfully.

At the desk, we're met with a beaming smile. I study the receptionist's round, friendly face, searching for even the slightest sign that she recognizes me or Strat.

"Morning! How can I help today? Do you have an appointment for an erasure?"

"No—no appointment," Strat says. "I actually had an erasure a little while ago, and I need the date for some forms. Can you look that up for me?"

She tucks a strand of hair behind her ear. "Of course. What's your name?"

"Strat Madigan," he says, spelling it out for her.

"Date of birth?" she asks, poised to type it into her search.

I go still. Strat doesn't show any outward sign of panic, but I know we're caught.

"July the seventeenth, 2007," he says.

The receptionist glances up. She looks conflicted for a moment, her lips pursed. "I'm not really supposed to give you any information without a parent here, but since . . . oh, I guess it's okay, since you're not in the system at all."

"What does that mean?" Strat asks. "That we had it done at a different branch?"

"No, it's all one records system. Let me check the spelling and date of birth again."

She does, and comes up empty again.

"What about me? Aria Lendell," I say, giving her my birthday too.

"No . . . you're not in here either," she says, frowning. I feel her goodwill ebbing, like she's wondering if we're pranking her. "Are you sure you—"

Strat slides in smoothly. "That's really helpful to know—we've just been having some weird stuff going on and wondered if that would explain it, but I guess not!"

"Oh, I—"

"We really appreciate your looking into it," Strat says, all charm, and somehow he manages to get us out before the woman calls her colleagues over to interrogate us or threatens to call our parents for being little shits.

Out on the sidewalk, Strat shakes his head. "Well, I wasn't expecting that."

"I don't understand. There's nowhere else we could have gone."

An unsettling feeling edges into my belly. This whole thing is getting more and more impossible. I *know* we erased each other.

So *where* did we do it?

When I get home, it's such a beautiful night that I stop for a second on my front steps, keys in hand.

The moon is a half-coin of silver-white light in the sky. Compared with the moons in our midnights, it looks small and hard, but there's still something wild and mystical about it.

When I lean back against the porch's wooden post, the peachy hairs on my cheek rise and a buzzing starts up in my temple.

I'm propelled back into the memory I saw in art—when Strat and I were here on the porch and he brushed the softest kiss on my cheek. I was leaning against this very post.

But this time, there's more.

He leans down. His kiss on my cheek is a warm press and sends tingles skittering through my whole body. He hovers there for a beat.

I shiver as his mouth skims to my ear. Shiver again when he murmurs, "Goodnight, Aria."

He withdraws, and I nearly stumble forward with the magnetic pull.

"I hope you had a good homecoming," he says.

"I had the best homecoming."

"Call me soon, okay?" Gently he takes my wrist, turns it over. Runs his thumb along the ten digits he printed there earlier with a Sharpie.

"You know I could have just put your number into my phone," I say, still a little breathless.

He smiles down at me, all easy charm. "Where's the fun in that?"

He tucks his hands in his pockets. His watch glints in the moonlight.

"Goodnight, Aria. Call me. Like in an hour, preferably. Less than that is fine too."

My smile almost breaks me open. "Goodnight, Strat."

The memory releases me, so staggering I have to slump down and sit on the top step.

We were so different than we are now. That was the old Aria, so quick to fall for a dashing wink and a smooth line. And he was more like the Strat I met in the forest. A little bit cocky, a little too charming.

I close my eyes and search my mind for more memories. What happened after that? When did I call him; when was the next time I saw him? I'm desperate for more details. But no matter how hard I try, I can't force my brain to serve me up any more memories of Strat.

That's the thing about memories. Time rubs the edges smooth until all that's left is a shiny riverbed pebble. First you can't really remember what you were wearing, and then the details of the hour that led up to the moment fade away too. And then all that's left is one searing image, or only a distilled, pure *feeling*. And then that becomes an echo too.

There's something odd about the front porch memory. Or rather . . . about how being in the same location triggered it.

I grab my phone and type wildly.

I pace nervously, waiting for a reply. Maybe he's still driving—

An incoming video call pops up on the screen. I answer right away.

"What do you mean?" he asks, without preamble.

I tell him about how being on the porch seemed to trigger the rest of the flashback.

"I saw another whole minute of that night." My pulse quickens as the idea solidifies. "Strat, I think we can coax the memories out."

"You think if we try going to the places we see in the flashes, the rest of those memories will come back?"

"Sounds far-fetched, I know," I say, my shoulders slumping, suddenly unsure of myself. "Never mind, we can—"

"Hey. Maybe it does sound far-fetched. But, Aria?" He gives me a wry smile. "Who are we to judge? Tell me where we're going."

CHAPTER SEVENTEEN

The parking lot outside my high school auditorium is a flurry of activity, buzzing with that special preshow energy that I used to love watching from the edges. Families stream from their cars into the building, flowing around my spot on the sidewalk like I'm a rock in a river. Little brothers tug on their mothers' hands; little sisters ride on their dads' shoulders. The sun casts a pink-orange glow over everything, melting the afternoon into night.

I shuffle the two tickets in my hand like playing cards. RIDGECROFT HIGH SCHOOL DRAMA SOCIETY PRESENTS: *PIPPIN*!

I scan the row of cars for Strat's station wagon. If he doesn't get here in time, I'll bounce; I don't really feel like watching a dozen of my classmates prance around in sequined unitards. There would have been a time when I'd have asked Arissa to score me front-row seats to every night of this show's run. Dean's playing the main role, as always, but despite all those weeks and months of pining for him, I'm not at all interested in watching tonight's show.

I shield my eyes and scan the parking lot again. I give it three more minutes, then shove the tickets in my purse. I'm halfway to my car when I hear Strat shouting my name.

"Sorry!" he says, jogging up to me, his edges vibrating. "I'm so sorry. Traffic."

I look up at him. It takes real effort to get a grip on myself. Strat in real life—it's like all the chemicals in my body start spilling and mixing together. I anchor myself on the fine-spun navy-blue wool of his St. Swithun's blazer. *Resist.*

"We need to go inside. Show's about to start."

In the lobby, two ushers are leaning over a cashbox sorting ticket stubs. A third, a tiny, birdlike blonde, is closing the last door into the theater. As Strat and I approach, she looks between us with a magpie-intense stare. Is it because she's seen us together before and is shocked to see us together again? Or does she just think he's tall and beautiful and is wondering where I found him? In his private school uniform, he's a different kind of boy from the kinds we have on offer here.

"I hope you enjoy the show," she says to him, ignoring me completely.

"Thanks, I'm sure I will," Strat says, and for the love of God, he *winks* at her.

I give him a little shove as we walk through the doors.

"What was that for?" he asks.

I raise an eyebrow. "Does that happen a lot?"

He grins. "Does what happen a lot?"

I roll my eyes.

Strat and I sink into our seats—back row, on the aisle— just as the house lights dim. The plan is to sit here for fifteen minutes, then sneak through the empty hallways to the rotunda where we met.

The sound system comes to life, and the stage manager makes her preshow announcement. The warm glow on the strawberry-red curtain fades out woozily.

For a second, we're in a darkness so complete it feels almost fuzzy. I sink into it. A moment of reprieve. A chance to steel myself against the Technicolor presence at my side.

But then Strat shifts beside me.

All at once, I'm tuned in to a frequency that is only *him*. I'm suddenly aware of every rise and fall of his chest, every pulse of heat through the arm that's propped on the armrest between us. He's so *close*. When he breathes out, I feel the stir of air on my bare wrist, on the slice of skin above my knee where my skirt hem falls.

I can't focus on the actors, who are suddenly faraway dollhouse figurines in a light box. I can't process a single word they're saying.

Strat's legs are spread wide, knees pressed into the seats in front of us. I have to sit on my hands just to keep myself from leaning into his side and threading my fingers through his or dropping my cheek to his shoulder. It's like my body wants to pick up right where it left off. My muscles remember him, even if the cells in my squishy, stupid brain don't.

With a huge effort, I force myself to get a grip. *Don't be stupid, Aria.* I shift to the far edge of my seat so I can't feel the heat of him radiating into me. We came here for a reason, and it wasn't to get lightheaded in the back row.

I glance around. The ushers lean against the side wall, raptly watching the show. In one fluid movement, I slide out of my seat and slip to the door. Adrenaline slides through me as if this is a bank robbery.

The lobby is empty, cast in the strange gray light that comes just before the last glow slips from the sky. Being out of the dark theater with a few healthy feet between us feels like a relief. Like I can breathe again.

Strat follows me out, hands in his pockets. There's that sly smile again, that amused look in his eyes. He dips his knees when he gets to me so he can put his mouth right by my ear. "Does that happen a lot?" he teases.

I huff. "Careful. Your arrogance is showing."

He laughs so loud I almost reach up to slap a hand over his mouth. But when I turn away and head for the hallway, I'm smiling too.

The auditorium is at one end of our long, narrow school. And when I say long, I mean it—end to end, it's an entire half a mile. The wide, tiled hallway stretches out before us, blocked by one of those metal-mesh gates that you pull down from the ceiling, probably to block off the rest of the school during public events. But right now, there's a two-foot gap at the bottom. Plenty of room for us to squeeze under. I don't know if there's a rule against roaming the school hallways after the doors have been locked, but before I can chicken out, Strat drops to the floor and rolls under. I go next, holding my skirt to my thighs so I don't flash him.

On the other side of the gate, we are silent as we walk down the dim hallway. It feels bizarre to be here, just us two, passing hallway after hallway of lockers that are usually teeming with my classmates.

We make it to our destination without incident.

The rotunda at night is an eerie, echoing space. With its high ceiling, it reminds me of the sequoia glade from our first midnight.

Strat tucks his hands in his pockets and looks at the enormous cougar face laid in mosaic tiles in the middle of the floor. "Intense," he says.

"What, no unnecessarily aggressive mascot at your fancy private school?" I ask in a half whisper, not daring to speak at full volume.

"Funny story, actually. Want to hear it?"

"Sure."

"So, Saint Swithun was this guy who lived in England in the 800s, right? His most famous saint miracle was when some workmen smashed an old lady's basket of eggs, and when he knelt to help her pick them up, the eggs became whole again."

"That is . . . the most ridiculous miracle I've ever heard of."

Strat nods. "He totally had some extra eggs rolling around in the pockets of his saintly robes."

"So wait—your mascot is the saint, right?"

"Nope." He grins. "Our mascot is *the basket of eggs*."

A matching smile breaks over my face. "Shut up."

"I'm serious. But let me tell you—they *are* unnecessarily aggressive eggs."

I laugh. I'm supposed to have my guard up, but he's making it difficult.

We pace around the edge of the rotunda, him clockwise, me counterclockwise.

"Do you think it would help if we re-create what we did that night?" Strat asks.

Everything in me does a somersault. "You mean if we dance."

His eyes settle on mine. "Yes."

My legs go hot.

"Worth a try, I guess," I say, trying to sound chill, like that's fine, like this is all totally fine.

He steps in close, hands still tucked in his pockets, eyes sparkling with mischief. "Where were we, exactly?"

I swallow. "The piano was over here, so I guess we were about . . . here," I say. "And you held out your hand—"

He drags his hands out of his pockets at last. "Like this?" he asks.

"I mean, less cheesily, but yes."

"Less cheesily?" he repeats, leveling a serious glare on me. But then he laughs and sweeps me into the dance. Thank God my feet know what they're doing, thanks to those YouTube learn-to-waltz tutorials I made Cady do with me years ago.

My brain is in panic mode. This tightening in my lower belly is too dangerous. I'm supposed to be resisting him, but I'm failing spectacularly.

"Close your eyes," Strat says softly, oblivious to the all-hands-on-deck alarm blaring DEFCON 1 in my head. "Try to remember something."

My memories of that night are jumbled, but I do remember standing at the edge of the cavernous cafeteria, starving for a glimpse of Dean. Two weeks before, I'd had to suffer through watching Hollis Oakley asking him to the dance during a rehearsal break. Hollis always looked as if she'd stepped right out of a seventies flower band, with her cowgirl boots and her swishy waist-length hair. But I don't remember seeing Strat.

I open my eyes. "I don't think this is going to—"

And then I feel the buzzy vibration at my temple. Something opens, and then there he is, layering over my patchy memories of homecoming and enchanting them . . .

Every boy in the cafeteria is wearing a variation of the same outfit: black suit trousers, a button-down shirt his mom ironed this morning, and a tie matching his date's dress. The ties range from emerald green to hideous yellow to Barbie pink.

But this boy . . . *this* boy has on a black silk shirt, undone one button too far. At each wrist, there's a spill of black lace that flutters over his knuckles as he plays. Instead of off-the-rack dress pants, he's insubordinately wearing jeans. A middle finger to the grand establishment that is high school society.

He's playing along to the song that's thumping from the other room, embellishing on it. His eyes are closed, and he sways a little as he plays. He's the kind of handsome that, when juxtaposed with the piano, has An Effect. Like Henry Cavill holding a puppy. Timothée Chalamet in pajamas snuggling a stuffed koala. Robert Pattinson bottle-feeding a spring lamb.

A loud tangle of energy pushes into the rotunda, led by Brock Wilson—the stolid blond linebacker I sit behind in English and often stare at, thinking, *How is the whole school obsessed with this absolute potato?* Brock and his cronies are punching each other on the shoulder. Lanky basketball player Trent Nguyen keeps a lookout as the guys pass around a flask.

"Hold up, hold up," Brock says, slowing the group when he sees the piano and the boy playing it. "Hey—nice cuffs, bro," he shouts across the rotunda. It's not a compliment.

"Thank you," the boy says without even opening his eyes.

"You won't get laid wearing shit like that," Trent adds, riffing off Brock, and their cronies laugh.

The boy does open his eyes at that. In this manufactured daydream of mine, they glow electric. He smiles slyly and says, "I haven't found it to be an issue so far."

Like magic, his response defuses whatever tension was building between him and The Jocks. That's a rare talent, and an attractive one.

"All right, man, all right," Brock says, laughing, as he holds up his hands. "You do you."

They leave, and the boy at the piano is alone again. I hover at the edge of the rotunda, unsure whether I should disturb him, wondering what I would even say.

But before I can step forward, the boy finishes the song he's playing and stretches his neck from side to side. He spots me out of the corner of his eye.

"Oh—did you want a turn?" he asks, gesturing at the keys.

"No, I don't play. I was just listening."

I step into the rotunda just as he swings a leg out, and he gets his first good look at me.

He's a shade less than graceful as he pushes the stool back from the piano, and something dizzy and hot blooms in me. The way he got up so quick—the way he's looking at me now—it makes all the hours I spent hunched over my sewing machine, carefully pedaling the most fragile fabrics through it, all worth it.

Because instead of a slinky, glitter-bombed dress with a cut-out over my spleen like every other girl in my school is wearing, I'm in a dress I made myself. It's fairy-wisp soft and palest green, point d'esprit lace and ten layers of tulle.

The heat that rushes to my cheeks is having an effect. Instead of clamming up into silence, I speak.

"I have to admit," I say, "your lace-cuff game is strong. Very Harry Styles. May I?"

He holds his wrists out.

I turn over the hem to study the needlework, how it's been bunched in three layers to make it bell out around his hand. "Chantilly," I declare. "Nice."

"Is that good?" he asks.

"Well, this is my favorite of the French laces," I say, swishing a fold of my own skirt.

"You seem to know a lot about lace," he says.

"Mm. I make dresses."

"Please tell me you made this," he says, touching my sleeve where it scoops down my bare shoulder.

I flush, and not just from the praise. "I did."

"It's beautiful. The green suits you."

It's why I picked it—I dyed it myself in a vat of Dylon until my fingertips turned green.

I let go of his wrist. "You don't go here, do you?"

He holds my gaze. "No, I don't."

My stomach sinks. Which means he's someone's date.

"But I'm not here with anyone," he clarifies, looking meaningfully at me.

"So . . . you just crashed another school's homecoming to . . . what? Play us some Mozart?"

"That wasn't Mozart, although I respect old Wolfgang's lace-cuff game immensely. But yes about the crashing. I go to St. Swithun's."

"Ah. The all-boys school. People say that all the St. Swithun's boys live in lakeside mansions."

His eyebrow rises. "Do they?"

"Mm-hmm. So I have to ask—what brings you to our humble suburban homecoming?"

"I wanted to meet someone new and interesting." Another look that heats me up from my toes, that seems to say, *Would you look at this? I have.*

Never in my life has a conversation with a boy gone so well—much less a boy like *this.*

The DJ announces that he's about to wrap it up, and the teacher-chaperones come into the rotunda to get ready for the spill of students into the parking lot. The thought of being tugged away, never to see this boy again, gives me a kind of courage I've never had before.

"My friends are going to IHOP after this," I blurt. "Do you want to come?"

"I . . . would actually love that. But I'd like to dance with you first."

He holds his hand out, and for a moment I wonder if he really is from St. Swithun's or if he's stepped out of time, from Regency England or seventeenth-century France or somewhere else romance isn't dead.

As if on cue, the music shifts into a haze of slow, glistening chimes. I place my hand in his and start to tug him toward the cafeteria to join the mass of slowly swaying bodies. He resists; pulls me back toward him. "Let's stay out here," he says.

And then I am in his arms, held as delicately as a glass princess, and we are dancing in the ugly fluorescent foyer of my mile-long high school, and suddenly it's the most beautiful place I've ever been.

I haven't waltzed since I made Cady practice with me when we were ten, her in one of Dad's suit jackets and me in my threadbare Belle costume, but he's good enough that it makes up for my shortcomings.

"Do they teach you how to waltz at St. Swithun's?" I ask.

"Funnily enough, they do," he murmurs.

The song finishes, but neither of us makes any move to step apart. Kids start to spill out of the cafeteria, flushed and laughing. The fluorescent lights snap on, but we stay still, eyes locked on each other.

He recovers first, a flicker of a smile at the corner of his mouth. One curl tumbles forward of its own volition as he looks down at me.

And then Cady is there.

My Cady. With a pang, all the twisted emotions I'm carrying with me in the present reach across my razed memory to study every detail of my smiling, blinking, breathing sister. Her hair, much shorter than mine and combed into a slick updo—a harsh contrast to my dark medieval spill. The toned muscles in her arms, the hardness of her abs (I have never had anything resembling an ab). The way she does her eyeliner. The way she smiles so brightly it feels like sunshine.

"Cady," I say in the memory, snagging her arm and dragging her close. Giddy and nervous and excited to introduce her to this boy I found. "This is Strat. He's coming to IHOP with us."

I didn't get a chance to warn him, but if Strat is thrown by meeting my twin, he sails over it. His hand is tracing heat on my back, and I can *feel* his attention on me. It's like my body has been hollowed out and filled with glitter.

"Nice to meet you," Strat says to Cady. "I have a car if you need me to drive anyone. Aria can ride shotgun."

Cady studies him for a long moment, her stare sliding back and forth between us. There's a weird look in her eyes I've never seen before.

"I can't just let her go off alone with someone I don't know," Cady says to Strat.

"Oh—of course. Totally get it," Strat says. He turns to me. "Should I—"

"You can meet us there," Cady decrees, linking her arm through my elbow. It's subtle, but she's pulling me a few inches away from Strat.

And I don't want to be pulled a few inches away from Strat.

We funnel out into the crisp October air. I was cold on my way in, but now I could walk through an ice storm and be warm and pink-cheeked with this sense of *possibility*.

As soon as we hit the parking lot, Trent Nguyen whistles at a cherry-red ragtop sports car. "Look at that ride, man! Whose car is that?"

Without a word, Strat digs into his pocket and produces a key fob. From a hundred yards away, he wakes the car up, turning on the lights, the engine, probably the butt warmers too.

Trent's so impressed his jaw's nearly on the tarmac. "No way. This is yours?" he asks.

Strat nods, and I feel a twinge of insecurity. I don't *love* the flashy car, and if I'd been able to choose the love interest in my big love story, a rich Swithun's boy would not have been it. My steps slow. Once he remembers that I'm not some California tech heiress, will he ditch me?

But then I see Britt Coleman, who's always made me feel stupid for believing in love the way I believe in it, staring at Strat's car with her mouth hanging open.

Maybe I can deal with the private-school-boy flashy-car thing if it helps me rub it in just a little bit. I smile at Britt, as if I'm saying, *See? All this time you thought I was pathetic for waiting for some drop-dead gorgeous boy to come sweep me off my feet, and here he is.*

"I'll follow your sister's car, okay?" Strat says in a low voice in my ear, hand lingering on my back, and then he's walking away.

As I watch him cross the parking lot, something tugs in my chest, like a tether being stretched too far. I don't want to be apart from him yet, not even for the five minutes it'll take to drive to IHOP.

I glance behind me. Cady's not looking, focused on cramming the train of Devyn's dress into the back seat of Tahirah Watkins's Volkswagen Bug. A rebellious flame leaps up in me—and then I'm pelting across the parking lot, high on the cold night air and the nip of whatever was in that Mountain Dew and my own brazen disobedience. I slam into Strat's passenger seat. "Drive, drive, drive!" I say, still laughing, gathering layers of lace and cramming them into the tiny space.

"Your sister's going to—"

"Just drive," I say again, eyes wild and daring, and we stare at each other for one long second. And then he grins.

He shoves the gearshift into drive, and on our way out of the parking lot, I see two things: Cady's face, slack-jawed with disbelief, and Dean, coming out of the building with Hollis on his arm. Hollis is wearing a plain silk tube dress, almost the exact color of her skin, held up with the thinnest straps, no shape except for what she gives it.

And I look at Dean and know—

This is the end of my obsessed crush on Dean.

Maybe I should be concerned by how easily Strat knocked him down off his pedestal and took his place. But I can't feel anything beyond the daring sugar rush in my veins, the press of Strat's arm against mine on the armrest between us, and the exhilarating free fall of my silly, romantic heart.

I hold on to every moment, because this is it. The start of my epic love story.

*   *   *

"It worked," I say, dazed. "Strat, I remember."

Back in the rotunda, he presses one finger to my lips, staring off into the space over the top of my head.

Oh.

He's remembering too.

He half closes his eyes, and I watch them slide back and forth under his eyelids. The tiniest smile tilts the corner of his mouth up.

After what feels like a century, he opens his eyes.

"Well," he says, voice a little hoarse. "That one wasn't bad."

"You saw us?" I ask.

"I saw us," he says gravely. "Aria . . . we were *glowing*."

For a moment, I'm lost, caught in his stare, and then I remember.

We erased each other for a reason.

I step back, desperate to get some space between us.

I replay the whole scene, scouring it for clues, but he's right. That one wasn't bad. That night . . . we were a fairy tale. We caught each other in an exquisite sliver of time when both of us were hitting every note just right, presenting our absolute best selves.

We were a fairy tale, but was it too good to be true?

CHAPTER EIGHTEEN

The next day at the hospital, I head straight for my chair by the window, brushing my hand along the metal rail at the foot of Cady's bed in lieu of a real greeting. I feel bad about how many afternoons I've been missing lately, but I need to work on this thing with Strat. We need answers.

I'm about to press Play on my ethereal ballet music playlist when my phone chimes with a text message from Strat.

I know you said you'd be at the hospital, so in case you need this:

Three dots appear, blinking, and then a photo bubbles onto the screen. A surprised laugh erupts from me. It's his school's mascot, the basket of eggs. To be precise, a person in an outlandish basket-of-eggs costume.

The basket circles the person's waist like a stiff tutu, and lewdly skinny legs poke out underneath, clad in shiny Lycra tights. The three huge eggs are made of thick upholstery foam covered with Nylafleece, the fabric they use to cover Muppets, and there are eyeholes cut into the middle egg under frowning black eyebrows. He wasn't kidding about the aggression.

I touch the smile curving onto my lips. If he'd asked how Cady was doing, it would have just made the weight settle heavier over my chest. But instead, it's lifting off. For the first time in a long time, he's brought a genuine smile to this room.

I type back:

> From a technical standpoint, I'm actually impressed.

> I thought you might be.

Another photo comes through, of a noticeboard in a hallway, zoomed in on a flyer that says DON'T PUT ALL YOUR EGGS IN ONE BASKET! GUIDANCE COUNSELOR APPOINTMENT TIMES WILL BE DISTRIBUTED NEXT WEEK FOR COLLEGE ADMISSIONS.

My thumbs fly over the keys.

> Wow, they're really milking it with that logo.

> STOP WITH THE DAIRY PUNS. I CAN'T BEAR TO LOSE YOU TOO

I press my hand over a giggle.

> St. Swithun is probably rolling in his grave right now.

Right? Bet he's wishing he hadn't pulled those eggs out of his pocket.

So wait, are you at your school right now, walking around taking pictures of all the egg-related things for me?

Would it make you feel better if I told you I had these photos in my phone already, in their own special album that I look through every night before bed?

It would make me feel infinitely worse. I've seen the legs on that mascot.

He sends a laughing emoji.

I shouldn't be smiling, but I'm grinning from ear to ear. He's chipping away at my defenses. How could I have erased this boy, the one who cheers me up and lifts me out of these difficult places when I need it most?

Something is bugging me about last night's homecoming flashback, though. Hesitantly, I pick my phone up again and type:

Hey, I meant to ask. What happened to your car? The red one you were driving at homecoming?

My fingers hover over the Send button. This feels important, but I don't know why. I'm about to press Send when the vibration starts up behind my left ear—another broken shard of our story.

In the memory, Strat's sitting across from me in a red pleather booth, laughing, more open and happy than I've seen him in our midnights or in real life.

He looks like he's in *love*.

There's a brick wall behind him, and his coppery curls look richer than ever under the glow of the kitschy neon signs of my favorite pizza place.

He leans forward and says, "I have a serious question for you."

I try to hold on to the memory, coax another minute out, but it slips through my fingers. I reach and reach, but I can't get it back.

We were at Wyldefire Pizza. I can re-create the layout of the restaurant in my mind, in a blended super-memory of all the times I've been there with my family to celebrate good grades and birthdays, or with friends once we were allowed to go out in groups without our parents.

I clear the text field—the car thing can wait—and send a different message.

Another memory came back. I saw us at Wyldefire Pizza.

Cool—let's go there tomorrow. See if either of us can remember more.

Out in the hall, I hear the click of high heels, and my mom's voice, saying hi to everyone as she strides down the hallway. I fumble to close out of my texting app, like I've been caught doing something wrong.

I give her a little wave when she bursts into the room, but she's in a strange mood. She drops her bag by the window and straightens her sleek ponytail, then she's beckoning me up.

"Don't I get a hug?"

"Um. Sure?" Warily, I set aside my stuff and let her wrap me up in a tight hug. In spite of myself, I melt into it. She smells like sunscreen and summer and *Mom*.

When I try to break away, she keeps holding on, which is unlike her. It's setting warning bells off in my head.

"We should be talking more," she murmurs, pressing a kiss to the top of my head.

I stiffen. Why? So she can sit me down and tell me that she and Dad are getting a divorce?

"In fact," Mom says, brightening, "why don't we hang out now? I can make us a bowl of popcorn, and we can watch a movie on my laptop? Barry the porter gave me the password to the cafeteria staff's Wi-Fi—"

"Uh—I'd love to, but I was just on my way out. Another meeting for that group project," I say, pulling a face to convey that it's a burden.

Her smile fades. "Oh. Right now?"

"Yeah—sorry!" I grab my backpack and flee for the elevator.

If she never gets a chance to tell me, it won't be real.

As I'm crossing the parking lot, I shoot off a text to Strat.

> Actually, can we go to
> Wyldefire tonight?

I'm in such a rush to get away from Mom and *divorce* and *we should talk more* that when I sling my backpack across to the passenger seat, it knocks into my travel mug in the cupholder. Raspberry iced tea sloshes everywhere.

"Crap," I mutter, shaking it off my hand. I open the glove compartment to grab a napkin, and an avalanche of junk slides out. Fast-food napkins, takeout menus, some of Cady's gross volleyball sweatbands, a melted tube of ChapStick.

I'm shoving it all back in when one torn scrap of lined paper catches my eye.

Something's up with him.

Lies!

The word *Lies* is underlined three times.

My stomach lurches. Who's "him"? Strat?

The worst part is—I can't tell if this is my handwriting or Cady's.

CHAPTER NINETEEN

Standing with Strat in the crowded entryway of Wyldefire Pizza Co. is . . . an experience.

I've been here more times than I can count, but never in a lilac fairycore sundress and espadrille wedges, clicked like a fridge magnet to the side of a tall, effortlessly attractive boy.

I'm trying to look like a pillar of calm and chill, but on the inside, my nerves are twanging like the strings of a steel guitar. I have spent *years* daydreaming about going out to dinner with someone, and it's finally happening.

As ever, Strat's hands are tucked loosely in his pockets, in a way that projects "totally comfortable in all situations, and in my own skin." Why do I have to love the way his arms look corded and strong with his sleeves pushed up to his elbows like that?

Good Lord, I need to get my shit together. We're here to trigger a memory, not go on a date. I dip my hand into my pocket.

Next to the double penny, I have the scrap of paper I found in the glovebox. *Something's up.* It's a good reminder to be more wary. We erased each other for a reason.

Strat steps up to the hostess podium. "We've got a reservation for two," he says. "Under Madigan."

The buzzy energy of the foyer becomes a distant blur, until the only thing I can hear is my heart pounding. No one's ever made a reservation for me. Well. Maybe he did, before. But this is the first one I remember.

Strat's hand slides to my lower back, just a shade too low to be the kind of touch between two people who don't really know each other. I inhale sharply. Our eyes lock, and I can tell by the flare in his pupils that he realizes what he's done. He stares at his hand like it's not a part of him, like it decided to curve around my hip of its own volition.

My face heats. I can't decide whether I'm glad I wore my one and only thong tonight or it was the worst decision of my life.

He springs away as if his palm has been burned. "Sorry. Sometimes it's like my body has a memory and it's doing what it used to do before my head can catch up."

Yeah. I've got the same problem.

I trail after the hostess. My mind is chanting, *This feels like a date this feels like a date,* over and over.

We slip into a cozy booth near the pizza ovens and order drinks. He slides my Shirley Temple to me when it comes, his eyes lingering on mine in a way that makes it impossible to look away. It's so much harder to think when he's here in real life.

With Ollie and Austin and Dean, I could watch from afar,

safe within my own imagination. But with Strat, this thing is plugged in at both ends—and it's terrifying.

After a shaky visit to the salad bar, I wince in pain as I slide back into the booth. My legs are killing me.

Strat notices. "You okay?"

"My hamstrings aren't. My PE teacher says he's going to fail me if I can't run a mile without stopping by the end of the year."

"You can't run a mile without stopping?"

I prickle. "I take it you're one of those freaks who can."

"By 'freaks,' do you mean ninety-five percent of people our age?"

"That's a generous and blatantly made-up statistic. But yes, everyone else in my class can. I'm the only one who can't. Bet you can," I say petulantly.

He's reluctant to admit it. "I'm actually decent at running, yeah."

"What's your mile?"

"Six minutes, forty-two seconds. Why, what's yours?"

I'm not about to tell him it's over twelve minutes. "You have an advantage. Look how long your legs are," I say, skirting the question.

He sticks one leg out into the aisle and wiggles his foot.

"See?" I say. "It's, like, in another zip code."

He chuckles. My nerves have loosened a little. I look around, savoring the familiar sights and sounds of Wyldefire.

"This is a cool place," he says.

"Yeah. I used to come here all the time with the team."

"Team?"

"Cady's volleyball team. They're who I hang out with, mostly."

"But you don't play volleyball."

"Nope. Hate it, actually. They're really Cady's friends more than mine."

"You don't have your own friends? Ones you vibe with?"

"Not really. The volleyball girls are nice enough, I guess." *Except Britt*, I think, but I don't say it out loud. "But, God, you wouldn't believe how many games I've had to go to, not to mention summer camps and workshops and after-parties."

"Why didn't you just tell your sister you didn't want to do that shit?"

"It's . . ." I frown, looking down at my lap, feeling tense all of a sudden. "You make it sound so easy. If I'd done that, it would have hurt her feelings."

His mouth presses into a line. "If you hate volleyball and you're not close to any of those people, maybe she should have let you branch out a little."

I prickle with irritation. "Look, it's a twin thing. We—we're just like that."

He wouldn't get it. Cady wanting me to be with her made me feel important and loved. I never had to worry about friends, because my best friend was built in.

He's quiet for a moment, then he says gently, "Is this like one of those things you were talking about, that feel too hard to do?"

I open my mouth, then close it again. I'm speechless. He's somehow hit the nail on the head, drawing a connection with my ineptitude at facing hard stuff to the real reason I spend so much time with Cady's friends. I'm not sure I was even really consciously aware of it.

"Let's practice," he says. "I'll be Cady."

"What? No, we don't have to—"

"I know. Just humor me. Pretend I'm asking . . . 'Hey, Aria, come to volleyball camp with me this summer.'"

I laugh nervously. "This is weird."

He leans over the table. "Come to volleyball camp with me," he repeats.

I stare him down. When it's clear that he's not going to let me off the hook, I huff and sit back, mumbling an answer. "Um. That's not really my thing . . . maybe I can just stay here and—"

"Too wishy-washy. Come on, you can do better than that."

I glower at him, frustration building in my chest.

"Come to volleyball camp with me," he repeats.

"Not this summer."

"Better, but that'll make her think you'll do it later."

Under the table, I squeeze my napkin into a ball. "Can we just not . . . do this right now?"

There's a tightness in my chest, like I feel bad for telling Cady I don't want to go to camp, and it's not even Cady asking.

He narrows his eyes. "Fine. We can practice more later."

My attention snags on something over Strat's shoulder: a couple who have just finished their dinner, standing up from their booth and waving goodnight to their waiter.

Dean and Hollis.

Hollis and Dean.

Dean smooths a hand through his thick, sandy hair. He's one of those seniors who seem to have already crossed the line into being a man, leaving most of his classmates stuck in the gangly bodies of boys. It was what drew me to him initially—that he had the deepest voice and most confidence of anyone I'd ever seen. He could read Shakespearean monologues off the cuff without a shred of self-consciousness. Tonight Hollis looks like a Stevie Nicks/Daisy Jones goddess, easy smile and twinkling eyes, long, wispy body. I'm ninety-nine percent sure she's not wearing a bra. Okay, make that a hundred percent.

Hollis spots us and tugs on Dean's arm. Identical flickers of surprise and confusion flash over their faces. And then, for some inexplicable reason, they start heading toward us. What alternate dimension have I slid into that Dean and Hollis are approaching me like we're friends?

I kick Strat's shin under the table. "They know."

"What?"

"They know about *us*," I hiss. But that's all I have a chance to say before they're at the end of our table.

"Hey, lady," Hollis says. Her voice is the same smoky purr I've always been jealous of, and her eyes are bright with history— like she *knows* me.

"Hey," I croak.

Strat stands, and it's probably socially awkward if I stay sitting, so I stand up too. Dean holds his hand out to bro-shake with Strat. It surprises me to see that Strat's taller, by at least an inch. I catch a whiff of pot on Hollis's and Dean's clothes, clocking their blown pupils and hooded eyelids.

"Sorry about the stage makeup," Dean says, waving at his face. "Dress rehearsal this afternoon and couldn't get it all off."

He's totally the kind of person who wouldn't take it all off just so he can talk about how he's Ridgecroft's rising star.

"It's really nice to see you two together again," Hollis says. She's stroking the inside of Dean's elbow—a move that would have provoked the most painful longing in me once.

My brain is working in overdrive. Okay, so we hung out together, but because Strat was there, my memory of it was wiped.

"So how does it work?" Dean asks. "Do you guys remember anything from your first go-round?"

Strat and I exchange glances. They know we erased each other?

Answers. We might get answers here.

"Nope, we don't remember anything," Strat says, even though it's not entirely true.

Hollis's eyes go wide. "That is *wild*."

"So you don't remember the beach? The bonfire party?" Dean asks. "You two were always hanging out on the ridge by the red swing set, but you came down that night."

"Did we say anything about why we erased each other?" I ask. I have to bite the inside of my lip to keep from trembling. This is it. We're going to find out why.

"Sorry, babe, no," Hollis says.

"Your breakup was a little out of left field when we heard about it, to be honest," Dean adds.

Hollis nods. "You two seemed *deeply* into each other, especially at the bonfire party. I mean—Strat, you shouted, 'I LOVE ARIA LENDELL!' out over the ridge so loud we heard it down on the beach."

"You should have seen the girls," Dean says. "All pressing their hands to their hearts, *Oh my God, that is so romantic*, then smacking their boyfriends on the shoulders."

"It was gorgeous," Hollis says with a dreamy smile as she shakes back her long, silky straight hair. "And it looks like you're on your way back to each other, which is so goddamn beautiful." Her eyes go a little misty, but it might just be because she's high. "Whatever happened to you guys before, you don't have to let that weigh you down now, right?"

"Sure, right," Strat says. I'm too dazed to speak.

The waitress comes with our pizza then, and Dean and Hollis say their goodbyes.

"We're having another bonfire party next weekend—you two had better be there!" Dean calls back over his shoulder, and then they're out of sight.

We sit in astonished silence. We almost had real information, maybe even a *why*, but of course it wouldn't be so easy.

And then Strat blows out a breath and pushes his hair back, and the brick wall's behind him, and the memory hits so hard I nearly knock over my drink.

Strat pulls his fingers through his hair, the loose waves springing right back into place, then leans forward over the small table and stares intently at me. I can feel the heat starting to spark and burn between us. Ever since our first kiss, when the delicate catch of his lips on mine stunned us both, I've been desperate to repeat the experience. Over and over, as many times as possible. And he seems totally on board with that plan. Maybe it's infatuation or instalove, but I don't care. I feel like I've swallowed sunshine. He's living up to every expectation I've ever had about a love story.

My phone lights up on the table by my elbow. I click it off.

"Do you need to get that?" he asks.

"It's just Cady."

"You can answer it, I don't mind."

"It's all right, I'll call her back later. If it's important, she'll text."

But when the text notification slides down from the top of the screen, I don't check it.

"Tell her thank you for letting me borrow you tonight," Strat says.

"I will."

I'm actually kind of pissed at her. She texts me *all* the time when I'm out with Strat but never seems to have anything to say to me when I'm not with him. And it's not just one message— it's a dozen, pinging in like I've gone viral. Stupid things too, like pictures of moths on bushes when she's out on a jog. Moths aren't cute. She knows I don't like moths.

Another ping. "Oh my God, she won't stop." I flick through my settings and turn off my notifications.

"I feel like I can't judge," Strat says. "I've been messaging you tons lately."

"Oh—that's different," I say, backpedaling. "You can message me as much as you want." *Please never stop.*

Truthfully, the messaging *miiight* be getting a little out of control. Every night, I fall asleep in the middle of our text conversations, usually around two or three in the morning. My parents, who have never had any real problems with our phones, had to lay down a rule about bringing them to the dinner table.

But I don't feel a shred of guilt. I'm going to savor every minute of this. Every minute of him.

Our pizzas come, and Strat lifts a slice without even glancing at the extra dipping sauce I ordered. They usually give you one tiny dish each, but I asked for five, clustered in a flower shape by our drinks.

"If you say you don't like Wyldefire sauce, we might need to wrap this up here and now," I tease, liberally dunking my first slice into the dip. His hand stops moving. I instantly want to take it back—I don't want to wrap us up, not over something so silly.

He slides a tub of sauce close and dunks his slice in, coating it with an unholy amount of dip. "We are not wrapping this up, Aria. I love Wyldefire sauce."

When we finally push our plates away, he clears his throat. "I have a serious question for you," he asks, leaning in close, voice low and melted-chocolate warm. Our hands twine on the table. My heart jumps into my throat.

"So, Aria Lendell, for this party later . . . I know it's only been two weeks, but can I introduce you as my girlfriend?"

The sunshine becomes a supernova burn, radiating out of my skin in a million shafts of light.

"Yeah. I'd really like that. Yes."

I have a boyfriend.

I murmur it again a little later, standing in front of the mirror in the restaurant bathroom, hands pressed to my cheeks, savoring this night. I take a quick, surreptitious selfie. *This is me, in love.*

A little smile curves on my lips when I check my socials and see the new comments under my latest photo. Everyone's clamoring about how gorgeous Strat is. This whole week I kept overhearing people talking about "Aria Lendell's hot private school boyfriend," and I must admit . . . I don't hate the attention.

When I leave the bathroom, I bump into a hard body in the hall.

"Hey, Aria."

I snap out of my love haze and force myself to focus on the person I knocked into. "Britt! I didn't know you were here."

"Yeah. Date with Marco. You and your boy certainly seem to be getting cozy."

I'm nearly shimmering with the news *I have a boyfriend I have a boyfriend*, but I don't want Britt Coleman to be the first to know.

"Yeah, it's going really well," I say. I want to star-shimmer-explode, because I've had so much practice loving boys from afar but now it's *requited*.

Britt shoots me a dismissive look. "You've known him for, like, two weeks."

I bristle. "So? Every couple you know had a day in their relationship where they'd only known each other two weeks."

"I'm just concerned for you. Cady is too."

I scoff, suddenly desperate to get out of this hallway. Cady is most definitely not concerned. She's my twin sister, so I think I'd know. I'm irritated that Britt's pretending her petty jealousy is tenderhearted concern for my well-being.

"I'm not trying to be mean. Just, like . . . maybe he's not all you've built him up to be."

A confrontational heat rises in me. I hate the lime-green feel of it in my veins. I yank my arm away from her. "Yeah, well, what if he is?"

I push past her and tell Strat I'm ready to leave. In an effort to recapture the magic of the night, I catch his sleeve outside the door and tug him to me, kissing him with a crushing desperation.

I have a boyfriend.

He laughs, walking me backward without letting me go, and he kisses me once more, up against the door of his cherry-red sports car.

I have a boyfriend.

The memory cuts off.

Strat knows right away that I've seen something.

"Tell me," he says.

"Not here."

Strat insists on grabbing the bill, but his card is declined, and then his second card is declined. He blanches. Rich private school boys don't blanch when their cards are declined, do they? I end up paying for it, hoping that there's enough left in my savings to cover the bill.

We sit in his car, and I tell Strat what I saw, leaving out the interaction with Britt.

"I just don't understand why we would have erased each other," I say, staring out of the window. "We seemed so happy."

"We're seventeen," Strat says. "What reason could we have had that would have been good enough?"

I can think of several, but probably only because I've been reading articles on erasures in my every spare moment. Among the top ten: trauma, bad breakups, witnessing murders, trips to war-zone front lines, death of someone close to you—but that one's sticky, and doctors will only do it if you can't pull yourself out of the grief after a set period of time, usually three years.

There's a long silence.

"Hey, Aria?" Strat says softly. "If it really does turn out to be something I did . . . if I didn't live up to your expectations, or if I broke your heart somehow . . . I'm sorry. In advance, I'm sorry."

The words on the scrap of paper tug at me. *Something's up with him. Lies?*

My body grows stiff with suspicion. Was Britt right? Did she know something I didn't know?

Could Strat have done something so bad? The more I get to know him, the harder I find that to believe.

Unaware of my inner turmoil, Strat plays chords on the steering wheel. "Well. Dean and Hollis seem . . . interesting," he says.

"Yeah." It is too bizarre to believe. Dean's brasher party attitude and that whiff of smoke caught me off guard. It's jarring to realize that the version of Dean I invented and pined for in my head is different from the Dean I saw tonight.

It's not the first time that's happened, though. A few months after the end of my crush on Ollie, I found out he was only into guys. I thought I'd been watching and loving these boys so closely, but I had no idea who they really were.

I cast a sidelong glance at Strat. Maybe I didn't really know him either, before.

Maybe I still don't.

When I get home, I flick through the stack of envelopes on the kitchen counter—still nothing from Sciarra Academy—then I go straight to my room and find an unopened pack of neon index cards. A roll of tape. A fat black marker.

The clock ticks us closer to midnight, and the anticipation of that, of where Strat and I might go this time, is tugging at me, but I want to do this first.

I shove Cady's shirts to one side of the closet. While the details are still fresh in my mind, I write on the first index card:

<u>3. Wyldefire Pizza Co.</u>
Laughing, in a booth, he sat against the brick wall
Was this our first real date?
Asked me to be his girlfriend officially

I get the feeling that it's going to be important to track these memories, to make sure the details don't fade in my mind. I add a few notes about the smaller flashes I've seen, but I still can't glean any location clues from those.

<u>1. Homecoming</u>
10 October, first meeting
Lace cuffs, waltz
IHOP after

Red sports car
Goodnight kiss on porch on my cheek

2. First Kiss
Sitting on dewy grass (where were we?)
Plaid shirt
At dawn—we'd been out all night
"Let's make this stratospheric" (omg)

I'm like an archaeologist, gently brushing dust away from the bones of what lived before. When I'm finished, I step back, satisfied: I have the beginnings of the timeline of us.

But there's something unsettling about all of it. Now that I've seen these snippets, I should feel closer to an answer. But I can't shake the feeling that the *why* is only getting further away.

All I see are reasons to stay.

CHAPTER TWENTY

The first thing I'm aware of, before I even open my eyes, is movement: a gentle rocking, like I'm bobbing in the middle of the ocean.

It's about to lull me back to sleep when Strat's voice floats to me, saying my name, soft and unsure. I feel a careful touch on my shoulder, the kind you'd use when you're trying to wake a person you don't know that well. Which I guess is what I am to him now. Even if I wasn't always.

This whole situation is such a trip.

When I finally drag myself up, the rocking motion becomes a woozy tilt.

We're on a narrow boat, like a canoe but longer. Strat's beside me on an upholstered bench seat at the back of the boat. "I would have let you keep sleeping," he says, "but I was getting a little restless." His ever-present blazer is nowhere to be seen, and he's rolled the sleeves of his crisp white dress shirt up to his forearms.

The boat rocks on slick, night-black water, but there is no shore. Instead, the water laps directly against the foundations of tall stone buildings rising on either side of us. A canal.

I sit up straight. "Strat? Are we in . . . Venice?"

The delight is too powerful to tamp down, a hot-pink surge of joy. I love Venice—or, I guess, the idea of it. I've never been.

"Looks like it," Strat says. "But why aren't we moving? Aren't the boats in Venice supposed to come with guys with sticks?"

The moment the words are out, the boat gives a gentle jolt.

Our startled eyes meet, and both of us grab for purchase as the boat lurches to life. I look behind me, but there's no motor and no striped-shirted person standing on the stern. It's like it's being steered by a ghostly gondolier. A delighted laugh burbles out of me. We're gliding through *Venice*!

Strat's chin tilts. "Oh—listen," he whispers.

Music.

His fingers play out one of the melodies on his thigh.

"Do you know this one?" I whisper, as if speaking will break the magic of the night.

"Monteverdi, maybe. Or Cavalli."

I stare at him. It always gets me, the piano stuff.

"You know, it's kind of . . . too perfect here," Strat says.

"Nothing can be too perfect."

"Where are the flaws? The chips in the stone from battles, lovers' names carved on lintels, windows broken by kids playing . . . that sort of thing. Life."

"You and your flaws," I say, shaking my head.

"I've been meaning to ask," he says. "At your homecoming—how did you know how to waltz so well?"

I flush. "Oh, I used to make Cady practice all sorts of weird things with me."

"What kinds of weird things?" His left eyebrow quirks up in amusement.

"It started out with the standard: weddings between our stuffed animals, mermaid soap operas at the pool in the summer, pretending our backyard playset was the *Titanic*."

I won't tell him how I used to make her hold me while I pretended to die, because dying in the arms of the love of your life is the most romantic thing of all.

"We even played Venetian gondolas once," I say. "We raided my mom's closet for striped shirts, then set a Barbie and Ken on one end of the sofa while one of us stood on the sofa arm being the gondolier." I sigh. "Barbie and Ken made out a lot back in those days."

Strat laughs. His eyes are bright pools in the Venetian moonlight, and I'm suddenly self-conscious.

"Sorry. I kind of used to be a hopeless romantic," I say quietly.

"Or maybe you just have an amazing imagination," he says.

A small, pleased feeling glows in me like an ember.

Imaginations are fine, until you get carried away with them. I think of Dean, of how different he was at the pizza place tonight than I thought he'd be. I daydreamed about him so many times and ended up building a version of him in my mind that didn't really exist.

Am I doing the same with Strat?

"I feel like I should know more about you," I blurt.

Strat cocks an eyebrow. "What, like my favorite color, or a rundown of my latest report card?"

"Yes."

He laughs. "Fine. Last semester I got B minuses all across the board, but I'm in easy classes. Nothing fancy. Oh, but I got an A plus in music theory, obviously. And my favorite color is gray."

"Whose favorite color is gray?"

He shrugs. "Mine. Why, what's yours?"

"Seafoam green. Or periwinkle blue. Slightly shimmery, if possible."

"That is very you," he says, and his smile is so full of fondness it makes my heart swell a little bit.

"Any siblings? Pets?" I ask.

His face brightens. I ignore the way it makes my heart clench.

"No siblings, and no pets anymore, but when I was growing up, I had the world's ugliest dog and the world's most beautiful cat. I picked my dog out myself—nobody wanted the poor little runt."

"And the cat?"

"My grandmother gave her to us, even though we didn't want a cat. She was very snooty. The cat, not Grandmother. Well, okay . . . they're both very snooty, and very beautiful. Not the kind of beautiful you are."

My blood thumps hard at my throat, just from that one word of praise: *beautiful*. I know I shouldn't latch on to it, but I can't help it.

"What kind of beautiful are they?" I ask quietly.

"Oh, the icy, untouchable kind."

"As opposed to . . . ?"

"I probably shouldn't say." His voice is a little lower now. "Got the impression you wanted me to hold off with the romance stuff until we found out why we erased each other."

I swallow. The air has changed, weaving around us thicker, tighter. I couldn't look away if I tried.

"Maybe one little slip wouldn't hurt," I say. "After all, we are on a gondola in Venice."

He studies me for a long moment. Like he's waiting for me to recant my decision.

"All right," he says softly. "You're wildflowers in a forest glade. You're warmth and dreams and pretty dresses." He touches the fabric of my skirt, just above my knee.

My heart is in my throat. I can't tell if this tingling in my skin is because my body still remembers him from before, or if this is all *now*.

The backs of his knuckles brush my skin as he lets go of my skirt. The touch has me flushing, but not nearly as hot as I would be if the magic of the midnight wasn't dulling the edges. It takes the pain off, but it takes the pleasure off too.

I'm surprised to find myself wishing that we were in the daylight.

No. *Crap.*

I can't want that. And I definitely can't be thinking horny thoughts like the visions that sprang into my head when I saw his hand on my knee.

The sooner we get answers, the better. Because it's getting harder and harder to remember I'm supposed to be keeping him at arm's length.

CHAPTER TWENTY-ONE

Violin notes cascade out of my phone speaker as I get ready for school the next morning, spinning from the starry Venetian night and the flowing conversation.

When it's time to leave the house, I pause in the hallway and brace myself for the dash to the front door. I have to go past the doorway to Mom's office, and I can hear her keyboard clacking away.

"Aria? Is that you?"

I wince. "Yeah. Just on my way out, see you later!" I yank open the door.

"Wait, I need to talk to you about—"

"I have to leave for school, Mom. Sorry, bye!"

I slam the door shut behind me. I feel awful, but not awful enough to talk to her. I can't let her corner me. I can't let her make what's happening between her and Dad real by speaking the word.

The car engine rumbles to life. Just as I'm about to put it in reverse, I look up at the house, at the garage door in front of me, and a patch of skin behind my right ear starts tingling. In sudden, striking clarity, I relive the memory of the night my dad moved to the garage.

There is a horrible pall over the house. Dad's been thumping up and down the stairs, carrying his clothes out of the master closet and trekking down to hang them on an old rolling rail in the garage.

Cady and I are on the couch in the living room, staring at the TV as a *Friends* rerun plays but not really watching it. We should have left, should have driven to Sonic or just *driven* to get away from this, but it's like my brain is in panic shutdown mode and I can't make a decision. I'm too scared to move, as if moving will make it real.

"This officially sucks," Cady says. "And I don't know why he's moving his shit downstairs. Extremely dramatic, if you ask me."

I stare down at my hands and see that I've scraped almost all the iridescent lavender polish off my nails.

Cady lays her hand over mine to stop my picking. "Aria. They'll be fine."

Will they? Our parents never used to argue. And they certainly don't spontaneously start moving to the basement.

The doorbell rings.

No one moves. Even the thumping on the stairs goes deadly quiet.

"I'll get it," Cady calls. "Probably an Amazon delivery for Mom," she mumbles.

I stay frozen in my spot on the couch—until my pulse jumps at the voice that travels down the hallway when Cady opens the door.

"Hey, Cady. Is Aria here?"

Strat? What is he doing here? Why didn't he text first?

"My piano lesson got cancelled so I thought I'd drive over and surprise her, take her to dinner."

"Let me check if she's here," Cady says, and I mentally thank her for buying me some time.

She comes back into the room with both eyebrows raised so high they might hit the roof. "Well? Are you going to get up or what?" Cady asks.

I glance down at my *Star vs. the Forces of Evil* pajamas and my greasy topknot. "I can't let him see me like this."

She throws me a judgmental look. "Seriously? You've been dating him for over a month. Go answer the door."

"Just—stall him, okay? Give me five minutes."

I bolt up the stairs just as she reopens the door and tells him to come in. She gets him settled, then comes up to our room. She leans against the doorframe, watching me as I drag a brush through my unruly hair. "You know, you can tell him it's not a good time. Because it's really not."

I feel a squiggle of guilt for forgetting all about our parents' argument. But I also have no interest in sitting on the couch and drowning in those emotions—not when I've got a ticket out. I give Cady a quick, hard hug. "Thanks for buying me some time.

You should get out of the house too—see if any of the girls are up for meeting you somewhere."

I don't wait for her response, just skitter down the stairs. "Going out. Cady knows the details!" I yell, banking on my parents being too distracted to come out and question me.

I stick my head into the living room. "Come on," I say to a bewildered Strat.

We're four blocks away when I'm finally able to speak. "Sorry that was hectic. I just really needed to get out of there. Thanks for coming over."

"Sure. Yeah."

He shifts in his seat, looking strangely uncomfortable. I'm still a little out of breath from throwing myself together so quickly. I smooth down my hair, my dress. Do I look all right? My hands are still shaking.

Strat clears his throat. "Is everything okay at your house?"

"Oh, yeah, fine!" I say brightly.

He looks askance at me. He's not buying it.

A heavy silence falls between us. *No, no, no.* I've pulled my parents' tension in here with me, and now it's sitting between us the way it was sitting between me and Cady on the couch ten minutes ago. I don't want to mix this toxicity into what Strat and I have. Our relationship is clean and shiny and sparkling, just like the inside of this snazzy car, just like the photos of us on my Instagram account.

Strat slows to a stop at a traffic light. He stares down at his hands on the steering wheel. "You know you can talk to me, Aria. You know. If . . . something's bothering you."

I don't want to talk about it. It's sweet of him to offer, but no one really wants to talk about stuff when they say that.

"Let's just drive somewhere and make out," I blurt.

He looks at me for a long moment. "We can do that," he says slowly. "If that's what you need."

I find his hand. Smile reassuringly. "Yeah. Definitely what I need. You know anywhere?"

"I can probably come up with something."

At the next set of traffic lights, I take a photo of our hands linked on the center console, because when I remember this night, I don't want to remember Dad's thumping steps on the stairs or the confused frown gathered between Strat's eyebrows. I want to remember the perfect way our hands twine together.

CHAPTER TWENTY-TWO

Two hours later, the sun beats down on me and my classmates as we line our toes up to the white starting line painted on the track. Coach Kapoor's whistle sounds sharp in the air, and within seconds my classmates are ahead of me by several yards.

By the end of the first lap, I'm so far behind it's embarrassing, but I have to plod on. My cheeks burn with effort and shame. This is officially the day from hell.

A rhythmic thud of footsteps pounds up behind me. Has Tahirah caught up to me already? She's the fastest in our class. Her fluorescent-yellow running shoes are usually a lot quieter than that when she laps me.

I shift a little to the right to make room for the runner. But instead of surging past, they slow, as if they're about to match my pace.

"Hey."

I almost trip at the sound of that voice. His voice.

"Strat?! What are you doing here?"

"Don't stop—keep running. Thought I'd come for a little jog with you," he says, as if it's no big deal, as if he's not missing some class like Catechisms for Strapping Young Boys or Medieval Catholic Architecture or whatever. Like he didn't have to drive forty-five minutes to get here.

He's in a St. Swithun's PE uniform, his long legs taut with muscles no piano player should have.

"I can't believe you're here," I say.

I'm going a little marshmallowy about it. It's kind of . . . chivalric.

"Talk later. Breathe now," he says. He matches my footfalls exactly.

Strat murmurs little encouragements as we power on.

"I feel like a dying cow," I say, the air whistling harshly through my desiccated windpipe.

"Halfway there," Strat says.

At one point, my footfalls slow. I'm in danger of converting this "run" into a walk—honestly, there is only a microscopic difference between the two—but his hand settles at the small of my back. I'm so mortified at the thought of him feeling my sweat that I find an unexpected surge of energy, crossing the finish line in what is actually a respectable imitation of a run.

There's a stitch in my side that makes me want to die, and I'm out of breath and shaking and sweating, but it's the most romantic thing anyone's ever done for me in my life.

Coach Kapoor jogs up. "Who the f—" He bites down on the word he was about to unleash. "I'm sorry, but who are you?"

Strat grabs my hand, ricocheting me back to him. For a second, I think he's going to grab my face and plant a kiss on me. Is this just another echo of what he would have done before, or does he want to do it now?

He smirks down at me, as if he knows exactly what I'm thinking. But instead of swooping me close for a world-tilting kiss, he squeezes my hand. "Gotta get back to school. See you at midnight," he says, and then he takes off running toward the locker rooms.

Coach Kapoor rises up on the balls of his feet, clearly at war with himself. He wants to chase Strat down and apprehend him, but he can't leave us to our own devices.

"I could catch him," he mutters to himself. "Second-fastest runner in the state."

"Coach Kapoor? I ran the entire mile," I say, clutching my aching side.

It barely registers—he's still staring after Strat. "Hmm? Oh. I guess you did. Guess I have to pass you."

Strat turns at the door to the locker rooms, his shirt a bright, dazzling white. He waves.

I lift my hand and wave back, unable to stop the smile blooming on my face.

I change out of my PE outfit and head for anatomy in a daze. Sometimes these wrenches from past to present are enough to give me whiplash. How we were in our first relationship feels so different from whatever it is we have now. How can a boy who turns up to help me run my mile have done anything to hurt me?

I'm not expecting another memory to hit so soon after the one this morning, but when Devyn Roberts from Cady's volleyball team whips her hair up into a messy topknot in the seat in front of me in anatomy, the smell of her apple shampoo tugs a scene from our past back into vivid color.

In the memory, there are twenty-four people in Devyn's living room, wedged onto the couch, the love seat, the papasan chair, and on pillows on the floor. Twenty-four faces glow blue in the light cast from a monster-huge TV.

Theoretically we're watching a movie, but there are so many side convos going on in the darkened room that I doubt anyone could tell me the plot.

Not that I could either. Strat found us a cozy place on the floor between the love seat and the papasan. He wedged himself against the wall and patted the space between his long, long legs. Now I can feel his heart beating at my back like my own pulse, and the heat radiating from his chest is a new kind of mesmerizing. But it's the way he's trailing his fingers up and down the softest part of my arm that has my thoughts scattering.

In return, I'm drawing tiny circles on the inside of his knee. I think he likes it, because he shifts the other leg every now and then, bending and stretching it out—the floor is not the most comfortable place to sit—but he's kept this leg still.

My head is in the perfect place, tilted back to rest on his left shoulder. My temple is touching his jaw, and occasionally he murmurs questions into my ear.

He's become an addiction. I never thought I'd be one to sneak out of my house or lie to my parents, but I find myself disabling the sensor on the alarm at one a.m., slipping out of the house to where Strat's parked around the corner to take me to a diner, or just to sit in the car and talk. Or not talk.

Last week I skipped three classes to meet him for coffee. My grades are tanking. I've never been especially aware of tests and quizzes, but now I'm so disconnected from that world I may as well be a dropout.

"PDA POLICE!" someone shouts, probably Brock Wilson, and a phone flashlight beam swoops over us. I wince in the light, and Strat holds a hand up to shield my eyes.

Embarrassment floods me. I start to move, even though losing contact with the heartbeat at my back is the last thing I want.

Strat stills me with the smallest touch. "Stay if you want to. Don't let them win."

Our eyes meet, and the world vanishes around us. Strat nudges my nose, and then he's kissing me.

"Oh my God, stop!" Ashley R groans, and then someone else is throwing popcorn at us.

"Is it bothering you enough for me to stop?" Strat murmurs. "I'll stop if you want."

"I absolutely do *not* want you to stop." This is what I've waited for my whole life. And if I'm smug about it, so what? I had to watch last year as Elliot Saxman shoved his tongue down

Ashley R's throat in the cafeteria after their fourth volcanic breakup/makeup.

"Everyone shut up and watch the movie," Tahirah Watkins says from the papasan chair. She leans over to pass us a bowl of pretzels. "Pay no attention to these heathens. I think you're a really cute couple."

I try to follow her advice, but I just find myself wishing we weren't here. I've always flitted at the edges of Cady's friend group, even though she insists I'm a real part of it. But it's never been more clear: My membership to this club is wholly dependent on my being zipped to her side and quiet enough to ignore. A shadow that follows Cady around and doesn't draw too much attention to herself. Now that I am drawing attention, they realize they don't know me. And maybe I don't know them.

It's then that it hits me: I don't know where Cady is. She was sitting on the couch a minute ago, but now her spot is empty.

"I'll be right back," I say, disentangling myself from Strat.

I search the kitchen, knock on the bathroom door, interrupt a deep philosophical discussion between two JV baseball players vaping on the back porch.

I weave back through the kitchen and see Devyn making herself a fresh drink. She's still got her volleyball jersey on, paired with fuzzy Elmo pajama pants.

"Hey!" She smiles at me. "Need a refresh? Jack and Coke, right? And what does your boy like to drink? We've got vodka, beers, even this extremely classy wine in a box."

I stare at the choices. I have no idea what he'd prefer.

"Oh. Um. Another Jack and Coke is fine, I guess."

"Cute dress. How long does it take you to make something like that?"

I launch into an answer, but I don't get very far before her eyes glaze over. I can't help wishing she was Arissa from my art class. Arissa would descend on the garment, deft fingertips checking the stitches. She'd understand how tricky it was to do the French seams, and she'd know just how many times I would have had to stop to press the pleats, and she'd commiserate with my tales of how my bobbins ran out of thread in the middle of this hem or that one.

I trail off and give Devyn a fake, uneasy laugh. "I guess the short answer is three or four weeks." I look down at my two drinks. "I'd better get this to Strat."

"He's really hot, and he seems so into you. I'm happy for you, babe."

"Thanks."

"What's he into? What's he going to study next year?"

My mouth opens, then closes. I'm blanking. Not because I've forgotten—because I don't know. He plays the piano, but is that something you have to go to college for?

"I'm not sure. He hasn't decided yet," I say.

She frowns. "That's cool. What schools is he considering?"

I swallow. "We, um, don't do a lot of talking," I say, trying to make it sound cool and suggestive.

Devyn holds her cup out to tap against mine, laughing. "Well, I can't judge you for that."

I take the opportunity to make my exit, but when I get back to the living room, I hover by the wall, watching Strat talk animatedly to Tahirah, his heavy watch reflecting the blue glow of the television. I should have known the answers to Devyn's questions. And I don't know other things about him either. Hopes, fears, dreams.

I clutch my drink and stare at the boy I've kissed dozens of times, and I worry that I hardly know him at all.

CHAPTER TWENTY-THREE

Late-afternoon sunlight streams into Cady's hospital room as I slide on my headphones and press Play on the *Swan Lake* album I've been obsessed with recently, visions of my ballerina hero Ayemi Onuki pirouetting in my mind.

It's not as difficult anymore, being here. Sometimes I wonder if Strat has a sixth sense for the moments when my thoughts creep closer to the edge of the abyss, because my phone always seems to light up the very next second with a *hi*, or a joke, or a link related to something we've seen in our midnights.

Last night's midnight started on the highest mountaintop in a jagged, majestic range and ended with us climbing into an honest-to-God hot-air balloon, drifting over endless purple valleys. Strat asked me about dressmaking, then listened to me talk for ages. And he *really* listened, instead of pretending, like most people do.

I have my tablet on my lap, open to a blank page, but my eye catches on my unzipped backpack and the shirt I can see inside. Strat's shirt. The one I found in my closet that made all this real. I've had it in my backpack for over a week. I keep telling myself I'll give it back to him the next time I see him, but I never seem to get around to it.

I tug the shirt out, smoothing its wrinkles. I wonder . . . After a quick glance to make sure none of the nurses in the hallway can see me, I bring it up to my face.

Breathe.

Sure enough, another one of those intoxicating snapshot-reel flashes comes back.

Strat, kissing the curve of my ankle after I rolled it stepping off a curb.

Running out into the sea on a perfect day, whooping, feeling his arms catch around my waist, lifting me up as waves knocked into our knees.

Sitting around a fire with St. Swithun's boys and their girl-friends, thrilling at the way he touches me when no one's looking.

Maybe this is the trick to making all the lost memories come back: I just need to spend an hour in his closet smelling all his clothes.

I keep the shirt on my lap but tug my tablet out from under it. For a long time, I just sit there, drifting in the new memories and thoughts of last night's balloon flight.

Without consciously thinking about it, my stylus starts moving on the blank screen of my tablet. Five minutes later, I'm looking at the rough outline of a dress.

The flare at the end of the skirt, the structured bodice, the

Bardot sleeves. And then—colors spring to mind: coral, with a slash of sunny, goldenrod yellow, embellishments of Grecian blue at the hem. I'll call her When the Heart Is Young, after my favorite Godward painting.

A dress. The first one in months.

I get so caught up in the design that I miss the sun slipping down in the sky. I stack the pattern books up and stuff all my fabric samples into my bag—I think I know what yardage I need to order. When I take my empty cups and chip bags to the break room at the end of the hall, the TV next to the microwave is tuned to the news channel. Normally I wouldn't give it a second glance, but then I hear the word *erasure* and I stop in the doorway.

"Let's take a look at our local business news, Sacramento. The biggest news is the surprise end-quarter results for Aracen Exradere. What's going on there, Oliver?"

"Well, we're not really sure. All we know is that it seems like suddenly fewer people are getting erasures, the first downturn in the company's twenty-year history. Aracen Exradere has long been criticized for its monopoly on the market."

"So what does that mean, that Sacramentans are getting fewer erasures than before?"

"I guess so, Tiff, because people certainly aren't going anywhere else to get them."

I frown.

"And this downturn—it's not happening anywhere else in the nation?"

"That's right."

"We'll have more on this for you after the break, including a statement from Aracen Exradere's founding CEO."

It cuts to a commercial, and for the entire drive home, I think about what it could mean. It's almost midnight by the time I pull into my driveway. Upstairs, when I switch on the lights in my bedroom, the memory sears into my mind's eye so abruptly that I flinch, as if I've been caught in an ultra-bright paparazzi camera flash.

Strat's at a keyboard, one of those portable ones on an X-stand. We're in an airy, painfully clean room. The signs of wealth are subtle but unmistakable: It's in the silence and the quality of the air, the sumptuous furnishings. The only sign there's a teenage boy living here is the row of band posters on the wall. The only one I recognize is a big rock band called Slydekick. I'm in a chair upholstered in beige velvet, my knees drawn up, ladylike, underneath my full skirt.

Lurking at the edge of the scene is a *bed*.

Strat's fingers float over the keyboard. I recognize the haunting melody even though I can't name it. It must be one of the greats: Bach, Beethoven, Mozart.

The memory fades as fast as it came, vanishing like a Polaroid developing in reverse. I scrabble for my phone to text Strat.

He responds right away.

What kind of room? Like a
practice studio?

I bite my lip.

No. A bedroom, I think.

A long pause. Minutes pass.
Strat finally replies.

Anything else?

I scour the image seared into my mind.

Just a poster. I think it said
Slydekick?

Aria . . . I think you were in my
bedroom.

His bedroom. I swallow. The way we were kissing in some of
these memories—I guess I should have seen it coming. The relationship was getting serious.

The desire to see more of the scene is sudden and overwhelming. Not because there might be clues about why we erased each
other, but because I want to see what happened after he stopped
playing.

OK, I type, fingers unsteady on the screen. Guess that's where
we'll have to go to coax the next memory out. When can I come over?

There's another long pause. And then: three dots, blinking.

I'm not sure that's the best idea.

Something in my chest clenches. Does he . . . not want to see me?

Is he hiding something?

A minute later, he sends:

I glance at the clock: 11:53 p.m. What will happen if I'm not asleep by then?

I brush my teeth at top speed, but before I can go to sleep, I have to do one thing. I dig an index card out of my backpack and write the memory on it before it fades.

<u>Strat's room</u>
Slydekick poster, keyboard
Bed was made
What was I doing there? Didn't seem like a study session

I add the index card to the wall in my closet, then dive onto the bed like it's a relay race. I wriggle under the stiff quilt and check the clock one more time.

12:03 a.m.

My heart sinks. What if I've missed it?

CHAPTER TWENTY-FOUR

Light glows on the other side of my eyelids.

My alarm bleats insistently, dragging me out of sleep. The light is dawn-soft instead of ultraviolet, and I'm staring up at my bedroom ceiling.

I missed our midnight.

I start to text Strat, but then I remember how he didn't seem to want me to come to his place, and I slide my phone into my pocket. On my way out of the house, I flick through the mail by the door. Still nothing from Sciarra.

After yesterday's creative surge, I'm uncharacteristically industrious in art. Arissa's usually working at an easel, but today she's sitting at her table with a huge taffeta dress draped over her lap. It looks like a costume—she must be falling behind on alterations if she's bringing theater work into class.

She's ripping out a seam, probably to let the bodice out for a taller actress, when she accidentally nicks one of the threads holding a string of tiny, pearly-white beads. They scatter over the floor, making delicate noises as they bounce and roll away.

I pick up the ones that land under my table and take them to her. "Need a hand with the rest?"

"That would be amazing. Thanks, Aria."

We get most of the beads rounded up, and I tip them into her hand. "Thanks again, babe," she says. "What are you working on?"

I glance back at my table. "A new design. First one in a long time, actually."

"Can I see?"

"Um—if you want to, sure."

She dumps the beads into a cup and follows me over.

"It's gorgeous! River, come here."

Before I know it, my desk is surrounded by my classmates, oohing and aahing over my work.

Arissa grins at me, tucking her hair behind her ears, and I grin back, one of those rare moments of *friendship* thrumming in my happy heart.

It tugs at a memory. Not a lost memory like the medically erased ones of me and Strat. This is just a very old one, its edges worn smooth.

I don't remember much from first grade. I can vaguely picture my teacher's face and a few bright pieces of the classroom, and playing "The Farmer in the Dell" for the first time in music and thinking it was the best game in the history of all games.

The school had, unbelievably, put me and Cady in different classes, and we weren't taking it well. My tears were a swift, violent storm that lasted three days, but then I met Millie. She wore her hair in two pigtails and Belle was also her favorite princess and she smelled like gummy bears. I remember giggling next to her in story time and grabbing her by the hand when it was time to line up for recess.

Cady's disappointment in our class assignments was a slow, angry, escalating burn. She went on a literal hunger strike, refusing to eat dinner until our parents went to the school and made them move her into my class.

And then she was there, right at my side like she'd always been, and I can't remember if it took days or weeks, but my new friendship with Millie just . . . faded away.

Maybe it was organic. But now I'm wondering if there was something more deliberate about that. Do I remember Cady frowning and taking my hand, pulling me away from our daily "Farmer in the Dell" game over by the swing set, or am I inventing that?

In the hallway on my way to my next class, my phone buzzes with a text from Strat.

I missed you last night.

A mixture of warmth and regret hits me square in the chest. I lean against someone else's locker to reply.

I guess if we're up past midnight it doesn't work.

He doesn't text again until after Algebra, but when he does, it's an address.

CHAPTER TWENTY-FIVE

The house slumping on the weed-choked lot in front of me looks nothing like where a boy whose family can afford private school tuition would live.

I stand in the driveway and double-check the address. Piano music drifts from a room inside, and it's a piece I'm sure I've heard Strat play before, so it must be right.

I decide to text him, just in case.

I'm here. I think.

A minute later, the screen door creaks open and Strat appears. Perfectly tousled hair and starched white shirt. He props the door wide open and leans against the doorjamb, seemingly unaware of the dichotomy between how he looks—*loaded*—and how this house looks—not.

Or maybe not so unaware. Is that a very un-Strat-like nervousness shimmering under the surface?

"How long were you planning to stand out here on my drive-way?" he asks, a teasing smile at the corner of his mouth.

"Oh, only fifteen or twenty more minutes, tops. Carry on with whatever it was you were doing."

He chuckles, then gestures for me to come in.

Stepping into his house is like entering a dim, stale cave. It's tidy, but everything is worn in a way that corroborates what I've been starting to suspect. The junky station wagon, the declined card . . .

Inside, there's a slouching leather couch with splitting seams and end tables that look like they came from a thrift store, but the thing that takes up the most space in the living room is a baby grand piano, slick and black and new.

"I don't like to practice when Dad is home, and you're a little early. Would it be okay if I kept playing for ten minutes?"

"Go for it," I say. I fold gingerly onto the black leather couch. It's so old that its wrinkles have wrinkles. "What's with the giant fancy piano?" I ask as he shuffles through a pile of sheet music.

"You mean why is the rest of my house a dump, except for this?"

My mouth opens like a fish, but he has mercy on me.

"It's okay. So you know that icy, beautiful grandmother I was telling you about? Her name is Annette Madigan, and she's kind of a big deal in the classical music world. She's a cellist with the Chicago Symphony Orchestra. She cut off my dad, hence the house. But not me, hence the very expensive piano lessons start-ing at age four. And this piano." He slides onto the bench.

"And the school," I conclude.

"No," he murmurs. "She doesn't pay for my tuition."

Before I can ask more, he presses a foot to one of the shiny brass pedals and arranges his fingers on the keys. A complex cathedral chord rings out, filling the room like a church organ.

I watch as he practices. I watch as he gets snagged up on a tricky section, playing it two, three, four times over. Each time the music crumbles abruptly into silence. And then he breaks through, playing that section fluidly, acknowledging the victory with a small, businesslike nod—only to get stuck on something else on the next page. He hits this block more than a dozen times, slowing down to rudimentarily plonk out each chord. Then he starts again at the top.

It's strange—he never seems to get frustrated. His focus is laser-like, and I might as well not exist.

I take the opportunity to look around the room. Have I been here before? I search my mind but come up empty.

When he finishes playing, he closes the lid over the keys carefully.

"How often do you practice?" I ask.

He shrugs. "I don't really keep track."

"But thousands of hours, right?"

"Probably."

"And it's always like that? You hit those blocks, but you keep chipping away at them until you break through?"

"Always." He sounds almost cheerful about it. It's baffling.

"You should probably know—I'm a serial quitter," I admit.

His eyebrow quirks. "What does that mean?"

"Like, you know when your parents stick you in all kinds of

little clubs to see what you might be interested in? I didn't last for more than a month in anything."

"Come here," Strat says, patting the bench. "Was piano one of the things you quit?"

"Yes." I don't tell him that I loved the moments leading up to my first lesson—the possibility, imagining that I would be instantly good at it, daydreaming about myself in a long black dress playing beautifully to a room full of people. Then the lesson actually started, and it was hard. I felt like I shrank an entire inch every time I hit a wrong note.

He lifts the lid of the piano again, then takes my fingers and arranges them on the cool, smooth keys.

"This is my favorite note," he says, pressing down on the ring finger of my right hand. "Because of this little chip right here." He runs his thumbnail over the jagged edge at the end of the key.

I swallow at the warmth of him beside me, his hand on mine.

Strat shows me a stupidly embarrassing piece: "Three Blind Mice." The kind where your hands rest on ten keys and don't have to move.

I try it. And mess up. I want to give up, but I don't want him to think badly of me. My cheeks flush. I pretend to laugh every time I mess up, but I hate it.

It takes about twenty tries, but I finally stumble through the whole thing.

"There, see? You just played an entire piece."

I shoot him a glare. "Great. Can I quit now?"

He laughs. "Sure. But hey—didn't it feel just a little bit good to work through it?"

I roll my eyes. "Maybe marginally."

"It doesn't have to be perfect," he says. "In fact, when I play concerts, or competitions, I always make one deliberate mistake."

"Really? Why?"

He shrugs. "Flaws are interesting."

"There's a difference between making a mistake on purpose and just completely sucking at something," I say.

I look down, poking at the keys.

"It's hard going to see your sister, right?" he says.

I pause. "The hardest."

"And you haven't quit going."

I haven't gone enough, though, I think, but I don't say it out loud. I plink out the notes for "Three Blind Mice" again, slow and stilted.

"You know," I say, "the only other lesson I actually kind of liked was ballet."

Mom and Cady and I go to *The Nutcracker* every Christmas, and a poster of my favorite dancer, Ayemi Onuki, is tacked up proudly on the wall above my bed.

Ballet is beautiful. Watching a show is like being in a dream, and I used to love sliding out of real life and into the glittering worlds on the stage.

"Cady and I used to take ballet classes when we were little, but we stopped going after fifth grade." I loved those lessons, loved my soft pink leather shoes and opaque tights and little pink leotard. Sometimes I wonder if that's the one extracurricular I would have stuck with.

"Why did you stop?" Strat asks.

I shrug. "Cady didn't want to do it anymore, and I guess I didn't want to keep going without her."

"Let me guess. Twin thing?"

"Yeah. I thought about starting some lessons again freshman year, but it didn't fit with the varsity volleyball schedule."

"Aria, you're not on the varsity volleyball team."

I look down. "I know. Cady wouldn't play unless I was in the bleachers."

He frowns. "Really?"

Outside the window, a car engine rumbles, crescendoing into a roar as it swings into the driveway.

Strat blanches and checks his phone. "Come on," he says, already tugging me to my feet. Keys jangle in the front door as we pass, and Strat practically pushes me up the stairs. "My room's on the right," he hisses.

Oh—he doesn't want me to see whoever this is.

Or he doesn't want them to see *me*.

He herds me inside and shuts us in just as the downstairs door opens. "I'm so sorry—it's my dad. Can you give me a few minutes to deal with him?" There's a pleading, soft look in his eyes. Apology and question all at once. *Help me out*, it's saying.

"Of course," I say.

He melts a little. "Thanks." For a second, I think he's going to lean forward and kiss my forehead. It's a strange feeling, like he's done that before.

And then he's slipping back out of the door, leaving me alone in his room, a pillar of awkward in this foreign space.

It takes two heartbeats to realize: This isn't the bedroom I saw in the memory.

It's smaller, for starters, maybe a third of the size of that airy, bright space. The wallpaper is browning, and there's a rust-colored water stain on the ceiling.

His closet door is open, and his St. Swithun's uniforms hang neatly inside: white dress shirts on the top rail and gray trousers on the bottom.

Some of the private-school-boy objects I expected to see are here: A shelf full of expensive colognes and hair products. A gleaming laptop—but there's a barcoded sticker next to the trackpad. School-issued. There's a basket with shoe polishes and brushes on the floor and an ironing board leaning against the wall. He polishes his own shoes and irons his own clothes. To keep up with his classmates? It makes my heart hurt to think of the things he's had to do to make it look like he fits in, when his classmates almost certainly have these chores done for them.

There is one shelf by the window that draws my attention. I step closer to make out exactly what's on it. Toys—but strange ones. A three-armed *Star Wars* figurine. A Hot Wheels car with no paint at all, just milky plastic and rough iron.

Flaws are interesting, he said.

I touch the double penny in my pocket.

A movement outside the window catches my eye. His dad is plodding to a worn garden bench, the wood gray and cracked.

He's an older, worn-down version of Strat. They're both tall and slender, but on his dad, the leanness looks gaunt and unhealthy. He's wearing a uniform, navy fabric with a badge on his breast pocket that I can't read from here. Mechanic maybe, or plumber? But his hands aren't grease-stained.

He twists the gold band on his left ring finger, and I remember something Strat said—that his dad's been having a hard time with the anniversary of his mom's death. My heart climbs up my throat. Is that the bench they used to sit on together?

The screen door squawks. Strat—still in his St. Swithun's jacket and looking like he doesn't fit with any of this—eases down onto the bench, leaving a space in the middle.

His dad attempts a smile, but it's so weary and watery it hurts to look at. He pats Strat's knee, then gets up like his bones are ancient, even though he's got to only be in his forties.

Strat stays on the bench for a while. He looks off to the side, his jaw working as if he's trying not to cry.

My heart aches for him.

I look around the strange, unfamiliar room, the one I'm starting to suspect he never brought me to when we were a couple. In all the memories from before, he was always happy and charming. And I know the old Aria would have been happy to never look beyond that facade. The Strat I know now is a real person, not a blank wall for me to project my daydream Prince Charming onto.

"I'm sorry it took me so long down there," Strat says. "If I don't make Dad something to eat, he won't eat at all."

"It's okay. I, um, found your toy shelf," I say, trying to lighten the mood. "Should I be concerned?"

That draws a smile from him. "I like to collect toys with manufacturer defects and stuff."

I reach into my pocket. "You might like this, then," I say, laying the double penny in his palm.

"Oh, wow," he says, inspecting it. "It's kind of eerie, right? Like an egg with two yolks."

"It's mine and Cady's. We found it at the beach, and we've taken turns carrying it as a good luck charm ever since."

"I love that." He puts the penny back in my palm and folds my fingers over it. "More meaningful than my three-legged Shrek."

"Yeah. Strat? Would now be a good time to tell you this isn't the bedroom I saw in the memory?"

He freezes. "Seriously?"

"Yeah."

He casts a glance over his room. "God. If I'd known, I wouldn't have subjected you to this dump." He scrubs a hand over his face. "But you said you saw a Slydekick poster."

"It was the same poster. But the room was . . . bigger."

"So you mean huge."

"Yeah. Built-in bookshelves. Two bay windows. The comforter on the bed was pale blue."

Strat sinks onto his bed. "I should have realized. That was probably Mick's room. He's loaded, in case you haven't guessed. Unlike me." He points at the poster on his wall. "Mick's dad is the lead singer in Slydekick."

I gape. "Seriously?"

"Yep. And he's one of the *less* wealthy kids at school. If I told you who else went to Swithun's, I'd have to kill you."

"Please don't tell me."

Wow. Slydekick. They're huge right now. Mick's dad must be

Bruce, the older of the two frontmen, because the newest member is only a few years older than me. Leo Sterling. The only reason I know of him is because his love story is kind of mysterious and epic.

Gingerly I sit next to Strat on the edge of his bed. "Strat . . . I don't think you brought me here before at all. I don't think you told me about your mom or your dad." Something's trying to connect in my mind. It feels important, but I can't quite grasp the edges of it. "I don't think I really knew you before."

We are silent.

"Do I know you now?" I ask in a small voice.

His eyes snap to mine. "Yes," he says firmly. "Yes, Aria."

"It's just . . . something's been bugging me. In the flashbacks I've had, you were never driving your station wagon. You were in this really expensive-looking red convertible."

He frowns. "That sounds like Mick's ragtop."

I feel as if I'm tiptoeing around landmines, and I don't know why. Something's not adding up. "I'm sure you said it was yours."

"Really?" He frowns with genuine confusion, trying to understand his past self's actions. "Do you think I borrowed it to impress you?" He slumps. "Honestly, it sounds like something I might do."

I swallow. "Strat, if I found out before . . . do you think that could have been why I erased you?"

He leans forward, elbows on his knees. "Shit. It's a solid possibility." Strat looks around his room. "So the chances of any memories coming back from here are pretty low, huh?" he says.

"Yeah." My shoulders sag. "There are still so many gaps. And still nothing to suggest why we chose to slice each other out of our heads."

"Is there anywhere else we can go? Any other places you've seen?" Strat asks.

"A few smaller flashes, but I couldn't place where we were."

Strat's quiet for a moment, then he sits up taller. "Wait, what about that place Dean was talking about? The swing set up on the ridge? He said we were up there a lot, right?"

"He must be talking about the art installation. That giant red swing overlooking Lake Tullanoch."

"No time like the present," Strat says as he stands, and I can tell he's eager to get out of here.

I take one last look around his bedroom, then follow him out.

CHAPTER TWENTY-SIX

The last tinge of daylight seeps from the sky as we pull up to the scenic lookout on the ridge above Lake Tullanoch.

The view from up here makes you feel as if you're perched at the top of California. The ridge has been dotted with larger-than-life art installations for as long as I can remember, but the giant swing set has always been my favorite. Up ahead, the red frame arcs high, the metal hammered into an arch that twists like a Möbius strip. It's twice as big as a regular swing set, and the seat is wide enough to comfortably hold three people. Or six, as we achieved one summer night back in eighth grade.

Strat pushes his blazer sleeves up to his elbows. "What are we looking for?" he asks.

I circle the swing. "I'm not sure. I haven't seen any memories of us here."

"Dean and Hollis seemed to think we were up here a lot, but yeah, it's not ringing a bell for me either."

I edge closer to the steep drop. Below, I can see the pale curve of the lake's only sandy beach. It's where the annual Ridgecroft Summer Beach Bonanza is held, and it's a favorite spot for pavilion weddings. It must be where we went to that bonfire party Hollis was talking about.

The swing wobbles as Strat and I nestle onto it, side by side. My feet barely brush the ground, but Strat's legs are long enough that he can plant his shoes firmly on it.

He stares down at his feet. "Sorry about my dad."

"You don't have to apologize. I've got family stuff going on too." We swing in silence for a while. "Is he going to be all right, though? He seemed so sad."

"He'll keep trucking, I guess. I don't remember his being any other way."

"And you take care of him, instead of the other way around."

He nods. "It's what I have to do."

"You don't *have* to," I say quietly. "But it says something about you that you do."

"Anyone would." He shrugs.

"I don't think that's true." The guilt tugs at me again. If Cady . . . *went,* I don't think I'd be the one holding my family together, cooking and cleaning and helping pay rent. I can barely look at her when I go to the hospital.

"My mom asked me to help." He pulls his wallet out of his pocket. His hand is a little unsteady as he passes me a folded square of paper. "It's a photocopy, so you don't have to be careful with it or anything."

I unfold the paper.

"She left it in my room, with a note on the envelope telling me to open it when I turned thirteen. I read it when I was eleven."

"Eleven? Oh, Strat."

"She knew Dad would take her death hard, but I don't think she realized how hard. He was a wreck. Lost his job. Wouldn't eat. Slept all the time. My grandmother got us through most of those years, sending money and then showing up twice a year, each visit culminating in her telling him he had to get his shit together. Instead, he'd just sink a little deeper, crying for days. I hated her visits. He was always so much worse after she left."

"Did he never consider getting an erasure?" I ask carefully.

"Never. He wanted to remember everything about her."

I touch the words his mother left for him, shocked that he's trusting me with this. Shocked that she even left this letter at all. Something about it seems . . . wrong. *Promise me you'll take care of him.* It's what she should have said to her husband. Not her son.

"I got Dad the job at St. Swithun's," Strat continues. "Made a CV and a convincing sob-story cover letter and dropped it off at the office. That's how I can go there: free tuition for sons of staff members."

"What does he teach?" I ask.

"He doesn't teach. He's a janitor." There is only the barest hint of defiance as he says it, as if he's used to other people judging him for it.

Oh. I can't imagine how hard it would be to be the janitor's son at a private school, but Strat soared above the odds to become popular and well-liked. That charm of his—I wonder how much of it is natural and how much he had to develop to survive.

My chest aches with admiration. He's been doing such difficult things for so long. I wish I could be like that.

I fold the note carefully and hand it back to Strat. It doesn't seem right that his mom saddled him with so much responsibility. There are other, sweeter things in the message, and it's clear that she adored him. She was sick, I tell myself; she might not have been making the best decisions near the end.

"Strat . . . I know she had good intentions, but don't you think asking you to do that was a little intense?"

"It's okay. Really," he says. "I like being what people need me to be."

What about what you need them *to be?* I almost ask.

What does he need me *to be?*

He tucks the letter back into his wallet. And then he reaches over and squeezes my hand where it's resting on my knee.

Strat sighs. "Well, if nothing's coming back, we better go before it gets any darker."

I nod, sliding off the seat. When I grab the red arch, my ring clangs on the hollow metal. I grab his arm. "Strat—look."

Scratched into the metal are letters, *AL + SM*, framed with a heart and a Cupid's arrow. There are hundreds of initials carved into the red paint—how strange that this is the one my ring would land on.

"Do you think this was us?" I ask, running my fingers over the letters. It's mind-blowing to think that we were here together months ago. That we scratched this into the pole and I have no memory of it.

My fingertip lingers on the letters. There's a memory hovering just out of reach, but I can't catch it.

We circle the swing set one more time, but we don't find any more clues, and no other memories resurface. On the way back down, Strat turns on his phone flashlight so we don't stumble on the uneven ground.

He walks me to my car door. I thought I was getting used to the hum of being near him, but when he looks down at me to say goodnight, I start vibrating with it again.

"The memories feel so real when they hit, don't they?" he asks. "There was this one where we drove out to Santa Cruz early to watch the sunrise, and afterward I gave you a piggyback ride to go get coffees, but then we . . ." He clears his throat. "We didn't ever make it to the coffee stand." His cinnamon eyes darken, and he stares down at me so intensely my legs turn to jelly. "I couldn't take my eyes off you, Aria."

I swallow. It's getting harder to separate the "before" feelings from the ones that are pulsing through me now. The emotions are so similar, an echo, like we've been set on the same inevitable path, destined to walk this story over and over again. I just have to hope this time it doesn't end the same way.

"Aria? I've got this thing tomorrow. A piano competition. I'd really like it if you were there."

I nod. I couldn't look away if I tried. "Just tell me where to turn up."

CHAPTER TWENTY-SEVEN

After the day we've had, I certainly don't expect to wake up in a children's indoor jungle gym at midnight, but that's exactly what happens.

I'm starfished on the surface of a ball pit that is bigger than an Olympic-sized swimming pool, floating on a million pearlescent plastic balls.

"Strat?" I call out. I flounder, rolling over ungracefully, surrounded by the smell of new plastic and the gentle clicking noise the balls make as they shift around me. I work my feet under me, but the pit is deeper than I thought, and I can't find the bottom. I struggle toward the edge of the pit like an uncoordinated toddler.

"Strat!" I shout again.

"I'm here," comes his voice, distant and muted.

I reach the edge of the ball pit at last and drag myself up the squashy blue steps.

"Up here," Strat calls from inside a play gym, peering at me through the netting. "I can't figure out how to get out of this damn thing. Hold on." He disappears.

I survey our surroundings while I wait. The place is cavernous, with towering climbing structures and glossy slides, trampolines and sponge pits stretching as far as I can see. There must be a ceiling, but it's so high overhead it fades into actual fog when I look up.

Instead of the clown-bright colors of the play gyms of my childhood, everything is softer. Dream colors, blues and pinks, laced through with a gleaming thread of ultraviolet purple.

Strat emerges finally, straightening his clothes. He still looks a little subdued, his shoulders a little heavier than usual. "This place is wild. There's even a space rocket," he says, staring up at the tower looming ahead of us. It's the cylindrical, shuttle-nosed shape of a bright-white NASA rocket. At the very top, there's one of those bubble windows—a half-sphere of clear plastic. It glistens at us, beckoning.

I glance at Strat. His house, his dad, his mom's letter—it was all so heavy. It aches, knowing that he's trying to be everything for his broken family but no one's trying to be anything for him.

He's always doing small, kind things for me, tugging me gently back to solid ground in a hundred tiny ways. The impulse rises in me like a balloon. Tonight, I'm going to do something kind for him. Tug him out of this heaviness and into something happier.

I shove my shoulder into his, knocking him off balance. "Race you to the top of the rocket."

Strat's mouth opens, but I don't hear his response. I'm gone. I plunge into the portal at the bottom of the space rocket, pushing through heavy hanging punching bags, hopping over lily pad steps, clambering up a ramp of spinning rods.

He catches the back of my dress, pulling me behind him, and slingshots past me into the lead.

"Hey, not fair!" I shout.

"Who said St. Swithun's boys play fair?" he says, deftly maneuvering across a rope bridge as I huff and puff after him.

"Show-off," I say, laughing.

The next plastic tunnel leads to a dead end, and I spin, looking for Strat. A hole in the ceiling. There's a rise of woven straps, layer after layer. I contort my body like a worm as I work my way up. I finally burst onto the final landing. We're so high up now.

I've caught up with Strat, but when I try to squeeze past him into the lead, he tackles me onto the foam-mat surface. Our skin sticks to the purple vinyl.

When his fingers tense on my ribs, on the spot where I have always—always—been the most ticklish, my reaction is instant and extreme.

Above me, Strat's eyes light like he's just discovered a trove of the most valuable treasure. "Oh, you're *very* ticklish."

I can't answer. My whole body tenses, and my laugh becomes a silent, airless thing. His fingers, strong from years of dancing over piano keys, dig in tighter.

I let him tickle me until I'm gasping.

He's *loving* it. My ridiculous reaction, or the squeaky awkward snorting noises I'm making, or just the fact that he's making it all happen with the smallest movements of his fingers.

When my oxygen levels get critical, I croak out, "Okay, okay, stop," and his hands instantly go still.

Everything goes still.

He's staring down at me, both of us grinning like maniacs. He's stretched out fully on top of me, almost crushing me save for the elbows he props himself up on, and when he breathes out, I breathe in, our bellies moving in perfect synchronization.

Suddenly, his fingers on my ribs don't feel ticklish at all. His hand is flattened on my side, a warm, solid press.

I've seen it in movies. When a moment pivots, when a laughing grin drops into awestruck lust. It's happening right now.

A sudden drop, low in my stomach. Our smiles fade to stunned seriousness.

His eyes flick down to my mouth, and the air becomes thick. My body is suddenly scorching under the weight of him. He looks back up, searching my eyes. His stare is smoldering.

How much better would this be without the airbrushed haze of the night lying over it?

A mischievous glint sparks in his eye. Before I can figure out what it means, he's lurching off me.

No way! He's making one last desperate attempt to be the first to the top of the rocket.

I shriek. "You low-down, dirty—"

He scrambles up squishy roller pins like a ninja warrior. I grab the hem at the ankle of his jeans and pull myself up after him. We spill into the circular room at the top of the rocket, collapsing on the slick white mat floor. The room glows, the UV light turning the space lunar bright.

We are both laughing. I'm smiling so wide my face hurts.

"I can't believe you did that!" I wheeze.

"Me neither," he says. "I'm not even a competitive person."

"You literally do piano competitions for a living."

"Yeah, but only so I can afford to keep the fridge stocked, not because I want to kick anyone's ass."

We're both still smiling ear to ear, and it's the unspoken conversation between our eyes that says, *This is the most fun I've ever had. This is joy.*

I press my hand to my chest. It feels like my heart is about to burst out of my rib cage. "Can you die from exercise?" I ask. "Because that's the most I've had in years."

It feels good. Cleansing and sharp. For the first time in a long time, I wasn't thinking about anything but reaching this place, and the getting here felt euphoric.

We crawl over to the clear plastic bubble. On hands and knees, I edge forward. Press my palms to the clear plastic. My stomach drops. We're eight or nine stories up, nothing but a little plexiglass stopping us from being splats on the UV confetti–flecked carpet below.

The structure sways under us. I remind myself that even skyscrapers have to move a little; they have to bend so they don't break. Fear has me reaching for him—and his hand is already there, reaching for me.

"The midnight wouldn't let us get hurt, right?" I ask.

"Still creeps me out that you think it's sentient."

I inch forward on my belly, looking down over the childhood paradise spread out under us. "Do you think it's just our minds creating these places?" I ask. That would make sense for the forest glade, Venice, Paris, but I've never been particularly obsessed with swimming-pool-sized ball pits or NASA rocket ships.

Strat glances up. "Oh, wow. Come here. Lie down."

Gingerly, I turn onto my back. We shuffle so we're shoulder to shoulder, elbow to elbow, hip to hip, our backs cradled by the gentle curve of the plexiglass bubble.

We look up at the hazy darkness together.

The backs of his knuckles brush mine. I hesitate. I know I should draw away—keep that distance I've been forcing myself to keep—but instead, I slide my hand into his.

Again the sensations go vague when all I want is to feel every inch of his palm against mine. I want desperately to get closer than this, but I can't figure out how.

"Ready to go to outer space, Aria Lendell?"

He's smiling like this is the best moment of his life. He's happy. I did that.

The euphoria of the tickle attack is fading, leaving behind something sweeter. He turns his face to me, and all I feel is a caramel-slow *fondness*, so deep, and swelling by the second.

I am *fond* of him.

And this midnight—it's not champagne in Paris or slow kisses in a gondola in Venice. It's not an impromptu waltz at homecoming or a hot-air balloon ride over misty canyons. It would have never been on my epic-romance bingo card, and I would have never acted out this ball-pit-rocket-ship-tickle-fest climb with Cady or made my Barbies reenact it.

But this has been my favorite midnight so far.

CHAPTER TWENTY-EIGHT

The blare of a car horn has my chin snapping up. I had one foot in the road, not looking before I crossed. I forget how much traffic there is in Strat's city, so different from my foothills town of twelve thousand people.

Where is the concert hall? I can't be late for Strat's competition after I promised him I'd come. The blue arrow on my map swivels this way and that, and I go an entire city block before I realize I've been going the wrong way.

My toes are throbbing in my vintage T-bar heels by the time I spot the modern white shell of the concert hall. Strat is leaning against the wall, looking like an album cover. He eats an apple as the diesel-scented breeze messes with his hair, and something inside me pinches tight.

I want to stay in this moment, watching him before he notices me, but he looks up as if he can sense me, his eyes snapping to mine so physically it's startling.

I wave and step—no, wait, look for cars before crossing this time—into the street.

He straightens, pushing off the wall. He's in a suit, and God, he looks amazing. His smile is wider and whiter than the building behind him.

"You should have worn the shirt with the lace cuffs," I say. That gravitational force is there again, tugging on us once we slip into each other's orbit.

"Believe it or not, the judges tend to frown on such frivolity," he says.

"Then they are totally missing out."

"Right? You should have heard the fuss they made about my hair. I believe 'unruly' was the word."

I reach up and twist one coppery spiral back into place. My chest grazes his in the process.

"I like unruly," I say. The words are out before I realize how it sounds.

"Believe me, I know," he says, his voice a little rough.

Strat pulls the gleaming glass door open for me like a doorman at an expensive New York City hotel. The lobby is five stories high, with an art deco chandelier and enormous banners hanging from the ceiling, huge overblown prints of dancers in motion, actors in velvet doublets caught in the middle of their most intense scenes, musicians with closed eyes, swept away by their own music.

"Let me take your coat," Strat says.

I shrug out of it, shivering a little as his hands land on my shoulders. Another first—no one's ever taken my coat for me before.

When I turn, Strat's focused on my dress. "You look stunning."

I bloom under his gaze. He said people usually dress up for the concerts, so I'm in the dress I named Afternoon Tea with Violet B. It's got Juliet sleeves and an empire waist, and the long skirt is printed with vibrant purple flowers.

I turn and spot the one banner I hadn't seen yet—the one with a three-story-tall print of Ayemi Onuki, mid-jeté.

"Oh," I whisper. I'm suddenly transformed into a wide-eyed little girl looking up at her idol. "I used to be obsessed with that dancer."

My memories of coming here every Christmas tumble into an Instagram-perfect blur. Cold and crisp air outside, Cady and I warm in the lobby in matching red velvet dresses. Mom always dolled us up and took us to a fancy restaurant beforehand, and we loved feeling like glamorous little adults.

I was enchanted by every ballet, starry-eyed at the opulence. But the performance sharpened when she leaped onto the stage. Ayemi Onuki, the company's prima ballerina, dancing the role of the Sugar Plum Fairy. I scooted to the edge of my seat, eyes glued to her. The way she floated over the stage, ethereal, perfect—it was like nothing I'd ever seen before.

Afterward I spent all my allowance on a charm bracelet and the poster of Ayemi Onuki in arabesque that's still hanging above my bed. Grace. Elegance. Beauty. Perfection. And there were a lot of flowers. I became enamored.

"Hold on," Strat says. "Let me check something." He taps through his phone, squinting at text too small for me to read from here. When he finds what he is looking for, he takes my elbow and spins me around. "Come on—we have time."

"Time for what?"

He takes my hand, and I have to try very hard not to let the world contract to the feel of his palm warm against mine. He leads me through the lobby's café to a half-hidden, unmarked door, then fishes a key card out of his wallet and taps it to the electronic handle.

"Am I allowed back here?" I hiss as we pass a storage room full of document boxes. It doesn't seem like this part of the building is meant for public eyes.

"Sure. I don't just play recitals and competitions, I gig for the ballet company too. I've been working for them on and off for about a year."

"In their orchestra?" I goggle. That seems like a big deal.

"No—I just help with rehearsals, when their music team can't cover everything. They have a conductor and two permanent pianists, so I usually only come in for half-hour rehearsals for smaller variations, while they're teaching sections to third or fourth casts. But I get sent all the rehearsal schedules. And guess who's rehearsing right now?"

I stop walking. Plant myself in the hallway. Our linked hands jerk like a rope pulled taut, and he ricochets back to me.

"Seriously? Ayemi Onuki?" I ask.

He grins. "They're doing a run-through for the show that opens next week. They won't be in costume, but the dancing is all there."

"I . . . don't we need to be getting ready for your competition? Don't you need to warm up or something?"

"Eh, I'm warm," he says, waggling his fingers like jazz hands. "And we've got a while before the stage manager starts freaking out and looking for me."

Still, I'm hesitant. Why don't I want to see this? There's something wrong with me.

We stop outside a door with a built-in viewing window. Inside the room, dancers mill around in plain rehearsal leotards and leggings.

"We'll sneak to the back of the room," Strat says, low. "Just stay quiet and pretend we've been invited, and no one will question it."

He opens the door, and we are enveloped in energy and sound and movement. We slide into hard plastic chairs against the mirrored back wall. Strat lays my raincoat across his lap, and there's something strangely intimate about seeing it there, handled so casually by him, that distracts me from my shaky nervousness.

Strat waves at a man standing at the side of a glossy black piano. He's got fluffy wheat-colored hair and wire-rimmed round glasses. He looks vaguely European, German maybe. "My boss," Strat whispers in my ear. "He's great."

A statuesque woman steps into the middle of the "stage"—just a square marked in colored tape. "We'll go from the top and break after the Grand Pas this time." She addresses the man at the piano. "Mr. Müller, take it away."

The pianist nods, lit with sudden purpose. A heavy silence falls as everyone settles into where they are supposed to be. The pianist strikes the first chord with a dramatic flourish, playing to the rapt room.

The corps de ballet trickles onstage. Their leotards are worn and faded. Their pointe shoes aren't even pink.

My body is almost straining for the door. I wonder if Strat would notice if I closed my eyes. With a surreptitious movement, he angles his phone screen to me. He's typed me a message in his notes app.

What's wrong? Do you want to go?

I take the phone, warm from his pocket, and type back: I'm not sure I want to see them like this. Not in costume, messing up.

Sweating all over the place? he types.

Exactly.

He chews on that for a moment. Why not?

I glance up at the stage. It's not beautiful.

He frowns. His fingers fly over the screen. Hands it back to me.

All those things—the costumes, the flawless execution—that's just set dressing. It's the movement that's the art. Watch.

And then Ayemi enters. Leaping out of a wing just as she did so many years ago, except there are no real wings in this stark, mirror-walled studio. Her rehearsal clothes are more ragged than some of the younger dancers', even though she's got to be making decent money. She's top billing. Prima ballerina.

Her tights are laddered, and her black leotard is faded to a fuzzy gray. Her pointe shoes are stained and tattered. Her face isn't caked in perfect, dewy makeup—it's just dewy. There are acne scars on her chin. Sweat already sheens her forehead, and wisps of hair escape her bun.

I can't watch. The veneer has been stripped away. The dancer who's been my hero for eight years, knocked off her pedestal in eight minutes.

Keep watching, Strat types, like he can read my mind.

It is painful to keep my eyes on her, for another wrenching minute. Another.

And then.

I watch her muscles flex and torque. Up close, they are more than graceful—they are solid and strong. I can see her collarbone rising and falling with exertion, something that's perfectly hidden onstage, but from this distance it's obvious.

In the theater, this solo will look effortless. Gliding. Buttery. Sparkly. But I can see now that it is *work*. And it might be more beautiful, because I can see the strength in it now. The control. The *effort*. The passion.

I am rapt.

Every eye in the room is glued to her. The pianist plays to an emotional crescendo, and Ayemi holds her final pose for five, ten, fifteen heart-in-my-throat seconds.

The moment breaks on a rush of applause, and I'm surprised to find myself clapping too, louder than anyone else in the room.

Strat catches my eye. He leans over, lips at my ear. "See? When you look past the surface, past the bells and whistles and polish, sure, there might be ugliness. But you might find something else too."

A deeper, more unexpected beauty.

"Shit," he says. "I really do need to get backstage now. Let's get you to your seat."

I follow him out in a daze, and his words linger for a long time after that.

I barely register the four people who play before Strat. In the darkness that falls like a blanket over the audience, I fold my program into a tight triangle and scrape it along my knee until an angry red line appears.

I am wrung out. Too exhausted for any more revelations.

Maybe that's why, when Strat crosses the stage with that casually confident lope I now know came from years of pretending that he belongs in a world he didn't come from, I feel like it's *my* heart that's walking onto the stage.

His first piece is a cheerful trot, his fingers popping livelily over the keys like a prancing show pony. He's good. Extremely good. The audience is with him from the very first bar.

And his hair *is* unruly. Distracting, even, bouncing along with the complicated, cascading rhythms. I'm sick with nerves for him, even though he shows zero signs of being nervous himself. I glance at the three judges seated at a table a few rows behind me, faces uplit by their little lamps.

The audience claps austerely, and I clap too. Was that good? The judges' faces are unreadable.

Strat shifts on the bench and rolls his neck, flexes his fingers. I wince—the other competitors were a little more . . . reverent. But they also looked like they were having less fun.

He knows where I'm sitting—he picked the seat and collected the ticket himself, but he doesn't look my way. I chastise myself for thinking that he would. He needs to concentrate. This is a big deal. A two-thousand-dollar cash prize.

His second piece starts with a timid, contemplative trickle. A question, an answer. He sways this time. Closes his eyes. The music pulls the room of people into an emotion. We follow blindly, heartbeats slowing to a melody composed a century ago.

When the last note lingers in the air, I'm holding my breath. The whole room is. Strat is motionless, still bent over the keys. The last note hums through the air, then fades out. In the moment before the applause comes, he has stunned us into silence.

Only someone who knows him well would catch it: the hitch of his spine. A breath taken too sharply. When he stands to bow, he presses a knuckle under his eye, and I realize that he's crying.

Oh, my heart.

I'm suddenly aching all over. This is a different feeling, so unlike the addictive exhilaration of infatuation. The pain of pining for Ollie, Austin, Dean . . . that was shallow, and almost *fun*. This, though—

This hurts.

The revelation hits with force. Love is not being starry-eyed when someone opens a door for you or makes dinner reservations or even asks you to dance in a cold rotunda.

Love is aching for the other person when they are in pain. Feeling your own heart break for them and wanting to make their sadness stop.

I love Strat Madigan.

Again.

CHAPTER TWENTY-NINE

The next day feels different. More vivid, the colors more saturated. I'm vibrating with the revelation I had yesterday, fizzing with the feelings that are taking up all the room in my body. As much as I want to go somewhere, anywhere, with Strat, I know I need to put in a few hours at the hospital.

When I get there, I hesitate at the doorway. I wonder . . . after yesterday, seeing Ayemi—maybe I can do this. Maybe I can make myself look.

I take a deep breath and step into the room.

I fight the urge to skate my eyes past her and head for my chair by the window. She's thinner than she was before, all the hard-earned muscles she got on varsity wasting away. I slide my hand over hers. No headphones, no distractions. Her skin is a degree too cool, but I know this hand. It's the one that held mine at our grandma's funeral, the one that played thumb war with me in the car when we were bored on long journeys, the one that passed me notes every day in freshman year English. During our Shakespeare module, I unfolded one that read:

I'd written *STFU* in giant all caps at the bottom and passed it back to her, and neither of us could stop silent-giggling for the rest of the class.

So sitting here, holding her hand—something's aching in my chest, but it's not destroying me. I can take it.

I'm proud of myself for facing something for once. Maybe I'm stronger than I thought.

"Why don't I sit next to you today, instead of by the window?" I murmur, letting go of her hand to drag my chair over. There's a thick packet of paper on it, and a cup of coffee sits on the windowsill, steaming into the air. Mom must be here already.

I pick up the packet to move it out of the way, assuming it's her work stuff. But then I spot the name of the hospital. Below it, horrifying words jump out at me, words like *in the event of a code red* and *persistent vegetative state* and *end of life care*.

The blood leaches out of my face as I sift slowly through the pages.

And then, on the last sheet, on heavier paper with words that look like they've been printed in rusty old blood, a form:

DO **NOT** RESUSCITATE.

The *click-click-click* of high heels staccatos into the silence. "Aria? I thought you'd be working on your group project again today."

Something sick and hot twists through my guts at the sound of Mom's voice. I turn, everything in me vibrating. I hold up the form like an accusation.

"What is this?"

She freezes.

"Mom? What's this?" I rasp.

"It's not signed."

"Why do you even have it?"

She blinks slowly, choosing her words carefully. "Baby, if things don't improve, we may have to consider—"

"No." I cover my ears. "No no no."

Are these the forms she and Dad were talking about, that night I first heard the word *divorce*? I feel sick. But that nausea is nothing compared to the deep shock that my parents could someday be *allowed* to make this decision. Shouldn't it be mine? She is half of me. DNA-wise, she *is* me. Don't they need my permission before cutting me in two?

It has always been a possibility that Cady might die. I've just been trying so hard not to stare that truth in the face.

It can't be just me.

I shove the DNR form at Mom. The hallway the elevator

the lobby is all a blur, the slam of my car door is an underwater echo. I can't be here.

I can't do this.

I came here to try to face reality, because I thought I felt stronger, but it was too much.

CHAPTER THIRTY

I'm shaking as I pull my car to the curb across from Strat's house. In my hurry, I misjudge the distance and run one tire up onto the grass, but I leave it. I don't care.

Come to your front door.

I text, fingers unsteady.

Why . . . ?

I don't answer, just stand on his doorstep with my arms wrapped around myself, trying not to throw up.

He opens the door twenty seconds later.

"Aria? What are you doing here?"

I'm trembling. I know I'm using him to escape, but I don't care. All I want is to push these horrible feelings down and sink into him. He's better than colors, better than daydreams, better than real life.

"Can I come in? Please?"

He glances back toward the living room. "Of course. Yeah. Just—be quiet."

His dad's weary voice travels out from the living room, barely audible over the sound of the TV. "Who was at the door, bud?"

"Just a friend, Dad. We'll be upstairs, but shout if you need anything, okay?"

Upstairs, I pace his room while he watches me with concerned eyes.

"What happened?" he asks.

I shake my head no. I can't. Not yet.

"Is there anything I can do?"

"Just—be you. What were you watching?" I ask shakily, nodding at the Netflix pause screen on his laptop.

He studies me. "Sit down. I'll let you pick something."

I don't watch the movie. I just close my eyes and let him put his arm around me and press my face into his shoulder. He strokes soothing lines down my arm.

"Talk when you're ready," he whispers.

I burrow deeper into his T-shirt. I'm not sure I'll ever be ready.

The next thing I know, Strat's nudging me awake.

It's quiet, and the lights are warm and low. I'm disoriented, untethered from time. Outside Strat's curtainless window, the sky is a flat black, and the red digits on his alarm clock click from 11:23 to 11:24 p.m.

I struggle to sit up. "I'm so sorry, I didn't mean to pass out on you."

"It's all right. Do you feel better now?"

"Much."

It's true. The nap helped, and so did being with him. I've pushed the worst parts of reality deep down inside me again.

"I was going to wake you up earlier, but you looked so exhausted," Strat says gently. "Do you want me to drive you home? Are your parents going to be upset?" There's genuine worry on his face.

I pick at the edge of his blanket. "They, um, think I'm at a friend's house," I say in a small voice.

"A friend's house," he repeats slowly.

"Tahirah's."

I risk a glance up, but I can't read the expression on his face.

I reach for his hand. "Strat? Can I stay here?" I whisper.

He stares at me for a long time.

Finally, he exhales. "You're going to get me into so much trouble. But yes. Yes, Aria, I would love it if you stayed."

He levers up off the bed. I'm about to ask if he has a spare toothbrush I can borrow, but the words die in my throat as he tugs his shirt off. I'd almost forgotten about the scar I saw by the waterfall. That second midnight seems so long ago. Back then, I still thought he was a dream. But he's real, and the scar is still there.

"Is that really from a skateboard accident?" I ask, the words sticking in my throat.

"It is. The sad thing is that I hardly ever skateboarded, and

I was so bad at it. But my cousin was egging me on to try this crazy trick in a grocery store parking lot. I had to get twenty-two stitches." His eyes narrow. "Why do you get all serious whenever you see it?"

A beat of silence unspools between us. I hold his stare as I lift my own shirt, showing him my scar.

He steps toward me slowly. Then he lifts his hand, running his fingers along the ridge. At his touch, goosebumps rise everywhere.

"I've had it since I was a baby. Cady has one too." I shove down the memory of what happened earlier at the hospital.

He draws his hand back, and I let my shirt fall.

"By the waterfall, I thought it meant . . . something." That he was a dream replacement for my sister. "But it was just a skateboard accident."

His eyes are tender. "Yes. Just a skateboard accident."

My skin is tingling where he touched me, and it suddenly hits me how intimate the moment was. He was touching my bare skin. I turn away to hide the sudden flush in my cheeks.

He finds me a toothbrush, and I get ready for bed in the tiny, orange-tiled bathroom at the end of the hall. When we meet back in his room—at his *bed*—he's arranged the comforter onto one side and thrown a ratty gray blanket over the other.

I didn't think this through. Watching a movie sitting on top of the bedding is one thing. This feels charged. Monumental.

I swallow down my nerves and slide under the covers. He gets in and twists over to turn off the bedside lamp. We're not touching at all, but it's as if I can feel his scar, pulling at mine like a magnet. I want to scoot over and lay my ribs against his.

We are silent as our eyes adjust to the thin gray moonlight. How many times has this happened before? Falling asleep together, waking up together? How much of our relationship have I seen? Half? Only a quarter?

"Aria?"

He shifts, turning onto his side to look at me. I swallow hard, then turn to him too. When our eyes meet, I am lost.

We lie on our sides and stare at each other for so long I feel like I'm a constellation spinning in space. We still have no idea what happened three months ago. But I know, deep in my soul, that this boy didn't hurt me. I trust him implicitly. When I'm with him, I feel . . . safe. Loved.

"Ready to escape reality for an hour?" he whispers.

Yes. More than ever, yes.

With the most delicate, deliberate touch, he reaches out to brush a strand of hair behind my ear.

"See you at midnight, Aria."

I feel his words as they are meant: a goodnight kiss, pressed softly to my forehead.

"See you at midnight, Strat."

CHAPTER THIRTY-ONE

The air tastes of salt.

I'm still lying on my side, still facing Strat, a mirror of how our sleeping bodies must be in the real world. I lever myself up on one arm to look over his shoulder. Behind him, an ocean churns, its waves cresting under the same purple-bright moonlight that floods all our midnights.

"You're lovely when you wake up," Strat murmurs, and my connection to the waves breaks.

He rolls up to sit beside me. We watch the waves together, digging our toes into the sand until they're breadcrumb-coated. There's something about the quality of the air—a thinness, and a harsh dryness that stings my throat when I breathe in. I think it's cold. I think it might be freezing, actually, but I can't feel it. My senses are blurred at the edges.

This.

This is what I needed.

Without a word, Strat stands and holds out his hand.

We walk along the stretch of sand, past beach chairs and striped umbrellas, sugar-soft dunes on our left and the roaring ocean on our right.

My steps falter when I look farther down the beach. It just . . . ends. The ocean seems to end too, dropping off into darkness. There's something deeply wrong about it, something that makes me feel queasy.

But then I see the faintest reflection of my own pale face. Two figures holding hands, getting larger and clearer with each step. It's like we're walking up to a mirror, or to—glass?

I raise my hands, palms out. When my skin meets the cold, slick curve, I suck in a breath. It *is* glass.

Strat's eyes lock onto mine. "Are we in . . . a bubble?"

"No. Not a bubble." The grin spreads on my face. Now that I'm looking for it, I can see the spherical curve vaulting back over our heads.

That's the moment it starts to snow.

The first flake lands on my nose. I look up, and thousands of them start floating down, falling so evenly and silently it feels like a movie.

"Strat, we're in a *snow globe.*"

In seconds, a soft white layer has settled like a blanket over the world, over the beach chairs and the striped umbrellas.

Some of the snowflakes aren't falling straight down—they're swirling, eddying in the air above our heads, like we're in that second right after the snow globe is shaken, then set on a table with a careful *clack.*

I am enchanted. Ringing with the joy of it. I throw my arms out wide and tip my head back, catching snowflakes on my tongue.

When I turn, I find Strat watching me. I see that fondness again, like my dreaminess is endearing, a spirit to be treasured, not snuffed out or hidden.

I laugh sheepishly and let my arms drop.

"No, don't stop," he says. "I love you like this."

He reaches out, catches me by the waist, tugs me in. We collide under the snowflakes, and my hands land on his chest.

Love.

There is a sudden seriousness now that we're pressed tight together. I don't dare speak. I crane my neck, searching his eyes.

"You know," I say, soft as snow, "I always dreamed of an epic love. To be adored. To be the only thing someone thinks about. For someone to be desperate to kiss me."

I'm about to say that I didn't realize how gorgeous it would feel being the one who adores. To be the one desperate to kiss *him*. But he chuckles in that low way that makes my insides tremor.

I look down. "I know. Stupid, right?"

"Not stupid at all. I'm just surprised you haven't seen it."

"Seen what?"

"Aria." He levels his gaze on me. "I am all those things."

My heart climbs into my throat.

He slides his hand to my neck, thumb resting in the hollow at the base of my throat. Slowly he slides his fingers up, a little unsteady as they curve around to cradle my head, tilt it back. His eyes are steady on mine when he says, "You are the only thing I think about."

His mouth, feather-soft on my jaw. "*You* are the person I adore."

I'm dizzy. The tip of his nose brushes against mine. "And, Aria? I'm *desperate* to kiss you."

The sensations are dulled, like they're stuck behind a thick pane of glass. I know that want is a fireball in my lungs, but it feels like a distant, lukewarm glow.

I duck my head. "Sorry. It's the midnight. It's—getting in the way."

We've kissed in here before, on the top of the castle. And it was lovely, and dreamy. But how much woozier would this feel in real life? How much hotter, how much more . . . real?

"I don't want this kiss to be in here, Strat. I want to wake up."

He presses his forehead against mine.

"Then let's wake up."

I close my eyes. Wishing for it. And, somehow, when I open them a second later, the unnatural quiet of the snowy beach is gone.

Oh—it worked.

The air hums with the mundane quiet of a house at night— air-conditioning *whoosh*ing, beams creaking, cicadas *chirrup*ing outside. It's all back.

And then I breathe in and my world *explodes* with sensation. Heat, and yearning, and oh, maybe I should have stayed in the midnight, because I think this might kill me, his hand warm on my jaw and his forehead pressed to mine. *In his bed.*

Strat's voice is hoarse. "Let's get up. I want it to be perfect."

"Stratospheric?" I ask as I slide out from under the covers, and he chuckles.

He guides me over to the window, where a slice of pale, real-life moonlight shines on the floor.

"Now," he says, catching my hips with his fingertips and pulling me close, "where were we?"

He brushes his lips along the curve of my cheek. The corner of my mouth.

And there is no longer a thick pane of glass between him and the sensations bursting through me.

This. This is *romance.* This is what I've dreamed of. And there's so much pure *chemistry* between us that it's almost dangerous.

I tilt my head up, lips parted. He's only a breath away. The want is so heavy in my lungs I feel like I'm about to pass out.

"If I don't kiss you right now," he says hoarsely, "I think I'm going to stop breathing."

"Better kiss me, then," I whisper.

And then his mouth is on mine.

He tastes like music. Like the quick, soft roll of mallets on timpani, like notes spilling from the piano in the forest. Like cinnamon and memories.

The hand cradling my head drags me deeper. His other is a hungry press at my back. Something rises up in me. With a roughness I didn't know I had, I grab a fistful of his shirt and haul him closer.

We are kissing, kissing, losing our balance, swaying. I scrape his lip with my teeth, and he responds with more heat. I can feel it in the hard press at my stomach. We pull back for one millisecond, wildly searching each other's eyes.

"Strat—I don't care why we erased each other," I rasp.

"Good. Me neither."

He surges back to me. We are a conflagration, blazing in the sliver of pale moonlight.

Eventually the heat melts into something softer, but even the counter-rush feels unbelievably good. Our last few kisses are slow and crystalline, as exquisite as this snowy night.

Afterward we cling to each other, stunned.

"Aria," he whispers, and there is so much in my name. Awe. Astonishment. He raises our hands, palm to palm. I watch as our fingers lace into one clasped fist. He rests his forehead against mine, sways me in the moonlight.

We're falling in love. It seems too miraculous, too much like unbeatable odds, to both feel this way at the same time. I found this boy, and he found me. Not just once but twice.

"Did you mean it?" he asks a long time later. "When you said you didn't care anymore why we erased each other?"

I meet his eyes. "I meant it."

I don't want to keep looking for answers. I love *this* Strat, in this timeline, and I want everything that comes with that.

CHAPTER THIRTY-TWO

Morning finds me standing in front of the mirror, trying to battle my hair into submission. Strat sneaks back into his room, carrying a gallon of milk, two cereal boxes, and two mismatched bowls. He sets everything out on his desk with a flourish.

"I'm mortified that this is all I have to offer the first time I get to wake up to you. Are you sure you don't want to grab breakfast somewhere?"

"I would love that, but I don't think we have enough time." It's still dark outside, but I know I have to get to school in time for the first bell.

He steps close, settling his hands on my hips. His chest is warm on my back.

"Next time, then," he says, holding my gaze in the mirror. The look has me flushing from head to toe.

I spin in his arms, and he's ready, his hands coming up to cup my face. I melt into him. Somehow I know exactly how to fit my lips to his. I guess that makes sense—we had months of practice, before.

It takes a concerted effort to pull myself away.

"I really have to go now," I say, flustered, smoothing my hair down again. "See you tonight, Dream Boy."

His smile is instant and blinding. "See you tonight, Girl in the Piano Glade."

I sail through my morning classes. My mind keeps replaying moments from last night. They're filling up my entire being, shimmering through my every nerve.

It's a relief to stop worrying about why we erased each other before. I'd much rather be hopeful and dreamy and in love instead of confused and miserable.

I'm in study hall, drawing snowflakes in my notebook, when the memory hits.

It's short, only five seconds, but it's as heavy as a punch. I can't tell where we are. Inside somewhere, in a huge room. It's dramatically lit, like . . . a party? Strat is dressed up—a real suit jacket instead of the Swithun's jacket, and a slim black tie. But his face . . .

His face is twisted with grief.

I'm about to cry too. I can't see myself in the memory, but I can feel all the emotions of the moment. The sob is a tightness expanding in my chest, threatening to erupt from me.

I watch as a single tear tracks down his cheek, leaving a shining trail of silver. It feels like something's . . . *ending.*

I slam back into study hall with a gasp. Grief pumps through my veins. I almost double over at my lab table. I reach up to check that hot tears aren't spilling out of my eyes.

It's the first time a memory has been less than lovely. I try to shake it away—I don't *want* this one—but the grief is a clinging, choking thing.

Why were we *crying*?

The rest of my classes are torture. I can't stop replaying the memory of Strat crying. I'm hurrying toward the parking lot after last bell when someone touches my elbow. I'm in no mood to talk to anyone, but when I turn, it's Arissa. The one person I might make an effort for today.

"Hey, glad I caught you," she says brightly. "A few of us are about to head over to the mall, maybe catch a movie. You wanna come?"

It's so out of the blue—did it have to be *today* that she's asking? I just stand there stupidly for a moment.

"I don't think I can today, Riss. I'm so sorry." There's too much going on right now, and I need to talk to Strat.

Disappointment flickers over her face. "Oh. Okay," she says, unsure, and maybe a little hurt. "See you tomorrow, then."

She starts walking away.

"Arissa, wait," I call after her.

She turns.

I clear my throat. "Thank you for asking."

She softens a little. "Hey, it's no problem. If you change your mind, text me. We'd love to have you." She smiles, then heads for the cluster of art kids who are waiting by her car.

But as I watch them drive away, I can't help but feel I'm losing the chance to be her friend all over again.

CHAPTER THIRTY-THREE

Strat's text comes through just as I'm sliding into the driver's seat.

> How was school? I couldn't concentrate for shit. Can I see you today?

I smile, biting the inside of my cheek.

> You already saw me today;)

> Not for long enough. Will you be at the hospital? Can I bring you a coffee?

I'm still rattled from the flashback, but I take a breath to center myself.

> Sure. I'd love that.

I hum along to *Swan Lake* as I sail down the highway to Sacramento. But when I pass the exit that leads to the part of the valley where the *really* expensive homes are, the homes where parents send their sons to St. Swithun's and their daughters to St. Ethelburg's, something tugs at my memory.

I'm not sure why I do it, but suddenly I'm flicking on my blinker and turning onto a road I don't remember being on before.

There's another place we had to have spent time at: his best friend's house.

Mick's house—and therefore Bruce from Slydekick's house—is dangerously easy to find.

Last month Bruce did a house tour for a design magazine's YouTube channel. (He also famously answered the door naked when the film crew arrived.) Doing a quick reverse image search on a screenshot of the front of the house led me directly to a real estate listing from 2003, back when Bruce bought it.

Getting close enough to the house to see inside is another issue entirely.

I stand outside the huge, wrought-iron gates. A long, manicured lawn stretches up to the house, and all the windows are lit, a dozen warm, rectangular glimpses into a life of luxury. Two security cameras are trained on the driveway, and fear spikes through me. Bruce's bodyguards are probably watching, preparing to come out and chase me off, or worse.

I'm about to traipse around the side of the lot to see if I can get a better view when I snap back to my senses.

Oh my God. What am I even doing here?

I told Strat that I didn't need answers anymore. I'm happy

with how we are now. I'm about to spin around and leave when a light flicks on in the palatial white marble kitchen, and a memory uncurls.

Strat and I stand side by side at the sleek kitchen island, transferring pizza slices from Wyldefire onto plates.

We've got the entire cool, humming mansion to ourselves for the night. I'm wearing a dress I never thought I'd have the chance to wear in a real-life situation—mainly because it's quite small. The velvet corset gives way to a perky, layered chiffon skirt. I took extra care with my hair, feeling rebellious and buzzy with anticipation.

But Strat's . . . distant. All evening we've been getting caught in long silences, and not the kind that feel easy or comfortable. He seems upset about something, but every ten minutes he takes my hand and squeezes it, so I don't think it has anything to do with me.

We take our pizza into the luxury home cinema, but the silence between us persists.

"I'm sorry I'm being miserable," he says. He pulls his hands over his face on a weary exhale. "I didn't get much sleep last night."

"It's okay," I chirp. "Let's just start the show."

I want my normal Strat back, the Strat who's easy and fun and loud and always peppering me with kisses.

Five minutes into the episode, he reaches for another slice and his mouth pulls into a small grimace. He uses his fork to push away the tub of Wyldefire dipping sauce. Like he can't even stand the smell of it.

"You don't like it," I whisper.

Strat looks over, puzzled.

"The sauce," I say. "You don't like it."

He looks down at the tub he'd pushed away. He sighs. "Yeah. Sorry. It's the only kind of sauce I can't stand. I had a bad experience involving garlic bread and a stomach virus when I was ten."

My body feels tight and strange. I'm sure I'm not misremembering that night at Wyldefire Pizza, and how I said I might have to wrap it up if he didn't like the sauce. I remember exactly how he answered: *We are not wrapping this up, Aria. I love Wyldefire sauce.*

He lied.

I'm not sure what to do with this small, insignificant piece of information. It's tiny, I know, but it's still a lie. And if he's lied to me about this . . . what else has he lied about?

For the next thirty minutes, I can't absorb a single thing the characters are saying. I'm too busy thinking, *Lie! Lie! Lie!* over and over in my head. I'm overreacting, I know—I need to sleep, and then I can think more clearly about this in the morning.

We are quiet as we clean up, and the heaviness clings to us as he walks me to the door. On the front porch, bugs buzz by the ornate lamp above our heads.

Strat pauses. "Aria . . . can we be real for a second?"

I work up a smile. "We're always real with each other."

"Are we?" he says, so softly I almost don't catch it. He shoves his hands in his pockets, studies the long run of the porch, the sheer rock-star opulence of the whole house. I've only been here a few times, and I've maybe seen a quarter of the rooms in it.

"If I didn't have all this, would you still be with me?"

"What? Of course."

His shoulders droop an inch, his eyes trained on the ground. "Aria . . . there's something I should tell—"

I grab his face and kiss him, harder than usual. He's surprised at first, but then he relaxes into the kiss. And because it's us, and it's the one thing I know for sure I can count on, the chemistry between us flares.

Some swooping fear caught me, and I had to stop the words coming out of his mouth.

When I release him, he looks down and tugs a hand through his hair with a small chuckle. It's the closest thing to a smile I've seen him haul up all night, which is so unusual for him.

"There," I whisper. "Better, right?"

"Better," he says.

He tugs me in for a long hug. We're fine. We're amazing. Happy and loved-up and in love.

I jerk out of the memory to the sight of a beefy bald guy in a black T-shirt rounding the corner of Bruce from Slydekick's house. He's headed straight for me.

Oh shit.

Running would look shady, so I shift my phone to my ear and start babbling. "Oh my God—you're at the house with the *fountain* out front? I'm such an idiot!"

I walk away quickly—not too quickly, *don't act suspicious*—and let out a few more peals of laughter.

My heart thuds out of my chest, but the bodyguard doesn't come after me. Once I'm in the safety of my car, I hit the lock button. I grip the wheel until my pulse steps back down to normal, then I start the car and ease away from the curb.

The kitchen memory is already losing its sharpness, the edges dulling as it knocks against the other memories on the shelves of my mind.

I'm trying to untangle the two timelines. After my visit to Strat's house in *this* timeline, I realized he'd been hiding some parts of himself from me on our first go-round. But past Aria didn't know that. Was she headed for a major freak-out about it?

I dip my hand into my pocket and pull out the scrap of paper.

Something's up. Lies?

Maybe it is my handwriting. Maybe that's the night I wrote it.

I drop my head to my hands. I think he was about to tell me the truth that night, and I shut him down.

It doesn't seem like enough of a reason to erase him, though. I didn't care about the car or the mansion back then, and I don't now.

Was there something else he was keeping from me?

That he's still keeping from me?

CHAPTER THIRTY-FOUR

My alarm bleats into the predawn dark. After hitting the snooze button twice, I pry myself out of bed and stumble to the shower, hoping that the hot water can erase the fact that I've had a fitful night's sleep.

There's a text from Strat waiting for me on my phone. During last night's midnight, we were in a vineyard, the rolling hills drenched in purple-blue moonlight. There was something smudged about it, like an oil painting that someone brushed their thumbs over before it dried. The air smelled like pasta flour and sweet ripe fruit, and we lay under a blanket looking up at the stars, but Strat could tell something was wrong. I almost told him about the two flashbacks, but in the end, I decided not to. I need more time to process what I've seen.

I nod off in my first three classes, laying my head on my folded arms and sinking into deep, drooly oblivion, not stirring until the bell rings. Every time I close my eyes, I see Strat's anguished face, that single tear tracking down his cheek, and I'm tugged under all over again by the waves of sadness that swamped me in that moment. It's nearly etched into the backs of my eyelids at this point, like when you stare directly at a light for too long and then see pops of yellow and blue afterward. I still can't figure out where we were. And I still have no idea why we were crying.

I get my first precious hit of dopamine in Art, when Arissa beams at me as soon as I walk in and comes to my desk with a container filled with doughy round lumps.

"My grandma made chapssal-tteok," she says. "I remember you liked them."

"Like them? I *love* chapssal-tteok," I say, grateful for the momentary respite from this hellish day. The gluey-sweet rice flour, the red bean paste filling—they're so satisfying. I select the plumpest ball. "You know I could eat all these in one sitting."

"Oh, I'm well aware," she says, grinning. Ms. Marley flicks off the lights and starts a video on neo-impressionism and Jean-Michel Basquiat. Arissa pulls her chair over to my table, the buckles on her raspberry-pink overalls clinking as she sits down.

"You have no idea how much I needed this pick-me-up today," I whisper to Arissa, savoring my second chapssal-tteok.

"Hey—slow down, those aren't all for you," she teases, tugging the container close. We snicker, and Ms. Marley scowls over at us. For a second, it feels like last year, sitting in the dark theater, whispering about costumes.

"Halmi made me a *mountain* of food for us to take up to the lodge for my birthday ski trip. You would have loved it," Arissa whispers.

"Oh," I swallow, some of the flickering happiness dying out. "Cool."

"I wish you'd been able to come," she says wistfully, poking at her rice cake.

"I thought . . . I thought you didn't want me to?"

"I invited you, silly. Of course I wanted you there."

"You—what? You never said anything. I never got the invitation."

She frowns. "What do you mean? I added you to the group."

"What group?"

"On WhatsApp—that's where I was sharing all the details, since there are so many logistics for a three-day weekend trip, and people's helicopter parents get testy if they don't get shit-tons of information. I saw you join, but then the next day you left the group."

I stare at her, utterly confused. "That's not possible." I literally have no memory of joining or leaving that group. I have vivid memories of *not* being invited, actually, feelings that churned in me every time I walked into this classroom.

This doesn't make sense. Arissa's birthday was before homecoming. Before I met Strat, and certainly before I erased him, so I shouldn't be having any memory problems about that far back. I had to have deliberately left the group, unless—

My stomach drops. There is one person who knows the password to my phone.

Cady.

CHAPTER THIRTY-FIVE

After school I'm not even remotely in the mood for the hospital. Instead, I find myself driving up to the swing set on the ridge.

The wind tangles my hair as I trace my fingers over the letters carved in red paint: *AL + SM.*

I can't shake the feeling that something happened here. That this place is important to us somehow.

I stay there for a long time, swinging slowly as I watch the sun melt down toward the horizon, but nothing comes back.

Later, when I'm tucked on the couch with a mug of hot chocolate, staring at the television but not really watching it, it's the taste of the chocolate that untangles another dormant memory . . .

"There you are," Strat says, closing the mountain lodge's sliding door, muffling the sounds of the party inside.

We're on a second-story patio jutting out over thick forest. Ten feet below us, a group of Cady's friends stand around a fire-pit, poking marshmallows close to the glowing embers. As we watch, Ashley R's marshmallow catches on fire for the *third* time. She squeals ineptly until Tahirah blows the flames out.

"Good news: I found hot chocolate," Strat says, setting two cups on the patio railing before drawing me to him. He's wearing a long, sharply tailored gray wool coat that makes him look like a dignified British billionaire. I find it unspeakably hot, and I've been smoothing my hands over the fine wool all evening, reaching up to latch my hands on to the lapels.

I burrow into his side for warmth. He dips down, catches me in a long, slow kiss. He tastes like chocolate. When my nails accidentally scrape over his ribs, he sucks in a breath. I've heard it before, in the back seat of his car, and hearing it now sends a bubble of pure oxygen straight to my head.

"Careful," he says darkly, and something in me thrills. We've been playing this game for a couple of weeks, skating the edge of something. It's a rush both of us are hooked on.

He dips in for another kiss, and I'm about to slide my hands up under his shirt when something vibrates against my stomach. "Strat, I think—your phone," I giggle.

Reluctantly he pulls away from me and tugs his phone out of his pocket.

And I watch as his good mood drains out of him.

"It's my dad," he says, his voice suddenly flat. "I just—I need to get this. You'll be okay here?"

"Sure," I lie, shivering at the sudden cool that steals over my skin now that I'm not wrapped up in him.

"I'll be quick," he says. And then, because he's Strat and he noticed the shiver, he slides out of his coat and drapes it around my shoulders.

The sweetness of the gesture, and being wrapped in the heavy wool and the cinnamon smell of him, makes me purr like a pleased cat. It's enough to keep me happy for ten minutes. Fifteen, maybe. I zone out, watching the campfire flames dance below.

But he doesn't come back. I finish my hot chocolate, and eventually the temperature drops another degree and the cold night steals through the thick wool. I sigh and plunge back into the party. I don't even know whose house this is—the girls played an away game and dragged me along to the rival team's after-party.

Strat's not in the living room or the kitchen. Not in the game room or the downstairs primary bedroom. Whenever I see one of Cady's teammates, I ask if they've seen him, but no one has. Something starts to coil in my stomach. I'm not about to find him in the guest bedroom making out with some other girl, am I?

I'm near tears when I knock on yet another closed door and finally hear his voice, muffled, saying, "I'll be out in a second."

For a moment, I consider turning away. If he is with some-one, I can't—I *don't want* to deal with that.

"Strat? It's me. Can I come in?"

"Aria? Yeah."

When I open the door, he's sitting on the edge of a kid's race car bed, staring blankly at the wall.

"Strat?"

He shakes himself out of his trance, then looks up with a forced smile. "Hey," he says. His voice is rough. Weary.

I close the door softly behind me and sit down next to him on the tiny bed. He looks down at me. He's fine for a second, but then his eyes water, and I . . .

I freeze. I've never seen him like this before. He's fighting back tears, and I have no idea what to do or how to help.

"Are you . . . okay?" The words seem inadequate and stupid. A knot forms in my stomach. Why does it feel so hard to talk about this stuff?

I have no idea what's going on with him and his dad. He hasn't told me anything, and I assume his dad's some unfeeling billionaire who doesn't exactly approve of his son playing piano and is pressuring him to go to business school or something.

"It's fine—we don't have to talk about it," Strat says. But there's something resigned in his voice that makes me wonder if he wants to. If he needs more from me than this.

The knot in my stomach pulls tighter.

I give him a useless side hug, my own hands trembling a little bit. "I'm going to go get us some more hot chocolate," I say, and then I *leave*.

I leave, as if he's a stranger, and not the boy I've been dating for months. As I make my cowardly retreat, I stumble on the edge of a shaggy rug.

I can't.

It's too real.

*   *   *

The memory ends. Becomes a hard knot in my chest. How I wish I could turn back the clock so I could be there for him when he so clearly needed me. I should have taken his hands in mine and asked him what his dad said, been there for him even if it was hard to talk about. But the old Aria was so desperate for her effortless, fairy-tale love story, and a boyfriend crying in a bedroom at a stranger's party certainly didn't fit.

The story is changing. The first two months of my love story with Strat were a fairy tale, but the cracks are starting to show. I wouldn't open up to him, and I wouldn't let him open up to me.

So much of the puzzle of Strat and me is pieced together now. I can almost see the entire picture: We fell for each other, fast and hard. Dived in headfirst in the way I'd always wanted to dive, ignoring everything else in our lives.

But for all we pretended to be loved-up and attached at the hip, we were keeping each other at arm's length emotionally. Strat wasn't showing me his real self.

I think about a very different conversation between the two of us, when we were on the swing set on this ridge, when he told me about his mom's letter. I didn't even realize it at the time, but I showed up for him that night, despite the knot in my stomach. I listened. It was uncomfortable for me, but I helped him.

Suddenly I realize that doing those difficult, uncomfortable things . . . it's like the difference between hiking up a mountain and watching footage of a drone soaring up alongside a mountain. A video might be beautiful and frictionless, but you're removed from it. It doesn't *really* take your breath away, and it doesn't change you. But when you hike up a mountain for real, climb for hours until your muscles ache and you're sweaty and exhausted, when you reach the top, there's *exhilaration*. Something deeper than beauty.

There's a text from Strat.

Hey . . . feels like you've been pulling away a little bit since the beach midnight. Everything OK? Was it too fast? We can slow down.

I take a steadying breath.

Not too fast. It's been a rough couple of days. Memories are coming back like crazy, even though I don't want them to. Tell you about them at midnight?

Do you want to talk on the phone? Or I can come over now?

No, it's OK. It can wait for midnight.

My eyes sting. Why couldn't I have stayed in that blissed-out, loved-up midnight on the beach? I don't want this mess.

CHAPTER THIRTY-SIX

My room is silent and velvet black, but I can't get to sleep.

I grope for my phone. The screen light floods harsh white over my nightstand, and I groan when I see that it's not even 10 p.m. yet.

My mind can't stop gnawing on all the things it's seen over the past two days. And I'm still trying to think of other explanations for how I could have joined and then left Arissa's WhatsApp group. Maybe I did it accidentally. I must have. Because why would Cady sneak into my phone, accept an invitation, and then leave the group?

I flop over, frustrated. I just want to go to sleep and get to Strat.

When the hum starts up, buzzing through my scalp, I clap my hands over my ears. I shake my head back and forth, trying to fight the flashback.

"No, no, no," I whisper. I'm angry, suddenly—I was happy

with Strat. We were dreaming of snowy beaches and kisses, and I was ready to just move on. I'm not even looking for these stupid memories anymore, and they're slapping me in the face.

I grab for colors. *Cadmium yellow. Cobalt. Viridian.* But the memory doesn't care—it comes anyway.

I'm kneeling somewhere outside, dirt and rain soaking into a gown I've never seen before.

Fingers clawing at mud. Digging—

The memory cuts off sharply.

I crack open an eye. Take a shaky breath.

It's definitely over.

I have no idea what *that* was, but at least it was short.

Maybe now I can get to sleep. I need to see Strat. I throw my pillow to the other end of the bed, searching for a cooler spot, and there, in the dark, another memory peels itself up from where it had been crushed down.

I am starfished on my bed, pillow at the wrong end, beaming up at the ceiling. Last night Strat took me to his piano teacher's wedding. It was like a fairy tale—festival lights and dancing under the stars, writing our names with sparklers against the night sky. As the celebrations wound down, Strat kissed me in a dark corner of the loveliest hotel I've ever been in and told me he loved me.

I was right about it all, about love being the best thing a person could feel. This is what I'd been made for all along. I love Strat Madigan, and we're going to have a life together, and . . .

I don't want to go to Milan.

I want to stay with him. I want to start my life *now*, here in California.

An idea forms, flaring into focus. I roll off my bed. My computer whirs as it boots up. Why wait until I get an acceptance when I'm just going to turn Sciarra down? Better to open up the slot for another hopeful who'll actually take it.

I run a quick search and find a rough guide for how to withdraw a college application. It says most schools have an automated form somewhere. I scour the Sciarra website for their automated form, but it's less snazzy than the big U.S. state school websites. I click around for a few minutes. There—in small print, it says you have to email their admissions address and explain why you're withdrawing.

No one else even knows I applied. Not Mom, not Strat, not Cady. If any of them knew how excited I felt when I discovered this program, how many hours I spent daydreaming about going there, how many more hours I spent preparing my portfolio and my application materials, they'd flip. Well, not Cady—she'd flip at the fact that I even applied in the first place, then she'd be relieved and happy that I'm withdrawing my application. If Strat knew how much I loved dressmaking, he would hate to see me give up my dream. But it's not my dream anymore, because he's come and eclipsed everything.

I hesitate on the Send button—it's almost *too* easy to unravel something that took so long to ravel—but my resolve doesn't waver.

I click Send.

*   *   *

"No."

My whisper ricochets off the walls in my dark bedroom.

"No, no, no," I repeat, louder now, sitting up abruptly in bed, blood suddenly pumping nauseatingly through my veins.

Please tell me I didn't do what I just saw myself doing.

I've been waiting for a decision from Sciarra. Checking the mail every day. Only now, when confronted with the thought of having that dream taken away, do I realize how much I still want it.

I scramble for my phone and open my email app, hoping that when I search "Sciarra withdrawal" it will serve me up a nice blank box and a message that says: *Searching All Mailboxes— Found 0 results.*

But that's not what happens.

It finds one email in the Sent section.

My words. Dated a little over three months ago.

> To Whom It May Concern,
>
> Please consider this email my official notification that I am withdrawing my application for a place in the program at Sciarra due to personal reasons.

I crumple to the floor. One email. A future thrown away with a click of a button.

How could I have been so utterly, utterly stupid?

CHAPTER THIRTY-SEVEN

There is piano music: light and soft and sweet. The notes trip and dance, each one as crystalline as glass.

The moment I open my eyes, I gasp. The midnight has taken a French ballroom and stretched it to an outrageous length—there must be a hundred windows instead of the usual ten or twenty. It's not the Hall of Mirrors at Versailles, but it could be its sister.

Hundreds of candles illuminate the space. Waxed parquet floors gleam underfoot, and outside the windows, the sky is heavy with stars, so many it feels like they'll cut your lungs if you inhale.

But the most astonishing thing about the ballroom has to be the clocks. Between the one hundred windows are one hundred grandfather clocks, eight feet tall and gleaming white, their hands all frozen on midnight.

There's an immense rustle when I heave myself up from

the floor. Layers and layers of organza and brocade and taffeta spill from my waist, which is cinched tight in a satin corset. It's the biggest ball gown I've ever seen, let alone worn. Gingerly, I reach up to touch my hair. It's finely braided and lifted from my neck as if I were a queen.

It's too much. The ballroom, the dress, the hair—this is the most beautiful midnight yet. This was made for the Aria I used to be, and there is nothing I want more than to sink into it.

But so much has changed since our last midnight. I've seen more of our past in these last two days than the rest of the memories put together.

"Aria."

I turn. Strat is at the far end of the ballroom, a hundred windows away. He moves, coming toward me as fast as he can. We meet in the middle of the long room.

"Tell me what's going on," he says, cupping my face in his hands.

He holds me as I tell him everything I've seen. The crying, the mansion, the party . . . that bizarre flash of me digging in the dirt. *Why was I digging?*

When I get to deleting my college application, my eyes well up with tears and I bury my face in his shirt. "I can't believe I did something so stupid!"

"Jesus. I would *never* have wanted you to do that, Aria."

"I know. I didn't tell you I'd done it. They're coming back so easily now. It feels like every time I look at something, it triggers a flashback. This isn't supposed to happen, Strat. No one else's ArEx erasures fail like this."

It feels like the memories are building up to something. Like this is just the beginning of a story about to go off the rails. The *why* is coming. I'm terrified it's going to break us all over again.

"I'm scared, Strat."

"I am too. It's getting hard, Aria." He draws back, looking down at me with serious eyes. "But we can handle it."

"Maybe."

"We *can*," he says firmly. "Will you promise me something? Whatever it is, when we find out . . . promise me you'll let *this* 'us' weigh more than the past?"

I'm not sure I can promise that. I want to. But—

All at once, every grandfather clock in the room begins to chime. Deep and resonant. Ominous.

Gong. Gong. Gong!

"I think it's coming soon, Strat," I whisper. "The why."

He nods, gathering me in his arms. "So we hold on tight. I'm not going anywhere."

CHAPTER THIRTY-EIGHT

I jerk out of the midnight, but the buzzing in my temples doesn't stop. The harder I try to fall back to sleep, the worse it gets. I can almost feel the neurons reconnecting, zips of electricity rebuilding the bridges my erasure burned down. I see it again—that flashback of me digging.

Kneeling somewhere outside, dirt and rain soaking into a gown I've never seen before.

Fingers clawing at mud.

The image throbs in my mind. Neurons fire. The humming gets stronger. With a gasp, the picture widens, and I see more of what's around me. Looming behind me, in the dark, I can make out a familiar shape.

The swing set.

I lunge for my phone. Strat answers his phone on the first ring, and my words start spilling out.

"I know where I was. In the digging flashback—I saw more of

the memory. The swing set was behind me, the one up on the ridge. I can't believe I didn't put it together before, that's why I—"

"Whoa, slow down," Strat says groggily. "Let me wake up."

But I can't slow down. This feels like the most important piece of the puzzle so far. The key to everything else. Maybe the last memory we made before we fried each other out of our heads.

I pace my room, fueled by nervous energy. "I want to go there, Strat."

"Right now?"

"Yes, right now."

"Aria, it's one o'clock in the morning."

"I won't be able to go back to sleep. I need to see why I was digging."

Was I burying *something?*

He's silent for a long, heavy moment.

My stomach sinks. "I—I'm sorry. It's fine. It's late, and you're half asleep, and I can go by myself, I—"

He exhales. "No way. I'm coming with you."

Strat maneuvers his station wagon down the dark, empty roads. He had the classical station on when I got in the car, but the piece that was playing—Grieg, he said, "In the Hall of the Mountain King"—had the tension of the night ratcheting tighter and tighter. It felt too much like the perfect soundtrack, so I reached over and turned it off. Now it's silent except for the hum of the tires on the road and the soft patter of rain on the windshield.

The answers are coming, hurtling toward us like a train and we're tied to the tracks. Part of me wants to turn back and forget all this ever happened, but another part of me thinks that maybe . . . maybe I can handle it.

By the time Strat parks the car, the rain has eased, so it's now just a gentle sheet of mist. The headlights shine on the swing set like a harsh construction spotlight.

Strat fumbles around behind my seat for an umbrella, and then hands me an old gardening trowel. "It was all I had," he says, holding up the soup ladle he's brought for himself to dig with. "Stay there—I'll come around to get you."

Outside, the night is black and slick. The ridge feels different in the dark, the drop-off sharper and more dangerous.

We huddle close under the umbrella. "Where do we start?" he asks, scanning the wet ground. There's no convenient telltale mound of dirt, no sign of digging.

"I could see the swing behind me, so I think I was on this side. Maybe . . . here?"

We move slowly, using our phone flashlights to comb over the ground. It all looks the same. Grass and weeds and rocks.

"Wait. The initials on our heart graffiti—usually the arrow points to the right on those cartoony drawings, right? On ours it was pointing left."

He frowns. "I don't think that really means anything, but we can try."

We run our fingers over the pole until we find our heart.

"Do you have any string?" Strat asks.

"I have this." I untie the pale blue grosgrain ribbon looped around my waist, the finishing touch to the white eyelet lace tea dress I wore today. Alice in Wonderland, down the rabbit hole.

Strat hands me the umbrella and squats down, stretching the blue ribbon in a line from the arrow we scratched on the swing set down to the ground. A shiver runs through me the instant the ribbon touches the grass—this patch is yellower and thinner than the rest, as if it's struggling to thrive. Like there's something poisoning it from the root.

We take turns digging. Before long, our fingers are slick with mud and my dress is smeared with dirt. Not the best idea to wear white tonight.

And then—the clink of metal on metal rings through the air.

We dig faster until a shape emerges: an old metal toolbox. I recognize it immediately—it sat in the corner of my garage, untouched, for years.

"Let's take it back to the car," Strat says, wiping away the rain that's collected on his brow. His curls are soaking wet.

In the back seat, we sit facing each other with the box between us. Strat's face is pale under the light on the ceiling of the car. His mouth is set in a grimly determined line. Something lurches in my chest.

"Wait," I say. "Before we do this, I want to—"

I catch his hands and press them between mine. Our foreheads meet, eyes closed. Just one moment like this, before the answers. Before the world turns upside down.

Strat's face goes a shade paler. "I'm so scared of losing you, Aria. I saw what losing my mom did to my dad. And look at me—I'm a completely besotted, piano-playing artist. It's not like

I can snort and spit out a wad of tobacco and say I'm fine. If I lose you again—"

I squeeze his hand. "You won't."

"I might." His shoulders slump. "But what are we going to do? Not open it?"

Strat looks at me, thumbs on the latches. "Ready?"

I want to vomit. "Yes."

He cracks the toolbox open, and lifts out—

A dress.

The fabric is gossamer light. The color of the moonlight in all our midnights. *Ultraviolet.* It's clear that it's a dress I made, although I have no memory of making it.

The buzzing starts up again, all over my skull. I grab for Strat's hand as memory after memory hits in a relentless barrage.

Cady bursts into our room, unzipping her backpack and dumping its contents on the bed. "Shit, I know, I'm late. But I packed my sleeping bag and most of my other stuff last night, I just need to get a couple of last-minute things in here and we can head out. We should still get to the minibus on time—"

She freezes, suddenly clocking the fact that I haven't moved, and that I'm in a flowing tulle ball gown that I've been working on for weeks. I'm so proud of it—it's my most whimsical creation yet. I've named her Ultraviolet Dreamgirl. Every time I imagine the moment everyone sees her, I feel a dizzy, bubbling delight in my chest.

"Why are you wearing that?" Cady asks, a hard edge to her voice. Her frown deepens when she sees my duffel bag empty on the floor by my bed. "What the hell, Aria? You're not packed at all."

I clench my jaw, gathering my courage. "That's because I'm not going to Spike Night."

Every New Year's Eve, the varsity volleyball team rents out a college gym for the entire weekend, usually one within walking distance of a beach. They play this dumb midnight volleyball game, then sleep in sleeping bags on the polished wood floor. A sports-themed lock-in, basically.

"What do you mean, you're not going?" Cady asks.

I force my shaking hands to steady as I clip a diamond barrette into my hair. "I told you I didn't want to spend New Year's Eve with the team."

She stares at me, eyes frighteningly wide and unblinking. "And we decided that you couldn't skip out on tradition. We've done Spike Night three years in a row."

"Well, for the last three years I haven't had a boyfriend who asked me to go to a winter ball."

Strat looked so sweetly nervous when he showed me the thick, creamy invitation, emblazoned with his school's coat of arms. It'll be the first time I'm going to step into his world. And it's a *ball.*

I don't want to spend the night in a gymnasium that smells like sweaty socks, and watch my sister play volleyball as if it's so much more fun to do it in the middle of the night than it is on a Saturday morning. And when her friends decide at two in the morning to find some raging frat-boy kegger, I don't want to tag along and stand awkwardly in a corner and watch people puke on themselves. That's not beautiful, and it's not me.

It's my first New Year's Eve as one half of a couple, and this night is supposed to be about champagne and pretty dresses and waltzing and knee-weakening kisses on the chime of twelve.

Cady's voice hardens. "And you thought it'd be a good idea to tell me *now*? When we're supposed to be getting on the bus?"

I glare at her. I tried to tell her a dozen times over the past few weeks, and she shut me down every single time. Honestly, I hoped I'd be gone before she got home.

Cady glances down at my dress again. "God, you really mean it." She shakes her head. "I can't believe you're going to stand me up for *him*."

My brow furrows. "Why'd you say it like that, all sneery? Strat's amazing."

Cady rolls her eyes. "What, because he's loaded and pretty and goes to some dumb private school? You guys are just ob-sessed with the idea of being this perfect, shiny couple. Do you even talk, or is it just kissing all the time?"

"At least Strat listened when I told him how I wanted to spend my New Year's Eve. He knows that Spike Night isn't exactly my scene."

Frustration roils in my chest as I think of all the times she made me do what *she* wanted to do.

Cady scoffs. "He doesn't know you. You won't let him see you unless you've perfectly curated your dress and your hair and your dreamy, spaced-out look. It's all on the surface with you two. He doesn't know you, Aria, so—"

"I hate volleyball!" I scream.

The room goes still and silent. Cady stares at me, stunned.

I've never shouted like that at anyone, especially not her.

"I hate volleyball," I repeat, shaking now. "I hate sports, and I suck at them. And shit like Spike Night is not who I am. So don't say Strat doesn't know me, because *you* don't know me either."

I feel hot and sick and awful, and my blood is scorching in my cheeks. "But maybe you'd know that if you weren't so busy forcing me to do whatever *you* want to do."

Something flares in her eyes. "Yeah, I *have* to make the decisions for us, because if I didn't plan things, you'd never do anything. You'd probably be sitting by the window right this minute, staring out wistfully like some deranged Miss Havisham, living in some fantasy land in your head."

"You *force* me to do stuff I don't want to do!"

"Excuse me? You've never once said that you didn't want to do something. But why would you stand up for yourself? That would take way too much effort."

"I didn't say anything because it was more important to be with you. I let you drag me to all that stuff because I didn't have a better option."

She goes cold. "But now you do have a better option, is that it?"

"Yes, and excuse the hell out of me for wanting to be with my boyfriend on New Year's instead of sleeping on a gym floor with *your* team. I wish I hadn't wasted four years hanging out with people I have *nothing* in common with."

"I always have to make friends for us, because you never want to talk to anyone."

"I can make friends for myself. You just never fucking let me!"

"You can't even remember what day of the week it is without me! You wouldn't be getting your high school diploma without me! So yeah, Aria, we're going to hang out with the people I want to hang out with, because I'm pulling all the weight and you're just bumbling around dreamy-eyed behind me."

My chest feels so tight I'm afraid my ribs are going to crack. She's demolishing me.

"You're wrong, by the way," I say, tears welling hot in my eyes. "I do make my own decisions. I applied to a dressmaking school in Milan."

Shock wipes the anger off her face.

"You *what*?" she whispers. For the first time in this entire horrendous fight, she looks hurt. "That's on a different *continent*, Aria."

I shrug, pretending it's no big deal. I won't tell her that I withdrew the application so I could stay with Strat.

"Okay, Miss Suddenly Decisive, I have a decision for you to make." Her eyes flash dangerously. "Him or me."

I look down at my dress. "I already made my choice. I'm going to the Swithun's ball."

"Not where you're going tonight, Aria. *Overall.* Him or me."

"*What?*" It knocks the breath out of me.

She just stares. There are bright blotches of red on her cheeks.

"That's such a messed-up thing to ask," I whisper.

"Choose, Aria."

Rage burbles up in me. *How dare she!*

"Fine. If that's the way you want to play it." I'm on the verge of a total meltdown, but something in me is hard as steel. "I choose him."

She stands there, stunned, swaying on the spot. She thought I'd cave. That I'd bend to whatever made things smooth and easy, that I'd be the carpet I've been my whole life, letting her walk all over me.

I choose him.

I've never felt so sick or alive or awful or powerful.

Cady's eyes glass over. So much hurt. *Good. She hurt me.* She takes one unsteady step backward. Then she snatches up her packed duffel bag and runs out of the room.

CHAPTER THIRTY-NINE

My hands won't stop shaking as I pull on my dress.

Don't cry don't cry don't cry.

This night was supposed to be my fairy-tale ball. Cady's ruined part of it, but I refuse to let her ruin the rest.

Somehow, even though my vision keeps going blurry, I manage to thread the thin metallic leather straps through the tiny buckles on my heels, pin my hair into a half updo, put a little makeup on my cheeks and lips.

I check my phone. I'm ready with fifteen minutes to spare before Strat gets here. There's a text from him, hovering at the top of my screen. When I read it, what little air I'd managed to get back into my lungs goes right back out again.

Maybe we should skip the ball.

The sentence stares back at me. There's not a trace of his usual sweet, teasing humor.

I drop to sit on my bed. I have no idea how to reply. After blinking at the screen for the better part of five minutes, I send a reply.

He types for so long I expect an essay to come through next, but his reply is short:

You don't really want to meet my
dumbass classmates, do you?
Let's do something else. Just us.

My eyes sting. He knows how excited I've been for this. Wired and nervous, because it's the first time I'll really be stepping into his world, but excited. It's been six weeks since he asked me if I would go with him to his school's Winter Fundraiser Ball. The moment he asked me, the vision of the dress popped into my head, almost fully formed. I've spent a hundred hours since then toiling over it. Choosing the fabrics, cutting the tissue paper patterns, draping it on my mannequin, sewing, sewing, sewing. Daydreaming about the moment we arrive, my hand tucked in the crook of his arm. Jaws dropping at the sight of my dress, swarming to ask where I got it.

Before I can convey the hopes I'd pinned on this night, another text lands.

Shit. Sorry. I'm being a jerk.
You've been looking forward to
this. I'm getting in the car now.
Sorry.

With shaky hands, I smooth out the petals of one of the flowers on my bodice. I was hoping that going to the ball would erase the tension my fight with Cady knotted in me, but now I'm not so sure this is a good idea at all.

Strat doesn't say a single word on the drive to St. Swithun's, not even when he maneuvers his glossy red sports car into the parking lot, pebbles crunching under the tires.

My mouth falls open when I see the Great Hall. The imperious stone facade is lit up against the night sky. English ivy crawls up to cradle leaded-glass windows. Suddenly I don't feel like I'm in Northern California at all. This is an old-world manor in some wetter, darker country.

"I'll get the door for you," Strat mumbles. My heart thuds as I wait in my seat, still staring slack-jawed through the windshield.

He pulls me up from my seat, and I grip his hand like it's a life vest. With each step toward the building, my nervousness grows. Music drifts on the air, and peals of bright laughter come from a cluster of long-legged, impeccably dressed boys on the lawn. It feels as if we've stepped into a photo shoot for a J.Crew catalogue. Maybe he was right. Maybe we shouldn't have come.

"Strat, wait," I say, halting at the bottom of the steps.

He turns.

"Do you think they'll like me?" I whisper. "Even though I don't really . . . *belong* here?"

The pained expression that flickers over his face makes me wish I could retract my question. I start babbling. "I'm sorry—you don't have to answer that. I'm being silly, I know." I do my best to put on a brave face. "It's okay, because you *do* belong. They'll like me because *you* like me."

I square my shoulders, but when I try to start up the palatial front steps, this time Strat tugs on my hand, holding me back. A muscle flexes in his jaw, as if he's bracing himself too, and then he starts up the stairs.

If I thought the outside of the Great Hall was impressive, it pales in comparison to the inside.

The room is vast, with cantilevered beams reaching up to the high ceiling. The walls are uplit with a thousand tiny blue spotlights, and a blanket of powdery snow shuffles underfoot. I know it's fake snow, but I can't help watching the way the hem of my dress sweeps it around in swirling little eddies.

Round tables draped in ice-blue silk surround a gleaming wooden dance floor. At one end of the room, a slideshow plays on a white screen. Boys on a field in pristine white clothes playing a civil game of cricket, boys on a muddy field playing a violent game of rugby, boys accepting medals and trophies and awards. One of Strat behind a grand piano.

"I'll get you a drink," he says.

My eyes snap to his. We just got here. I want to say, *Don't leave me*, but there's a tightness at the corners of his mouth that makes me let him go. I melt to the side of the room and hover by a table of canapés. I smooth my hand down Ultraviolet Dreamgirl.

Our entrance went entirely unnoticed.

Nearby, a girl and a boy murmur to each other in low

conversation. I recognize the boy—he was at that party Cady dragged me to months and months ago. Stew. I try to turn my body so he doesn't see me, but he does a little double take and steps over.

"Sorry, do I know you?" he asks.

"Um. I don't think so."

The slinky, ghostly-pale blond girl slides a hand onto Stew's shoulder. "She came in with Strat Madigan."

"Ah, so *you're* Strat's girl," Stew says. His smile is wide and friendly, but under it there's an edge. Like he's entertaining himself with some joke I'm not in on.

The girl drapes one limp, cool hand out toward me. "Aveline," she says. I reach out to shake hands, but she gives me only the barest lazy touch of her fingertips.

"Aria," I croak out.

"I love your dress," she says, but there's something in her sliding pitch that makes me think she means the exact opposite.

"Thanks," I say. "I like yours too."

I fist one hand in my tulle skirt to keep my nerves from collapsing. Every other girl in here is wearing body-hugging sheaths in luxurious metallics, as if they're toned, sporty statues dripping in liquid gold and quicksilver. Most of the gowns have thigh-high slits, and some are fitted with mesh panels in strategic spots. The few who aren't wearing metallics are in black or white. My lavender-and-electric-violet concoction is the most colorful, maximalist dress here. The bell of my skirt swishes over the floor in a near four-foot radius, and the lush flowers I tacked in a swathe from waist to foot glitter in the dramatic lighting.

I was right. I don't belong here.

Stew and Aveline drift away without saying goodbye, his hand trailing crudely over her ass as they go. I scan the cavernous room for Strat. *Where did he go?*

Finally I spot him by an arched door, talking to a guy with spiky black hair and a black leather jacket. The boy claps Strat on the shoulder, laughing.

I wonder who he is. A friend? Strat's never really talked about the boys at St. Swithun's. This guy looks more out of place here than me, but he's owning it. Everyone who passes him says hi in a fawning way, like he's famous or something.

I take a deep breath and head for the two of them, pushing through the crowd. Strat glances up and spots me coming, and a strange expression flits over his face. I'm sure it looks like— *guilt?*

"Hey, I'll see you later, man," Strat says to the other boy, who hesitates for a moment, then disappears into the crowd.

"You didn't want to introduce us?" I ask weakly.

"To Mick? Um, no, it's okay."

He's so tense and on edge. So unlike his usual self. He looks . . . *afraid.* He passes me a flute of sparkling punch, and we stand awkwardly for a few minutes. My eyes prick with tears. I wish I knew how to fix this night, to get us back on track to our normal selves, but I don't even feel like touching him right now.

We're jostled by people milling around. Strat doesn't introduce me to anyone. At one point, Stew passes us, clapping his hand on Strat's shoulder without stopping. "Out of curiosity, did you bring the Lambo or the Lotus tonight?"

Strat shrugs his hand away. "Fuck off, Stew."

Stew's laugh booms as he makes his way deeper into the room away from us.

"Shit," Strat hisses under his breath, seemingly to himself. He takes my elbow and guides me into a smaller room. He pinches the bridge of his nose. "This was a mistake."

Something horrible starts churning low in my belly.

"What was a mistake?" I ask feebly.

"Coming here . . . us, everything." He tugs a frustrated hand through his hair. "Aria . . . this isn't working."

I go still. "What?" I whisper.

He looks anguished. "This—us. It's not working."

The words feel like a knife to the kidney. I clutch my hand over my stomach. I can't breathe.

My mind reels. What did I do? Is this because I didn't stay in the room with him when he was upset about his dad? Deep down, I know—I know things aren't perfect between us. Maybe there are cracks in us that run deep, but there's nothing really *wrong*, right?

This isn't working.

"Strat . . ." My voice is shaky. "Are you . . . are you breaking up with me?"

He squeezes his eyes shut, pressing hard at his temples. "I can't—I just can't see how it's going to work."

"I don't understand," I say, tears clogging my bewildered voice. "What did I do?"

His mouth twists down. I watch him try to fight the tears gathering at the corners of his eyes, but it's a losing battle. One spills down over his cheek, leaving a long, silvery track.

We're caught there, drowning in awful, aching feelings. I'd give anything to make them stop.

I'm in shock. How is this happening? We were fine, right? What's going on?

That's the moment I realize that nearly everyone in the room has gone silent—and they're holding up their phones.

And—there's a weird echo to our words. Like a time delay.

With a sickening drop, I look over Strat's shoulder. On the projector screen in the other room, two figures loom, larger than life: me and Strat.

Someone's AirPlaying this to the projector screen. Our heartbreak broadcast for all to see.

Strat turns around. Sees the screen. Grief turns to anger. "What the fuck? Who's doing this?"

He moves through the crowd, searching for the culprit, and I crumple without him next to me.

And then Strat's growling, "Put that the *fuck* away, Stew!" to someone in the crowd. Strat shoves him—not quite hard enough to start a fight, but close.

"What? It's entertainment," Stew says with a cruel smirk.

"I'm fucking serious, put it away."

He makes no move to end the AirPlay. Strat grabs the phone right out of his hands and drops it in a punch bowl.

But the damage is done.

A hush falls over the room. A hundred, a thousand, a million eyes watch me, beady and hungry and glistening.

Strat just broke up with me, and it was broadcast for all to see.

Someone covers a cruel snort of laughter, and I see Aveline bringing one lazy hand up to her mouth to cover a nasty smile.

Humiliation.

Streaking hot through every cell in my body.

"Aria, wait!" Strat reaches for me, but at his touch, a sob starts to rise up through me, threatening to burst out of my throat. This pulsing, mortifying moment will only get worse if I let that sound out.

I yank my arm out of his grip. I don't need his help to flee.

CHAPTER FORTY

I push through the crowd, battling my way to the front door.

The hall coughs me out of its grand front doors and into the cool night air, and the effort to keep it all in breaks. I can barely see, barely think. I pull up Uber on my phone and shakily tap in my details.

I didn't know it would hurt like this. It's taking every last shred of my strength not to crumple like Cinderella on the steps.

A sob catches me like a punch in the back. I sink down. I'm losing more than just a boyfriend. When Strat and I met, that night at homecoming, the starry-eyed romantic in me swelled to bursting. Now that sweet, hopeful girl who believed in great love is lying in a lifeless, broken heap inside me. It's a terrifying feeling: to know that I might never be able to revive her. A whole part of *me*, cut out.

All my years dreaming of love, I had no idea how it would feel when it went wrong. I can feel this night reshaping how I feel about love altogether.

The app pings, letting me know that my Uber will be here in four minutes. I look back at the hall, still teeming with noise and light. A few people linger outside vaping, flicking nosy glances at me. I can't stay here.

I start walking up to the main road, Ultraviolet Dreamgirl's hem trailing over the dirt. The Uber slides up, and I collapse into the seat. As the driver pulls back into traffic, I slump down in the dark back seat and break, silent tears streaming down my face.

With a sickening twist, I remember my fight with Cady, less than an hour ago. I chose Strat over my sister, and it was a colossal mistake.

The harsh streetlights pulse as we pass under them, then glare brighter as the driver turns onto the highway. Huge billboards loom over my head, and I press my forehead to the window and wonder how grief can make you feel *ill*.

In the distance, the huge LED ArEx billboard burns brighter than the others. I stare up at the ad playing on it as we get closer and closer to it.

DO YOU WANT TO FEEL LIKE YOURSELF AGAIN?

BREAK FREE FROM EMOTIONAL PAIN?

My breath catches in my throat. For one blissful second, the grief loosens its grip on me.

Could I . . . ?

The idea is gaining momentum. I feel the tug of it. The temptation. Save myself the heartbreak. The path of least resistance.

It doesn't have to hurt like this.

Wouldn't it be easier if Strat and I had never met at all?

Yes.

Anything would be better than feeling this horrible, gut-slashing pain of loss.

Something inside me loosens. An erasure. Better than the strongest painkiller.

We zoom past the billboard, and the decision is made. When I wake up, he'll be gone. All the pain will be gone.

I wrench my attention back into the car and lean forward to speak to the driver. "Sorry—can you actually take me to ArEx? The one by the medical district?"

I burst into the ArEx lobby with such a crazed energy I'm lucky they don't call the police. I quiver at the counter for ten minutes, begging them for an erasure, but they refuse to give me one.

"I'm so sorry, but we can't help you without a valid ID proving you're over eighteen," the woman at the desk repeats. Her voice is dripping with pity and kindness, and I hate it. I'm sure she's trained exactly for this situation, handling difficult customers late at night.

"Please." My voice breaks. "Isn't there anyone I can talk to?"

"We can call a parent or guardian for you, sweetheart, but other than that, there's really nothing we can do."

"It's okay," I say, fear thrumming through me at the thought of explaining this to my parents. I back away, wiping my dripping nose. "It's fine. I'm sorry I bothered you."

I make it through the doors before the pain kicks into me again. Outside, I slump down against the wall, gripped by another wave of grief.

This isn't working.

The automatic doors slide open, and a man with salt-and-pepper hair and an ArEx lab coat steps out.

I swipe the tears out from under my eyes and try to stand. I'm only embarrassing myself sitting out here sobbing.

"Ah, there you are," the man says, in a kind, fatherly voice. "You left this inside."

He holds something out to me. Something I don't recognize. A white business card, faintly glowing in the light from the ArEx ads on the side of the building.

"Oh, that's not mine, I didn't—"

"You know, ArEx isn't the only place you can get an erasure now," he says. He holds the card out to me again, and this time I take it.

On it is a strange blue symbol that looks a bit like a crescent moon, and an address.

"Have a nice night," he says, tucking his hands into his pockets and disappearing back into the ArEx building.

I wipe my eyes and flip the card over. There's a QR code on the back. When I scan it on my phone, the landing page reads:

STEPS TO PREPARE FOR YOUR ERASURE.

I hear Strat's words again, slicing me in two.

This was a mistake. This isn't working.

I call for another Uber and tell the driver I need to make two stops. The car idles on the curb as I run into my house, gathering things like a wild tornado, leaving my side of the bedroom in shambles. I strip out of my dress, ball it up. I leave a note for my mom.

And then I'm running back out to the taxi, a toolbox cradled
in my arms. The only thing I could find that would hold it all.

Up on the ridge, by the swing set, I sink to the ground. Dig
until my arms ache with it. I clamber back into the taxi and pass
the business card to the driver.

"Take me to this address, please."

I come back to myself in the back seat of Strat's junky station wagon up on the ridge. Rain patters softly on the night-dark windshield. The two of us sit as still as tombstones, the dress between us, clenched in our hands.

I drop it on a gasp, clutching at my stomach. The pain from the recovered memories floods through me as if it just happened. As if it was mere minutes ago, not months.

After weeks of wanting to know, I finally have our *why*.

"I saw everything." My voice comes out broken and raw. "I know why I erased you."

"The ball. I saw it too." His voice is dazed, heavy with the same ache.

I don't understand.

"Why did you break up with me?" I ask in a tiny voice.

I never got a chance to ask that night, didn't force him to explain. I was too blinded by the hurt. And then the next day, I was wiped clean.

Strat meets my eyes, and there is only devastation there. "I was freaking out, Aria. I was so scared. I didn't pull you into that hall with the intention of breaking up with you. I just got carried away, and I was—I was panicking." He plows his hands through his hair. "God, I loved you so fucking much. I didn't want to break up with you."

"That doesn't answer my question," I whisper.

He presses his eyes shut. "I was so scared it would all come out that night. All my stupid lies. I'd just been digging myself deeper and deeper with them. I was terrified that you'd find out I'd been lying, and you'd leave me."

"You were only lying about using Mick's car and mansion to impress me, right? Nothing else?"

"Nothing else, I swear."

In the silence, our heartbeats pound, pumping out *pain, pain, pain.*

"Strat, why did you think you had to lie about those things to make me like you?"

"It was so fucking stupid," he says, slumping forward and putting his head in his hands. "I just—everyone was so impressed when I showed up to your homecoming in Mick's car. And the way you looked at me—it was like a drug. I couldn't get enough."

"That's not why I was looking at you like that," I whisper. "It was the way you played the piano, and your smile, and the way you looked at *me.* I never cared about the car, or that you went to St. Swithun's, or that you wear this dumb watch all the time."

He looks pained. Like I'm stabbing him all over again. "I

didn't know that then, Aria. I just . . . I just wanted you to love me. I thought you were radiant, and so special, and that if I was just normal Strat, I wouldn't be good enough for you."

My chin wobbles, and I fight back tears.

He lied, but I did this too. My expectations. The pressure I put on him.

"I'm so sorry," I whisper.

"I'm sorry too. What a fucking mess, right?"

I let out a shaky breath and turn to face out of the front window, tipping my head back against the headrest. We know what happened, finally.

I feel almost . . . disappointed by the revelation. There's been such a crazy buildup in my head. I imagined so many awful things. I was expecting some huge, awful betrayal, something dramatic and shocking that would have made the erasure make total black-and-white sense. Well, the breakup was huge, but the catalyst for it wasn't.

Us falling apart wasn't the work of one moment. Sometimes relationships die on a whisper, after a slow descent through misunderstandings and miscommunication and turmoil.

I can see it all now. I was infatuated with him, so focused on being his girlfriend that I let my other relationships slide. I was projecting my rose-colored vision onto him, just like I did with those other boys, convincing myself they were something different than who they really were. Worst of all, I was so caught up in him that I withdrew my Sciarra application. I gave up my *future* for him.

In a way, it all fell apart because I was too scared to face the difficult parts of us. The parts of us that were real. I didn't let Strat see me at my worst, and I didn't let him show me his deeper feelings when he was dealing with his own pain about his parents. I was trying to build our relationship on a foundation of daydreams.

We both screwed up, but not in an unforgivable way. A sad, realistic way.

I press my eyes closed, and a tear tracks down my cheek. I hate realistic.

Strat reaches for my hand, and I cling to him even though my bruised, wounded heart is telling me not to.

After being immersed in the emotions of three months ago, it's so difficult to remember that this is us *now*. I force myself to pick it all apart in my mind. This Strat is different. This is the boy I hated when I walked into that moonlight glade, the boy I started to soften toward in each progressive midnight, the boy who told me his secrets and fears and dreams and who listened to mine.

He pulls his hands through his hair. "Aria? When did I erase you?" he asks.

"I have no idea."

He smashes his palms over his eyes. "Do you think . . . do you think I got one too so I wouldn't end up like my dad? I mean, I know it's different, that he and my mom were married for six years before she died . . . But do you think I did it so there wouldn't be two heartbroken, useless people in the house?"

The thought makes my own heart ache.

I slide down in the seat and press my hands over my eyes. I'm dizzy and exhausted.

"Maybe I should get you home," Strat says miserably. "It's after three."

I nod. We don't speak during the drive. It feels like there are a hundred questions, but all of them are too big to voice out loud. He holds my hand the entire way, and I grip it like a life raft.

Strat pulls the car up to the curb two houses down from mine so we don't wake Mom. There is so much between us now. It feels too complicated to lean over and kiss him, so instead I just drop my forehead to his shoulder and breathe him in.

His fingers stroke through my hair. "Aria? We're okay, right?"

"I think so. It's so much. But I'm trying to detangle the old us from *this* us."

"We made so many stupid mistakes. It was all surface, before."

"I know," I whisper.

"But it isn't now."

"No, it isn't now."

He presses a kiss to the top of my head. I let the warmth radiate down through me, let the cinnamon smell of him envelop me.

Inside I lean against the door until I'm sure he's gone. I swear I can almost feel the connection to him stretch taut, then snap when his car disappears around the corner. Like we're planets in orbit and he's gone far enough to escape the gravity of me.

CHAPTER FORTY-TWO

An ache takes up residence in my chest, somehow hollow and heavy at the same time. I keep having to stop and remind myself to breathe around its tightness.

The TV in the living room is on, and the clicker is in my hand, but I've been here since Strat dropped me off at 3 a.m. and now the sun is high overhead and I couldn't tell you what I've been watching.

My phone is lying on the floor. I'm ignoring Strat's calls. The text that says, Don't shut down on me, Aria, please. You can handle this.

But I'm not sure I can. I can't stop *feeling* the things I felt that night. The horrible tangle in my throat during my fight with Cady. And then the humiliating, heart-shredding breakup with Strat . . . it was like I'd had my insides ripped out. I'm feeling it all as if it happened yesterday. It's like erasing it all just put it on hold, and now I'm having to feel the fallout.

And the guilt . . . I'm an awful sister. I chose Strat over Cady. She shouldn't have asked me to, but I shouldn't have chosen him.

The news is on, but the TV's muted. I stare at the ticker tape that scrolls headlines across the bottom of the screen. I'm about to change the channel when one of the headlines has me pushing up from the arm of the couch.

SACRAMENTO AUTHORITIES FINALLY LOCATE AND SHUT DOWN ELUSIVE UNDERGROUND CLINIC THAT PROVIDED THOUSANDS OF ILLEGAL MEMORY ERASURES.

I jerk up. Grab the remote and click up the volume until it's booming through the room. They show a clip of a windowless metal door with a blue logo above it. My whole body goes stiff. That logo—it's what was on the business card with the address that led me to the erasure. And that's the same door I went through to get my erasure.

Illegal? Am I going to be arrested for what I did that night?

My heart is pounding hard. Behind the polished blond reporter, cops are perp-walking a dark-haired man in a white doctor's coat out of a building.

A chill runs down my spine. Because the man getting perp-walked out of the building with the crescent moon above the door?

It's the man who was outside ArEx the night I begged for an erasure.

The reporter turns back to the camera. "Authorities have not yet released a name, but many are speculating that the brain behind the underground clinic is the founder of an upstart biotechnology company that has long been trying to unseat Aracen Exradere as the nation's most beloved—and only—erasure provider.

"Obviously many Sacramentans have fallen victim to this medically dangerous scheme. If you think you or a family member may have received treatment from this facility, please call the hotline at the number below. The City of Sacramento's Department of Health and Public Safety has established the hotline to connect with those who had erasures. They have expert neurosurgeons on hand to advise you of your rights and next steps you need to take. They say it's very important you speak to them, as unregulated procedures can have medically negative side effects that can be life-threatening."

Life-threatening? Could there be something wrong with me? I reach for my phone. Shakily I type the phone number in. A woman with a smooth, professional voice answers right away.

I clear my throat. "Hi, I, um—I think I may have gotten an erasure at the place they're talking about on the news."

"Thank you for calling. The first thing we'll need to do is confirm that you were a patient at the clinic. Can I take your last name, please?"

I hesitate for a second, then decide that if they have my name on file anyway, I won't be able to escape the consequences, if getting an underage erasure really is illegal. "Lendell." I spell it for her.

"Let's see . . ." the woman murmurs. "It looks like there are two of you in the system. What's your first name?"

I open my mouth to answer, then stop. Did she just say there were *two of us*? I tell myself Lendell isn't an unusual last name, and Sacramento is a big place. Probably a coincidence. But I suddenly have a weird feeling.

On a hunch, I give her my sister's name instead of mine.

"Cadence. Cadence Lendell."

A flurry of quick keyboard taps. "Yes, I can confirm that, according to the clinic's records, you did undergo an erasure procedure, on—oh, on New Year's Eve. December thirty-first."

My heart skips a beat.

"Are you sure about that date?" I ask.

"It's here in the system. The City of Sacramento seized the underground clinic's records in the interest of public safety, and we have their computers and all their data here at City Hall. The records indicate that you had an erasure procedure at 9:37 p.m. on December thirty-first."

Oh God. Cady wasn't home when I stopped at the house that night, before going up to the ridge. I thought she was just at Spike Night . . .

But she never went. Instead, she went to this clinic—the same clinic I went to, and only two hours before me.

My breathing ratchets up. Adrenaline spills in a sick wave through me. What did she erase? Our fight? Strat?

Oh my God. *Me?*

I shake my head. She couldn't have. She wouldn't have.

"I need to take some details from you now, Ms. Lendell," the operator says. "At the end of the call, I'll be able to give you more information and contact details, and an appointment to come down to City Hall. There will also be further information for you regarding what legal action you can take."

"Wait," I blurt. "On TV, they said it was . . . dangerous. Potentially deadly."

"That's right. The clinic wasn't licensed to be performing these types of operations. But we'll get to that when—"

"Sorry, this is important. I was born with a malformed blood vessel in my brain," I lie, pretending to be Cady. "Would that make an erasure more dangerous?"

The phone operator pauses for a few seconds. "Hold on. Let me check with our consulting neurologist from Aracen Exradere."

She puts me on hold. Weird jazz plays while I wait.

My temples pulse with a fierce headache. *Cady had an erasure too.* I can't stop thinking it, over and over.

The line clicks and the music stops. "Are you still there, Ms. Lendell?"

I clear my throat. "Yes, still here."

"Our doctor says that at an accredited facility like Aracen Exradere, they would never operate on a patient with an arteriovenous malformation, because the likelihood of its rupturing is extremely high. Usually systems are in place for doing a preliminary scan to ensure that the brain is healthy enough to undergo the erasure procedure, but due to the nature of the facility you went to, those checks were likely not carried out. Hold on—"

I hear a man's voice in the background.

"The doctor is strongly advising that you go see a neurologist as soon as possible. There's a chance that even though you're symptom-free now, the experimental procedure you underwent could have caused further damage to your AVM, weakened its walls, and you could be at risk of rupture. He's—he's actually quite adamant about this. He recommends that you call as soon as we get off the phone."

"Okay. Yes, sure. I'll call them right after this."

"Miss Lendell—he says you're lucky the malformation didn't rupture during or shortly after your erasure at the clinic."

She takes more information after that, but I zone out, auto-piloting my way through the answers.

You're lucky it didn't rupture.

Oh God.

I think back to the awful day of Cady's hospitalization—January first. The day I now know was the day after the St. Swithun's ball. That morning I woke up feeling tired but blank—I didn't realize the exhaustion was from my breakup with Strat and my midnight erasure. I just felt blissfully clean.

Cady was rolled over, facing the wall, her back to me. Her hair was in a messy topknot on the pillow.

I crossed the room in three steps and sat on the edge of her bed. I touched her shoulder gently. "Cady? It's time to get up."

Her arm slid backward under my touch, flopping like a doll's. It fell back until it was crooked behind her at an odd, unnatural angle.

Fear slid through me then.

"Cady?" I shook her harder, but she didn't respond. She

was breathing, but she wasn't waking up. She was limp, and pale, and—

That's when I screamed.

The rush to the hospital was a neon blur of horror.

Ambulance sirens, waiting in a cold white room, my parents watching the door that led to the operating rooms. It was the worst place I'd ever been. I couldn't stop replaying that limp, bizarre fall of her arm, couldn't stop hearing myself screaming, *Mom Mom Mom!*

Two hours. Three. Four.

A man in operating scrubs and a PPE mask came out of the double doors. He was stout and heavily bearded. He tugged his mask down. "Mr. and Mrs. Lendell?"

We jolted up and went to him.

"She's out of surgery and her vitals are stable," the man said.

Dad exhaled hard. Mom pressed a hand over her chest. My whole body started trembling.

"Your daughter had an arteriovenous malformation in her brain—it's when the blood vessels are enlarged and tangled. Earlier this morning, or maybe last night, the AVM ruptured, and she began to bleed into her brain, which increased the pressure inside her skull. Right now we're keeping her in a medically induced coma. It's too early to tell whether she'll wake up when we take her out of that. It's also too early to know whether there is any damage to her brain or what the extent of that might be."

I watched in a daze as Mom nodded, as Dad's face went slack and vacant.

"Miss Lendell? Are you still there?" The voice is small and tinny, coming from the phone I've dropped in my lap.

I blink, snapping out of the memory and back into real life. Now, back in my bedroom in the aftermath of everything, it clicks:

Cady got an erasure right after our fight.

Maybe *because* of our fight.

CHAPTER FORTY-THREE

The nurses are busy with other patients, so no one sees me slip into Cady's room. It's dim, lit only by the lights on the ArEx building next door.

I stare at my sleeping sister, taking in the dry, cracked skin at the edges of her mouth. The greasy sheen at her temple. The way her skin drapes over her shoulder bone.

I start to shake.

I did this to her.

She did this to me.

"Why?" I whisper. Why did she make me choose? Why couldn't she just let me have my romance? I'd been following her around for years, doing what she wanted. And the minute I started spending time with someone else, she couldn't get her jealousy in check?

Maybe I should have seen it coming. Now that I'm looking for it, there were small things scattered through our history.

The way she pushed in between me and my new friend Millie in first grade. The way she subtly pressured me into quitting ballet and then made me go to every single one of her volleyball games. Dragging me to parties I didn't want to go to, to athletic summer camps I didn't want to go to. Driving wedge after wedge between me and my interests and the people who shared those interests.

I'm sure now that Cady was the one who screwed with the group chat for Arissa's party. She didn't want me having friends outside the group I'd been roped into for all of high school.

Why?

I might never be able to ask her.

I slump in the chair, defeated.

"God, Cady. What am I supposed to do with all this?"

Her machines *whoosh* and *beep*, but no answer comes.

CHAPTER FORTY-FOUR

The numbness sets in. Like when you break too many bones at once and your brain can't handle the pain, so it just switches off entirely.

I'm lying on my bed facing the wall—facing away from Cady's side of the room—when an unfamiliar number pops up on my screen. Thinking it might be Mom at the hospital, I force myself to answer it.

"Could I please speak with Aria Lendell?"

"That's me," I say, dragging myself up to sit.

"Ms. Lendell, my name is Dorothy, and I'm with Aracen Exradere's corporate office. We're reaching out to everyone affected by the Sacramento crisis. We understand that you underwent an erasure procedure on December the thirty-first, is that right?"

"Yes, that's right," I say. Fear jolts through my belly. Am I in trouble?

"We're pleased to share that we are offering everyone

who had an unsafe erasure a free ArEx erasure, as a gesture of goodwill."

I stare at the wall. *What?*

"Ma'am? Are you there?"

"I'm here. But—why? Why would you do that?"

The woman pauses at the unexpected question. But then it clicks. It's clearly a PR stunt, to win over anyone who might disapprove of their monopoly on erasures. It'll make the company look great compared with all the bad press that's coming out about that man who opened the clinic in the alley.

"Never mind, it doesn't matter," I say. "I'm not eighteen yet."

"We're offering this program to anyone over the age of sixteen. It's perfectly safe—we were about to roll out our full array of procedures later this year to that age group, and there have been intensive studies done. If you'd like me to send you materials—"

"No thank you. I'm not interested in another erasure."

"I'll send a voucher to the email we have on file anyway," she says brightly, "and we hope to see you at a clinic soon. ArEx takes patient health—"

I hang up on her.

Before I toss my phone down, I catch a glimpse of the red notification badges. A dozen texts and two missed calls from Strat. I'm not ready to talk to him yet. I'm not ready for a midnight either. Everything is too raw, and I can't seem to get a grip on my emotions.

*　*　*

The clock blinks at me: 10:43 p.m. I rub my eyes. I'll never be able to stay awake tucked up warm in bed. I swing my legs out from under my blankets, but when I try to stand up, the room tilts and I knock over the stack of fashion magazines on my bedside table. Fatigue settles over me, as heavy as an antique quilt.

There's a strange pressure in my head, like I've been drugged. I stumble to the bathroom and splash cold water on my face, but the pressure is so intense it feels like it's dragging me down.

A cold weight settles in my stomach. Is this the midnight? Is it . . . trying to forcibly drag me back in?

It can't be. The midnights *aren't* sentient. They don't have intentions.

But on my next blink, my eyes close for a full four seconds and I sway on my feet.

I can't—

Stay awake—

I open my eyes to heat and cracked clay under my cheek.

The ground is lunar-pale in the moonlight, and there is nothing here except for three spindly black trees, reaching up to the sky like grasping claws.

This is a desert, and these trees are dead. Petrified and black.

Strat's sitting with his back against one of the dead trees, his eyes closed. He looks *wrecked.* Like he's aged five years since I last saw him. His eyes open when he hears me, and there must be so much pain on my face that he shifts into action, coming over to help me sit up.

He brings one hand to my cheek. "Oh, Aria. Will you let me hold you?"

I nod. He's the boy who broke me, but he's also still the boy I'm in love with, and this is all so fucking confusing.

He wraps his arms around me, and for a long time I just listen to his heartbeat, the steady rhythm of it under my ear.

"I got a call today from ArEx," I say, my voice weirdly flat.

He exhales. "Yeah, I did too."

I press my eyes closed, letting him sway me a little, soothingly.

Suddenly he stops rocking me. I can hear him thinking. And then he shifts, drawing back to look in my eyes.

"Aria . . . we could do it."

"What?"

"We could do it. If we get the erasures, we can start over. Try again."

I try to process what he's saying, but it feels like I'm thinking through a wall of water.

"I keep thinking that if there was any way I could undo what I did back then, I would. And there is a way. The erasures can do that for us. I could give you the love story you wanted us to have."

I press my hand over the tight knot of pain and pressure in my chest. The pain of our breakup is lodged there, the wreckage of our tailspinning first relationship still stuck inside me. I'm so terrified that in my heart, he'll always be the boy who lied to me and then dumped me at a ball.

Imagine what it would feel like if it was just . . . gone.

Strat and I could start over. Cady and I could start over. It would be easier with a blank slate, wouldn't it?

My heart thuds. Aching for rest. To not feel like this anymore. I thought I was getting stronger, but I was wrong. I want to sink back into nothing.

"Okay," I whisper.

Strat's eyes go wide. "Really?"

"If it makes it stop feeling like this, then yes. Really."

He brightens, speaking faster now. "We can write ourselves notes, to find each other again. And tell ourselves not to dig into the past. Just start over clean."

I catch his arm. "Wait—what if we don't have midnights this time?" What if they were tied to the bad erasure somehow?

He considers it. "We might not have them anymore. Is that a deal-breaker?"

My eyes drink in the moonlight, the vast expanse of desert. I've loved all our midnights. They are beautiful, empty canvases. But . . . the midnight could serve me up a million of the most exquisite places and they'd all feel empty without him. It was Strat who made the midnights wonderful all along.

"No," I say. "It's not a deal-breaker."

For the second time this year, I prepare for an erasure.

This time, it is quiet and methodical. Not a whirlwind, no impulsiveness. Something is ending, but it's so that something else can begin.

The hangers in my closet screech when I push the clothes

aside. There we are on the wall, our story written in index cards, the whole arc of us, everything so bright and sweet—until it wasn't.

I take the cards down, one by one. In some places, the tape peels flakes of paint away, but when I slide the clothes back, you'd never know. Whole months of love reduced to a few patches of exposed drywall.

CHAPTER FORTY-FIVE

The ArEx lobby is bustling with smiling staff and flashing with bright advertisements, but Strat and I sit in tense silence, not speaking, both of us just staring into space as if we're in a zombie trance.

There is a strange airport feeling here that I've only just noticed, written on the faces of the patients nervously awaiting their procedures. A sense of departures and endings, a tight weave of worry and relief and regret.

They call Strat's name first. A bored-looking ArEx technician in a bright uniform hovers by the door to the treatment rooms. "Strat Madigan? This way, please."

He stands. I stand too.

"This is it," he says softly, looking down at me. "You sure you still want to do this?"

I nod. Anything to put an end to this horrible tightness in my chest.

He seems to want to say more, but I can't look him in the eye.

"Okay." He squeezes my hand, then lets go.

And then I'm alone.

I bend down and unzip my backpack. Pull out the stack of index cards I took off my closet wall. I look around for a trash can and spot one by the coffee machine. I drop the cards in, onto a bed of empty foam cups. After my erasure, I won't remember that they're here.

But there is one index card I keep. I sink back into my seat and turn it over in my hands. I'm going to tuck it in my pocket so, after, it will be the first thing I read.

You might start dreaming about a boy named Strat. He's real. Find him. Start over. Don't dig into what happened before.

Strat has an identical card in his pocket.

"Aria Lendell?"

I snap out of it to see another ArEx technician waiting by the door with a clipboard. She's early.

I hesitate. "I'm not scheduled for another half an hour," I say.

"Well, we're a little ahead of schedule. That okay?"

"I guess." I follow her down the hallway and through a set of imposing, windowless doors. Fear closes in on my throat. Not because they're about to point a proton beam at my brain—thousands of people get ArEx erasures every day without a second thought—but because this feels too much like an ending. This isn't like last time. ArEx is good at what they do, and these memories are never coming back.

The technician guides me through a freezing-cold prep room, and then, after signing another form, into the ER.

The Erasing Room.

Inside, everything is white, and so futuristic it feels like a spaceship. There are three technicians at a counter of monitors lining the far wall, preparing whatever data needs to be prepared. In the middle of the room is the machine. There's a glowing blue circle of light on the wall behind it, making it look like we're inside some enormous mechanical eye.

Music is playing, trying to make this seem fun and casual, but it sounds tinny and hollow. The gantry moves, bringing the bed down to a height I can reach. The technician helps me onto it and starts strapping me in. Chin, neck, forehead. My head can't move even one millimeter while the proton beam is pulsing. The technician is kind, introduces herself as Claire and attempts to make small talk, trying to catch my skittering gaze with her warm brown eyes, but I feel only fear.

Finally, all the restraints are in place. The table hums as it raises me up, positioning me under the machine. I squeeze my eyes shut. When Cady and I were little and didn't want to go to sleep, Mom always told us to close our eyes and think of our happy place.

I close my eyes and try to sink into the forest, that first midnight. The curling fog, the electric-purple moonlight. The snowy beach, the Ferris wheel, the castle turret . . .

It's not working. I'm still so tense, so wound up. I squeeze my eyes shut harder and try again. And this time, what I see isn't a place.

It's Strat.

Strat, dancing with me at homecoming. Teaching me "Three

Blind Mice" on his piano. Leaning over to whisper to me during Ayemi's ballet rehearsal. Running next to me in PE.

Strat Strat Strat.

Fear kicks hard behind my ribs. Is this how I want to spend my life? Making baby steps of progress with him, and then, when it gets too hard or messy, or one of us makes a mistake, making another trip to ArEx? Index cards in our pockets, *Find me again*? Forgetting and falling in love over and over again, a cycle that never ends?

Or do I want to face the things that feel too hard to face? Learn from our mistakes and . . . work on them? Change. *Grow.*

The blue ring of light pulses, and suddenly I know:

This isn't right.

Erasing all those moments won't fix our future. We'll make the same mistakes all over again, and maybe some new ones too.

We will never be a perfect fairy-tale love story, and that's okay. Life is messy. Life *is* the mistakes you make. Nothing will ever be effortless, or exactly what you expect. You just have to keep building on top of the mistakes.

My body rings with the clarity of it. This whole thing with Strat is so different from what I pictured, but I want it. I want our whole history.

And that means I have to get out of here.

With a horrible stomach drop, I realize—it might be too late. I'm trapped on this table, strapped down, with a huge proton beam pointed at my head.

"Wait!" I cry. It comes out sounding stiff because of the strap buckled so tightly under my chin. "Let me down! I can't do this, please, I can't do this."

The machine above me lights up, the blue ring glowing.

No, no, no.

"Stop!" I yell.

The machine whirs like a helicopter gearing up for takeoff, and there is a horrible, sickening moment—

And then the whirring clicks, winding down. The blue ring fades out. With a jerk, the bed starts to move down and hands start working at undoing my restraints. There are voices, questions, but I can't answer. As soon as the bed gets close enough to the ground, I sit up.

I rip the electrodes off my arms. Scramble down, heart suddenly pounding. I have to get to him before he erases me.

I'm pushing through the door when one of the technicians picks up a phone. "We've got a runner."

I explode into the corridor with the kind of urgent force that, if it were a bank, they'd be pressing the red button under the counter to call for the police.

"Miss!" A man appears out of nowhere. A navy uniform and tools clinking at his belt. A stern voice. A hand gripping my upper arm tightly. "I'll escort you back to the lobby."

I wheel around wildly, trying to shake the hand off. "Please, I need to just—" I crane my neck to look into every room he drags me past, searching for a riot of cinnamon curls. *Please please please.* He's not in any of them.

Where are you, where are you?

And then we round the corner and everything in my body stops.

There he is.

He's not running. He's standing coolly, thanking the nurse,

using that charming prep school grin. The one I know he had to practice, the one that makes him look like a cocky young Kennedy. *No, no, no!* He looks lighter than he did the other night. Like the weight has rolled off his shoulders. Like time has rolled back for him, and he's the boy I met at homecoming.

Something inside me buckles. I'm too late. He's already had the procedure.

Nausea sweeps through me.

If he turns, he'll see some frizzy-haired, frantic-eyed girl standing in the hallway staring at him like she's unhinged. He won't know who I am. Inside, an earthquake tremor starts. This is going to break me.

He looks up from the paperwork.

But instead of a blank sweep over me, a passing glance he'd give to any stranger, there's only *recognition.*

And then. One word.

"Aria?"

CHAPTER FORTY-SIX

The second hand ticks.

The world takes a breath.

Relief floods me so intensely I must look like I'm going to throw up or pass out. Maybe both simultaneously.

"Is this the girl?" the nurse asks with an eager smile.

Strat doesn't take his eyes off mine. "Yes. This is the girl."

The security guard finally lets go of me. The urge to fling my arms around Strat and bury my face in his shirt is overwhelming.

I take a step toward him, shaking. "I came to stop you," I say.

His eyes burn into mine. "I was on my way to stop *you*."

I'm desperate to cover him with apologies, let it all out in a rush, explain why I bolted from that treatment room, but the ArEx technician is puppy-dog-eyeing us like she's watching some matchmaking show, and the security guard is frowning.

Desperation wells up in me. "Can we get out of here? Please?"

The corner of his mouth curves up. "I would love that."

On our way out, I make a quick stop by the trash can in the lobby, and then the ArEx building is spitting us out into the sun. I scan our surroundings, frantic for a place to go, bubbling with all the words I need to say to this boy. We walk until the bustling city-sidewalk crowds thin, walk until we find a sliver of privacy at the corner of an empty parking lot.

In my pocket, my phone vibrates. I reach down and decline the call without looking at who it is.

I turn to face Strat, crossing my arms against a hot blast of wind. There's an AC unit juddering on the back of the building beside us, and the air smells like machinery and Freon. It's not quite the view from the castle midnight, but now I know it's not about how it looks. We're here, and it's real, and that's all that matters.

Our eyes lock. A thousand emotions well up between us.

"It wasn't the right thing to do," I say.

"No."

I fling myself at him then.

He catches me. I press my face to his shirt, just holding on to him. Here is relief, and here is comfort, and here is love.

"I want to show you something," I say, pulling back a little, hands trembling to get the index cards out. They are garish in the daylight, neon green and fluorescent yellow.

His brow lifts. "Are those cue cards? Are you going to make a speech?" There's the faintest tug of amusement at the corner of his mouth.

"No, not cue cards." I grab one of his hands and turn it palm up, laying the index cards there. "Every time a new memory came back to me, I wrote it down."

He flicks through them, to where I ran out of yellows and greens and started writing on hot pink.

"At first, I only wrote down the flashbacks. But then I started writing down things we did together after the midnights began."

Our story, in his hands, stacked as neatly as flash cards for a test. But when you look closely, it's tangled, bizarre, complicated.

"Strat—I don't want to start clean. If we erase our mistakes, we'll only make them again. Or make different ones."

We were a bad combination before. A girl who had impossible romantic expectations and a boy who would have done anything, changed anything about himself, to meet them. We should have just been ourselves and been honest with each other. Enjoyed the love but not let it take over everything.

"Out of all these moments," I say, laying my own hands on top of the pile of cards, "my favorite ones are the ones that felt real. When you came to run next to me so I could finish the mile without walking. When you told me about your mom's letter. When you kissed me by the window in your bedroom."

"I'm pretty fond of some of those too," he says, smiling down at me.

"All my life, I hoped for some fairy-tale-perfect love story, one I could tell people about that would make them coo about how romantic it was. But now I just want this one. Our whole twisted, winding way to each other, erasures and all. I want *you*. No matter how messy it gets."

"Aria—"

"Wait—let me get it all out." I press my hand over my ribs. "The pain of that night at the Swithun's ball is still fresh. It hurts, but I can take it, Strat. Difficult things are going to happen to us, and we might have rough patches, but this is my promise to you: that I won't stick my head in the sand and pretend they don't exist."

In my pocket, my phone vibrates again. *Not now.* This time I glance down and see Mom's face on the screen before clicking to silence it.

Strat steps closer. Frames my face in his hands. "My turn, okay?"

"Okay," I whisper.

"Aria, we had no idea what we were doing before, and we screwed it up. But we figured some stuff out too. And somehow we got this second chance. I didn't want to erase it all again either. Maybe we're not going to be Elizabeth Taylor and Richard Burton, or Antony and Cleopatra. Maybe we're just going to be a guy who plays piano at a bar to an audience of ten people and a girl who designs lacy, romantic, bohemian dresses. And who are just . . . good to each other. Honest. Who face it when things get hard, and get through it together."

"I like the sound of that," I whisper.

He kisses me then. He kisses me until I forget where we are, until I forget everything but the taste of him and the beat of his heart under his soft shirt.

He pulls back a long time later, pressing a breathless kiss to my forehead. "*Annnnd* there's still that. Jesus, Aria."

"There's still that," I murmur, dizzy-drunk on him.

The AC unit whines. "This really is the least romantic place I can think of to be declaring our everlasting love," I say, glancing over at it. "But . . . I'm okay with it."

"You fell for me the first time dancing on the face of an unnecessarily aggressive cougar, so I think it's on brand."

"True."

My phone vibrates again.

"Sorry—maybe I should get this. Just a second." I answer the call.

"Aria? Where are you?" Mom's voice is pitched with emotion. A strike of panic lances through my gut.

"Mom? What's wrong?"

"I'm on my way to the hospital. Cady—" Her voice cracks on a sob. "Just come, Aria."

CHAPTER FORTY-SEVEN

End the call

drop my phone to my side

where it hangs from my fingers, listless.

Strat's looking at me, a question he's too afraid to ask on his lips. The sky is painfully bright, and all the oxygen in the world has turned into something too thin to breathe.

I run.

I run like I'm an Olympic track and field star, like my lungs aren't burning. I run in a way that would make Coach Kapoor's jaw drop. My shoes pound on the pavement, the hospital impossibly far away. I don't stop to walk, ever.

And then, when I'm twenty steps away from the front door, dread rises in me and my feet come to a halt, as if I've hit an invisible brick wall.

I can't do this.

I can't face this.

My breath comes harsh, too fast. *Indigo chartreuse vermil-ion phthalo blue.* I double over. The ArEx building is a hundred yards away. Maybe I should go get an erasure and just erase my whole life, and move to a different state and get a fake name and I'll never have to feel this ever again.

I squeeze my eyes shut.

No. I have to face this. No matter how awful it is.

I draw myself upright. I hear Strat's footsteps behind me, but I don't turn. I'm off again, through the lobby, up the stairs because I can't bear to wait for the elevator.

I smack into the door to the fourth floor with the full weight of my body, exploding onto the ward. But my forceful entry is nothing compared to the hubbub in the hallway today, noise and industry and energy, all concentrated around room 408. Cady's room.

A doctor I don't recognize stands in the doorway. He tries to stop me. "I'm her sister," I growl, in a way that is so unlike me. I push through into her room. There's Dr. Tsukino and the lead nurse, Julia, moving quietly but efficiently around Cady's bed. The blinds have been pulled almost all the way down, casting the room in a cool blue.

Cady is propped up. Nothing is different except her eyes.

They're open. And blinking. Tired, long blinks.

She looks over. Sees me.

Her eyes water. Her mouth shapes a word that I can't hear, but I've always been able to read her lips.

Aria.

And something in the universe clicks back into place.

                                   *   *   *

Thirty-five minutes later, my parents rush in. Within seconds, my unshakeable, practical mom is a mess, eyes glassed over with tears and hand pressed to her mouth. Cady's still kind of woozy and out of it, and I'm sure she's wondering why we're losing our shit. To her, it feels like she's woken up from a long nap.

She's awake.

But it's Dad's reaction that is the most shocking of all. For the first minute, he's a statue in the doorway, unmoving as he watches Mom and me fuss over Cady.

And then he takes a step forward. And *breaks*.

He staggers to the bedside and clamps onto Cady's pale hand. I have never seen my father cry, but he weeps now. Silent tears spill down his cheeks, and his chin quavers. Wrinkles I barely noticed before become deep trenches of emotion.

Mom reaches out for my hand, and suddenly, for this one moment, we are a family again, linked in a chain, Meredith Cady Aria Michael, and something in my heart heals.

The next few days are a jumble. Mom and Dad and I are at the hospital from dawn until dusk.

Three months of sleep have not been kind to my sister's body. She can't take more than a few steps at a time, and her voice, always a rusty thing, is even rougher now, scarred by tubes and mechanically humidified air. She can't wrap her mind around how much time has passed.

She's tired. Flat. Not the Cady I know. But she is here.

Every time she looks at me, her eyes glass over with tears. I can feel the dark edges of the rift between us. There is a reckoning coming—but there always seems to be someone else in the room.

And then, one evening as the sun is setting, casting shadows onto the ArEx building next door, we're alone for the first time.

"Three months," she rasps.

She's been saying that a lot. As if she's hoping one of these times we'll say, *Oh, just kidding, you were only asleep for a couple of days.* Her chin goes taut and dimpled. One of my earliest memories is of snatching a doll out of her hands, and her chin did exactly this. It sends the same lance of panic through me as it did back then. I shoved the doll back into her arms, and the chin dimple went away. But now I can't shove the three months she lost back into her life.

Her eyes glaze over with tears, and she looks out of the window. The doctors are saying it's completely normal to feel intense, overwhelming waves of emotion, but watching her go from a headstrong, confident athlete to a girl who cries several times a day has wrenched my heart in more directions than I thought it could be wrenched.

"We should get you ready for bed," I say. I'm about to get up to get her toothbrush and her earplugs, and whatever else she might need so she can sleep, when she stops me.

"I'm sorry," she whispers.

I pause. The room suddenly feels tight, and the seconds tick by with excruciating slowness.

"Sorry for what?" I ask carefully.

She swallows hard. "That night. I shouldn't have made you choose."

I let the moment hang.

"No. You really shouldn't have," I say.

A tear squeezes out of her closed eyelids and rolls down her cheek.

And it wasn't the only time she tried to come between me and someone. Before, I would have backed down from this whole conversation, but now I need to know.

"Cady, did you mess around in my phone and delete messages from Arissa so I wouldn't go to her birthday party?"

There—a skitter of guilt. And I know immediately that my hunch was right.

"That pretty much ended that friendship, but that was what you wanted, right?" I start to shake with nerves. Just because I can handle a confrontation doesn't mean I have to like it.

"And there have been other things," I continue. "I didn't notice them at the time, not really. Millie in first grade. Making me go to every one of your games or you'd pout and sulk. Not letting me stay in ballet after you quit."

"I'm sorry. I just wanted . . ." Tears swim in her eyes. "I just wanted us to be *us*. Cady and Aria, two peas in a pod. And it got so much worse after you met Strat. You were drifting away from me, and it felt horrible, and I just wanted us to always be side by side."

"That doesn't make it okay. It's seriously messed up that you did those things."

"I know," she whispers. Her chin wobbles. "Do you hate me? Will you ever be able to forgive me?"

My heart thuds. I've been thinking about this since the moment she woke up.

And I think I need a break from being a sister for a while.

I take a steadying breath, about to say the words that will gut her.

But then I look at her, tears welling in her eyes, and the words crumble.

Cady and I . . . we are a tapestry too tightly woven to unpick the good from the bad. She's in my every childhood memory. Holding hands at the top of the stairs on Christmas morning, both of us fidgeting with excitement. Fighting viciously over a toy a few hours later. Looking over in third grade at the picture she drew of her favorite thing in the world and seeing two stick figure girls with long brown hair holding hands. Feeling waves of rage when she wouldn't listen to me, or made me do things she wanted to do. Sneaking downstairs in the night to watch our favorite cartoons on mute and thinking we were being so devious. Singing along to music in the car the day after we passed our driving tests, and late-night runs to get ice cream.

Cady was the one who put up with me when I decided we needed to know how to waltz like Disney princesses. She's the one who let me pretend to die in her arms in some sweeping reenactment of old-school romance.

She's also the one who sulked until I relented to go to her games, who didn't let me stay in ballet after she quit, and who deleted the messages about Arissa's party to sabotage my friendships with other people. She's made mistakes, and I have too.

I chose to move *forward* with Strat, instead of taking the easy way out.

Now I know: I have to do the same thing with Cady.

We can't change the past. We could erase it, but I don't want to. I'd rather try to build from here, to evolve from where we are.

"Please say something, Aria," she says, fear swimming in her eyes. "Is it really too much to come back from?"

"I think . . . ," I say slowly, "I think we're going to have to work on it."

Relief swamps her. She reaches for my hand, gratitude shining on her face. I shift and dig my hand into my skirt pocket. "And to answer your other question—no, I don't hate you." I pull out the double penny and press it into her hand. "I could never hate you."

I exhale, pressing my eyes closed. "And I'm not blameless. I should have stood up for what I wanted every once in a while. And I shouldn't have gotten so wrapped up in Strat that I ignored you. I'm sorry too. So sorry, Cady."

We hug for so long I start to worry I'm hurting her, but she won't let me go. My eyes sting. "I'm so glad you're awake," I whisper into her hair. "I was so scared."

After a long time, we let each other go, wiping our eyes with our sleeves.

"Aria? I did something stupid. After our fight."

"I know."

She frowns. "What?"

I sink into the chair by her side. "I know you didn't go to Spike Night on New Year's Eve. I know you went to get an erasure instead."

She goes pale.

"Cady—what did you erase?"

"I only wanted to erase the fight we'd had. I felt so awful about it. But it obviously didn't work, because I remember every second of it. Why didn't it work?"

"Because the place you went was shady. After I found out you'd gotten an erasure, I asked if that could have exacerbated your AVM. They said yes."

"So I did this to myself?" She looks down at her emaciated legs, her muscle-less arms.

The guilt that's been clinging to me since I called that hotline wraps tightly around my neck. "I think maybe I did it to you," I say.

"That makes no sense."

"If I'd chosen you instead of him, you wouldn't have skipped Spike Night to get an erasure, and it wouldn't have ruptured your brain." My throat clogs up.

"Aria. Hey. Look at me." There is a flash of the firm, protective sister I knew. Seeing it is a small thrill. "No one told me to get that erasure. No one but me forked over that cash and signed that sketchy form. You are not allowed to blame yourself. I refuse to allow it, okay?"

"But—"

"Nope. Not allowing it."

I didn't know I needed her to say it, but the guilt releases its chokehold on me, and I take the deepest breath I've taken in days.

I grip her hand tightly in mine.

"Are you and Strat still together?" she asks quietly.

"Yeah. Yeah, we are."

"Good," she says. "You were right to choose the ball over Spike Night."

I press my lips together. I'll tell her later what a disaster the ball was—we've had enough emotional turmoil for the day.

My phone buzzes, lighting up on the windowsill.

"You can get that," Cady says, exhaustion creeping into her voice.

"It's just Strat. I'll answer it later."

Cady turns on her side and nestles farther down under her covers, eyes drooping a little. "You know, I had a lot of strange dreams when I was under," she murmurs sleepily.

That grabs my attention. "What kind of dreams?"

"I only felt like I was asleep for a night. A long night, maybe. The whole time, I just felt . . . guilt. It was like I was made of it, like that was all there was to me. I don't even think I really understood what I'd done, but I knew I'd done something awful to you. And I felt this . . . presence."

I go very still. "Like . . . Fate?"

She stirs enough to roll her eyes. "You know I don't believe in all that crap."

"No," I murmur. "No, you don't."

She snuggles down again. "Anyway, whatever it was, I could feel it all around me, but like . . . it wasn't paying attention to anything in particular. But I begged it to help you. Begged, and begged, until finally . . . it felt like it turned to me. Looked at me. And I felt better after that."

The force Cady felt . . . could it be the same as the force Strat and I saw? Would it have paid any attention to us, or dragged us into our midnights, if Cady hadn't intervened and asked it to?

I pick at the edge of the hospital blanket. "Cady—I've been having weird dreams too."

She doesn't ask what I dreamed of, though, because her eyes have drooped closed. She inhales, and her gently purring snore reassures me she hasn't slipped back into a deeper sleep.

I sigh and kiss her temple. It's probably too soon to tell her about the midnights anyway. I've decided I will. She'll be the only other person who knows the *whole* story. Strat's fine with my sharing it with her.

Speaking of.

I roll carefully off the bed and slip into the hallway.

I find Strat exactly where I expect to find him: in the lobby on the ground floor, at the grand piano. To exactly no one's surprise, he's charmed the front desk team, and they let him play whenever he wants, even if it's two in the morning.

A few weary relatives sit in the café chairs nearby, listening to him play even though the café has long since closed. Two women in scrubs sway in the simple peace his playing brings to these late, empty hours.

He looks up as soon as I arrive, as if he can sense me. I lean against a column to watch him. His lips curve up, and he holds my stare, playing all the while.

I wait, listening for the deliberate flaw he'll work into the piece. It's familiar to me now, this Rachmaninov prelude, so maybe I'll catch it.

He looks down for a second, playing a few wrong, beautiful notes in between the others, and when he looks up, the smile that unfurls when he catches my eye is everything.

CHAPTER FORTY-EIGHT

Strat leans against the doorframe, a lock of hair falling into his eyes as he passes me a paper bag of takeout food.

"I got an extra order of fries in case she was hungry," he says, keeping his voice low.

I glance at Cady. She's staring down at her blanket, looking ashamed.

"I'll take off," Strat says. "Just wanted to make sure you had something to eat."

"Thank you. Seriously, thank you for being so awesome."

"Anytime."

He pauses. It's clear that he wants to lean down and kiss me goodbye. I feel my own body leaning into it, but then he flicks a glance toward Cady's bed.

I close my eyes and take a deep breath. I can't keep the two of them apart forever. We need to face this so we can get on with our lives.

"You should come in," I say softly, lacing my fingers through his and tugging him the rest of the way into the room, positioning us at the end of Cady's bed.

I brace myself. "Cady, you know Strat. Strat, this is . . . my sister."

"Hey," Strat says, pushing a hand through his hair. His Adam's apple works in his throat. Nervous.

"Hey," Cady mumbles.

The tension in the air coils tighter. Maybe this was a bad idea.

"Obviously you guys have met before," I say, "but he doesn't remember a whole lot of it."

Cady looks down. "But he knows that I wasn't super friendly before, right?" she says softly.

"Um. Yeah."

She doesn't say anything else. The lump in my throat grows. How am I going to fix this? I need them both in my life.

Cady speaks so quietly that at first I don't hear it.

"I'm sorry." Then she seems to rally, looking up at Strat. "I owe you an apology, for not supporting you guys before. For trying to come between you."

Strat nods. "I get it. I want to keep her all to myself too when I'm with her. She's incredible."

Their eyes lock, and an understanding seems to pass between the two of them.

Suddenly a cluster of loud voices comes from outside the door, and then a head peeks into the room. Devyn, still in her volleyball jersey and her sweatband, her ponytail messy from a game.

"Heard our captain was awake!" she sing-songs, and then they're all flooding in, all twelve members of the varsity team. Everyone's dancing around the bed, giving Cady careful hugs. There are GET WELL SOON balloons and flowers, and someone's playing some music on their phone.

The room is crowded and alive, girls sitting on the window-sill, two or three squeezed on a chair, two perched on the end of Cady's bed. Cady's smiling, the first genuine smile I've seen from her since she woke up. Britt Coleman hovers in the corner, and I catch her glaring at Strat and me more than once.

Tahirah passes, squeezing my shoulder. "Don't let her bother you. It's not personal, trust me. She's just a sourpuss."

The girls stay until the night nurse kicks them out. As they file out, Tahirah stops me by the door. "It should come as no surprise to you, but we are headed to IHOP."

I laugh. "Nothing comes between the varsity squad and their pancakes."

"You should come, babe. We miss you tagging along."

I'm about to automatically agree when I realize . . . I don't want to tag along.

I roll my shoulders back. "I'm not going to come, T. Thank you for the invite, but I've never been super into sports. I'll be at Cady's games when she plays, but you don't have to make room for me anymore."

"We weren't making—"

"It's okay," I assure her. "It really is. I've gotta work on my dress stuff, and there's a girl in my art class who's amazing at helping with that kind of thing. I'm going to have to buckle down to get my final project done by the end of the semester."

She squeezes my arm, beaming. "Hanging out with the art kids. Love that for you. See you at a game sometime, then."

"Yeah, see you."

Once everyone's gone, Strat slides up behind me. "Heard that. Very well done."

"Thank you, glad to hear it was up to your exacting standards."

"We never got around to practicing again, did we?" He drops a kiss on my shoulder.

"Yo—lovebirds? I fully support your relationship, but I'm afraid I must draw the line at making out in my hospital room," Cady says, mockingly shielding her eyes.

I throw a French fry at her. Finally, there's room to sit down. I take out my phone and find Arissa in WhatsApp.

> Hi Arissa! I'm putting that dress together this weekend—I would love to have you take a look at the pattern! Are you free Saturday afternoon?

She responds a minute later.

> OMG yes! Did you decide to go for the mint tulle? And please tell me Bardot sleeves? I'll bring chapssal-tteok!!

Strat leaves shortly after that, and Cady, exhausted from the excitement, falls asleep before I can help her into her pajamas. I clean up a few pieces of trash the volleyball girls left and head for the break room at the end of the hall.

As I'm approaching, I see Mom's ponytail. She's at one of the small tables, staring at her laptop but not typing. She sighs, then drops her head to one hand in a way that makes my heart ache.

My whole body tenses, urging me to slip away without saying anything. But there's something I need to do. I press my hand over my stomach and step into the break room.

"Hey, Mom? Is there anything you want to tell me about you and Dad?"

CHAPTER FORTY-NINE

In the dim blue glow of my bedroom, I touch my phone screen to trace the one rogue curl that's fallen across Strat's forehead. His eyes drift closed as if he can feel my touch through the video call.

"I wish we were really lying next to each other instead of just FaceTiming," I whisper.

"Same," he says, voice rough with exhaustion. "But we'll see each other in"—he drags his arm up to check his watch—"fourteen minutes."

"I'll let you sleep, then."

"Mm. See you at midnight," he murmurs.

A smile tugs at my lips. "See you at midnight, Strat." I reach out to end the call, but something makes me hesitate, finger hovering just above the screen.

A thought blooms, an idea taking shape.

It's so tempting to sink back into the midnights. I used to try so hard to willfully ignore anything difficult or ugly. But real life can be incredible even when it's not postcard pretty.

"Strat, wait. Don't go yet."

He drags his eyes back open. "What's up?"

"I don't . . . I don't want to dream tonight."

He frowns, then props himself up on one elbow. "What do you mean?"

"I would rather be awake with you."

The realization is so powerful it sends a shiver sweeping down from the top of my head. "I want to see you in real life."

I would rather live in all the grittiness and electricity and imperfection of reality than run away to a place where everything is pretty but nothing is real.

"You mean now?" Strat asks.

"Yes. Right now."

His grin spreads slowly until it's beaming over his whole face. "Who are you and what have you done with the girl I love?"

I laugh. I realize then—I would never have smiled at him like this that first midnight, when everything he said in the sequoia forest made me grit my teeth and want to stomp away from him.

No matter how complicated this has all gotten, reality with him is a thousand times better than the most perfect fantasy midnight without him.

"Also . . ." I add, "kissing you in the midnights is nice, but there's always that weird haziness. I can never seem to get as close to you as I want to get. When you kiss me in real life, it . . . well, it pretty much wrecks me."

He throws off his covers and reaches for a T-shirt. "Then let's get wrecked, Girl in the Piano Glade."

*　　*　　*

He catches me at the waist just as the waves crash over my bare toes, swinging me around until I collide with him, chest to chest. He lifts me off my feet and presses a searing kiss to my lips.

My heart soars. It's the middle of the night, but I am made of light.

When he finally puts me down, I stumble back dizzily. He looks at me, the corner of his mouth quirking up. He winks. That confident prep school boy, all easy charm and charisma. And everything underneath.

"Sit with me," he says, and then he's tugging me down to the sand and tucking me in front of him so both of us are facing the ocean.

"Hey, Aria? I have another confession."

"Uh-oh. Here we go." He's been doing this lately, making sure I really know him and I'm not warping him into a flawless boyfriend in my head.

"I don't like that actress you like, the one with the super sharp cheekbones," he whispers in my ear.

I twist around, eyes wide with mock shock. "Ugh, are you serious?!"

"Very serious."

I settle back into him. "Oh well. I guess I'll just have to accept that you're not the ideal boyfriend."

There, nestled in the circle of his arms, with his chest warm at my back and our feet burrowed into the sand, we watch the waves.

The moonlight is thin and lunar white instead of the pulsing ultraviolet of our midnights, but there's still a hint of that twelve o'clock magic here. We've got all the best parts of a midnight—that quiet, magical hour, the easy honesty. But now when he traces his fingertips up the soft part of the underside of my arm, I can feel it magnified in every nerve in my body.

Before all this, I was trying to live with both feet in a fantasy version of my life. Maybe a lot of us are, when we're children. We want life to be like our favorite lift-the-flap book, bright and per-fect. We want our love to be just like our favorite love stories. But life is a balance between living with your feet on the ground and keeping *just* enough of your head in the clouds to not be beaten down by the pragmatic, day-to-day difficulties. Go too far either way and things start to go off the rails.

I'm so grateful for the midnights, not just for their beauty and their magic but for the chance they gave us to fix the mis-takes we made the first time around.

"I have something for you," Strat says. He tugs his bag over and pulls out an envelope. "So . . . you know how this illegal clinic thing has been getting a lot of exposure on the news, and it's blow-ing up on Reddit and socials and stuff?"

"Yes," I say slowly, wondering where he's going with this.

"I know you applied to that school in Italy. I know how upset you were when you realized the old Aria withdrew the applica-tion. So . . . I called them."

My eyes go wide.

"I explained the whole situation, and they'd heard of the era-sures crisis over here. They weren't that impressed with my sob story, unfortunately, but it turns out the head of the department you applied to had back surgery last month and wasn't able to read through all the applications by her deadline to choose an incoming class anyway, so we got you back into the pile, and then . . . well, here," he says, pressing the envelope toward me.

Somewhere in the middle of his speech, I clapped my hands over my mouth, not daring to hope this means what I think it means.

My hands tremble as I open the letter.

Dear Ms. Lendell,

Felicitazioni and welcome to the class of 2028 at the Sciarra Academy for Fashion and Design.

The rest of the words blur.

"You okay?" Strat asks, ducking his head to peer under the curtain of my hair. I nod, but I can't speak. It's huge, in my chest, this feeling.

"You did this for me?" I whisper.

"Of course. And your mom was super helpful—she's, like, intimidatingly efficient. Oh, wait, that's not all." He unlocks his phone and taps around, then turns the screen to me.

"Remember my icy untouchable grandmother? She's performing with the Vienna Philharmonic the week before your classes start, and I asked if she could help us with tickets to come see her. I scheduled us a cheeky stop in Paris on the way. I thought that might be a city you'd be interested in seeing."

I squeal and launch myself at him, knocking him down onto the sand, climbing on top of him, and covering him with kisses.

After an interesting interlude, we roll onto our backs and stare up at the moon.

"We've had kind of an unbelievable month, haven't we?" he says.

"We certainly have."

The memory stuff makes sense. I've been following the news about the busted underground clinic like a hawk. Turns out that because the clinic didn't use ArEx's tested, high-quality technology, it only damaged brain cells instead of fully destroying them. As our brains—miraculous, mysterious things that they are—healed or compensated for the micro-damages, our memories healed too, and came back in flashes. Just like how amnesia patients recover memories. Memory is an incredible, complex thing, and I've only begun to scratch the surface of understanding it all.

Strat weaves his fingers through mine, resting our hands on my knees. "What I still don't get is . . . what are the midnights?"

The question hangs in the air between us. I haven't told him about what Cady said yet, what she saw and felt when she was asleep for three months.

"You know," I say cautiously, "back when I was a hopeless romantic, I really did believe in things like . . . destiny. Soulmates, maybe. Fate."

"Sounds on brand," he says teasingly.

I elbow him. "But I guess I thought Fate was more like . . . a map that had already been laid out for everyone, or that some connections between certain people were stronger and would always pull them together somehow. I never really thought of it as an entity, a being with its own thoughts and goals and motivations. Or three entities, like the Grecian Fates with their threads and scissors."

"But now?" he prompts.

I think of the way we were pushed back together by the midnights. The way the ground rose up and kept us from walking away from each other, the way I could *feel* the midnight's personality when the fireworks rained over Paris, the way it tried to pull me back into those last midnights no matter how hard I tried to stay awake . . .

"Maybe something is out there, but it can't get involved on a daily basis. Maybe it only corrects people when they go way off course," I say.

"Hmm. So we were meant to be, but we screwed it up so badly that Fate had to step in and do something dramatic to shove us back together?"

"Maybe." I tip my head back onto his shoulder, exhaling. "And . . . that sounds absolutely ludicrous."

But secretly the hopeless romantic in me—although she's a little wiser, a little more willing to buckle down and put in the hard work and face the tough parts of life—would like to think that that might be what happened.

"Maybe not everything has to have an answer," Strat says. "Maybe I'm just happy we got here in the end."

"I'm happy too," I whisper. So happy.

There's no midnight the night after that, or the following night. After a long run of dreamless sleeps in a row, I start to grapple with the idea that midnights aren't going to happen ever again. We're tramping through the sequoia forest—the *real* forest, twenty minutes from my house—when I mention it to Strat.

"It's been ten nights without them, Strat."

He stops and pulls me into his arms. "Maybe when you decided you wanted real-life me instead of Dream Boy me, it broke the chain."

"Or maybe the midnights achieved what they set out to achieve," I say quietly.

I crane my neck to look up at the sequoias, breathing in the scent of the forest, savoring the clarity of the vision even if it isn't as misty or airbrushed as our dreams. I've decided that as soon as I have enough money, I'm going to buy a used piano and put it out here for someone else to stumble upon. Maybe I can give them a sliver of the wonder I felt when I saw our piano glade.

"Still, part of me wishes they didn't have to end," I say.

"Aria." Strat shifts so he can look me in the eye. "Our *real* midnights are just getting started."

ACKNOWLEDGMENTS

First thanks must go to my brilliant agent, Chloe Seager. You were the earliest believer in this story, and without that glow I would never have found the courage to keep at it. I'm so grateful for your enthusiasm and support. Thank you also to everyone on the fabulous team at Madeleine Milburn, particularly Hannah Ladds, Hannah Kettles, Valentina Paulmichl, and Kelly Chin.

Immense thanks to all the publishing teams around the world that worked on the many different editions of this book. I'm always honored to send out a story that weaves another thread into the web between nations and languages.

Huge thanks to Kelsey Horton and the fabulous team at Delacorte Press for working to bring Aria's dreamworld into the real world: Emma Leynse, Trisha Previte, Kelly Thompson, Sarah Lawrenson, Kristin Guy, Colleen Fellingham, Alison Kolani, Cathy Bobak, Liz Sutton, Tamar Schwartz, and Wendy Loggia.

Thank you to Polly Lyall-Grant for your work in helping me shape this story—I loved working with you and your team on this!

Jaw-droppingly grateful to Lauren K. and Kat R. for loving Aria and for giving me my swooniest author career moment so far. Still in disbelief!

Huge thanks to my brilliant writing group, MUG—Taylor Ross, Ana Ellickson, J. C. Peterson, Aleese Lin, and Genevieve Sinha. You are stunningly talented and ferociously intelligent women. I feel so lucky to be a part of the group and to have you all in my writing life.

Lily—I am so thankful for your unwavering encouragement, wisdom, and general badassery. You are a sunshine goddess!

Christina—no one can get me giggling uncontrollably quite like you. Your friendship has kept me (and this book) afloat in all weather.

To all my family on both sides of the pond—you are the best! No one has put in more hours of support to make this book possible than my incredible mother-in-law, Terry Bourne—thank you. And to my parents—I'm so glad that out of all the parents in the world I get to be your daughter!

Deepest thanks to my sweet daughters, L + M. For someone who doesn't have a sister, I write about them a lot. I think that's because I'm so inspired by the sistership I am witnessing between you. Thank you for showing me a whole new kind of love.

Henry—I find it hard to express how deep my gratitude is. Thank you for being my teammate through three books, two kids, and one international move. You make my daydreams come true. Can't wait for whatever's next on our horizon.

And lastly: Thank *you*, reader. For picking up this book and coming on this surreal and swoony trip with Aria and Strat. I hope you had a magical time living in the pages of their story.

♥

ABOUT THE AUTHOR

BRIANNA BOURNE writes books about teenagers who meet in impossible situations—and then try very hard not to kiss. Her debut novel, *You and Me at the End of the World*, was recommended by *The New York Times* on their summer YA reading list and was called "stunning" by bestselling novelist Emily Henry.

Bri's heart-wrenching sophomore novel, *The Half-Life of Love*, was nominated for the Carnegie Medal, shortlisted for the Cybils Award, and placed on several statewide master lists. Originally from Texas, Bri grew up in Indonesia and Egypt and just returned to Houston after living in the UK for many years.

@brianna_bourne_writes